Hiroshima Bugi

Native Storiers: A Series of American Narratives

Series Editors
Gerald Vizenor
Diane Glancy

| Hiroshima Bugi: |

| Atomu 57 |

| Gerald Vizenor |

| University of Nebraska Press | Lincoln and London |

Vizenor, Gerald Robert, 1934–
Hiroshima bugi : Atomu 57 / Gerald
Vizenor.
p. cm. — (Native storiers)
ISBN 0-8032-4673-0 (cl.: alk. paper)
ISBN 978-0-8032-3284-6 (pa.: alk. paper)
1. Hiroshima-shi (Japan)—Fiction. 2.
Racially mixed people—Fiction. 3. Indians of North America—Fiction. 4. Japanese—United States—Fiction. 5. Alien-
ation (Social psychology)—Fiction. I.
Title. II. Series.
PS3572.I9H57 2003
813'.54—dc21
2003042696

In memory of Miki Sawada and Will Karkavelas

Contents

To starve a child of the spell of the story, of the canter of the poem, oral or written, is a kind of living burial. It is to immure him in emptiness.

George Steiner, *Real Presences*

An easygoing conscience, however, cannot remain untroubled except by intentionally refusing to listen to the stories that come out of Hiroshima.

Kenzaburo Oe, *Hiroshima Notes*

The streets were deserted except for the dead. Some looked as if they had been frozen by death while in the full action of flight; others lay sprawled as though some giant had flung them to their death from a great height.

Michihiko Hachiya, *Hiroshima Diary*

The first atomic bomb destroyed more than the city of Hiroshima. It also exploded our inherited, outdated political ideas.

Albert Einstein, *The New York Times*

Hiroshima Bugi

1   Ronin of Rashomon Gate

The Atomic Bomb Dome is my Rashomon.

Come closer to the stone, over here, out of the rain. You are the first person to visit me in these ruins. This is my unearthly haven in the remains of the first nuclear war. Only the dead rush their stories under this dome.

The gate of ruins.

The rain, the moody rain, a reminder of that bright and vicious light that poisoned the marrow and forever burned the heart of our memories. Rain, rain, and the ominous stories of black rain. No one can ever be sure of the rain.

The park ravens break that inscrutable silence at the wispy end of a rainstorm. Listen, the shadows of dead children arise from the stone and shout back at the ravens. They mock each other, a parade of ghosts forever teased by the rain.

Sit here, near the ropes.
Twisted reeds?
My kabuki theater.
Raven sumo.
Kabuki of the ruins.
Fierce beauty.
Shadows of the dead.
Ghostly souvenirs.
Atomu war.
Curse of black rain.
Hiroshima by chance.
Kyoto preserved.
Twice by irony.

The Rashomon Gate was in ruins too, more than eight centuries ago. Brutality so old it has turned aesthetic, the fierce cruelty of beauty. We might have been there, waiting for the rain to end just as we are today.

Akutagawa wrote our stories.

Kyoto, a grand city of shrines and willow trees, was wasted, as you know, by natural disasters, war, and wild fires, and that once-mighty gate was taken over by animals, thieves, and ghosts.

The warrior ghosts.
Kabuki scenes.
Memory is our gate.
The Atomic Bomb Dome has been registered as a World Heritage.
Preserved, as you can see, for the tourists, sentimental bystanders,
and, of course, for the cryptic outriders and politicians of peace.

Early in the morning, every morning since this river city was deci-
mated, at this very site, the ruins of the hypocenter, shadows of the
dead gather in a ghost parade. The children of incineration, and
the white bones of an empire war, arise in a nuclear kabuki theater,
and the slender shadows come to light in a ghost parade at eight
fifteen, the very same moment of the explosion on August 6, 1945.

My life ended before the bomb.
My life started with the occupation.
My father sent me away.
My father was an army sergeant.
My mother was a cripple.
My mother was a bugi dancer.
My only friends are lepers.
My only friends are orphans.
Our stories are eternal, and the ravens are wise not to break the ab-
solute silence of the ruins in the morning. Stay overnight and you
may see a theater of human horseweeds and perfect memories.
This is our new story.

Chrysanthemums?
My shirt of tricky shame.
Printed flowers?
Mocks the emperor.
Ruth Benedict?
Story of guilt not shame.
The government poisoned our prize chrysanthemums because of
their fear of leprosy. The mere touch of a leper shamed the great
beauty of the flowers.

The empire of shame.
Crown stigma.
Sovereignty of the ruins.
My theater is liberty.
Hiroshima arose out of the nuclear ruins to become a testy, pros-
perous city of peace and victimry. Millions of tourists treasure

the origami cranes and forever recite the tragic stories of Sadake Sasaki.

Discovery is the cure.

Never leprosy.

Listen to the distant thunder. The air is thick, heavy, black in the distance. A few days ago lightning struck the dome and demons sizzled down the beams. Have you ever thought about being struck by lightning?

Lightning evades me.

The perfect death is by chance, and the thunderous, terminal turn of a conversation in the rain. The last perfect vision is a burst of bright light, and then the mighty rage of memory.

I pray for lightning.

For death?

Yes, a natural liberty.

Stop praying.

Suddenly, bright, and true.

I was tormented by terrible dreams the first few nights alone here in the ruins. The horror was inescapable. I was caught in the same nightmare, night after night, and could not scare myself awake. The children and lonesome dead crossed over the circle in the ruins.

My nightmare lasted sixty years.

I was surrounded by white bones and burned, puffy bodies. The river was packed with bodies that never floated out to the bay. I was dead, a heap of ancient white bones, and could only reach out for bits of passing flesh to cover my bones, to create a new memory.

I caught a white pigeon with burned feathers. Suddenly the pigeon turned into an angry ghost and scorned me. Then my bones were mounted in a museum, with my broken, burned watch beside me, probably as punishment for my resistance and tease of time.

My body had deserted me, and my remains were displayed in a diorama of victimry to promote peace. I raged over the passive notions of peace, and then, in the last scene of the nightmare, the museum was destroyed in an earthquake. My bones were liberated by chance and my shadow was cast in a ghost parade, a nuclear kabuki theatre. I awakened in the ruins, and every morning since then there has been a ghost parade that starts abruptly at eight fifteen ante meridiem.

My body is a nightmare.
Old war wounds?
Yes, but not military.
Samurai?
No, leprosy.
Where?
Oshima, an island of lepers.
Another ghost parade.
The rain is over.
Nasty sores on your face.

The caved nose and sores are the shame, the black rain of culture and disease on my face. No, not the ecstatic fear or perverse pleasures of stigmata. There was nothing aesthetic to bear by reason or creative poses.

My father reported the sores to save my sister from social scorn and separation. No man would have her with a leper brother at home. My face was erased by disease, and my name was erased by fear and family. The police snatched my body and confined me on an island for sixty years, even after there was a cure for leprosy. My war, you see, never ends, there is no surrender, no occupation, no reformation because my body and eroded bones are the ruins of this nasty, cruel, empire culture. My stories are separations of time and family.

Oshima, a perfect nickname.
No, no, too severe.
The samurai of leprosy.
Death in that name.
Tricky stories are liberty.
Try my leprosy.
Oshima of the ruins.

Oshima was my prison, and by torment and desperate loneliness we cared for each other to the end, a wounded and abandoned family. Many of my close friends died of loneliness. Three elders, about my age, and a younger blind woman, the philosophers on the island, died in the same week.

Death by silence.

For many years we had nurtured prize chrysanthemums on the island. Strong, beautiful flowers gave us courage in the morning. Then, reluctantly, we agreed to cut some of the chrysanthemums for sale in a nearby town, across the Inland Sea.

Happily, the trade developed slowly, but then we were told that our prize chrysanthemums had wilted and died in a single day. My friends died too, outcasts, suicide by desolation, when we learned that the chrysanthemums had been sterilized because we were lepers. Those beautiful blooms died because of our terrible, devoted touch of leprosy.

I reach for the lightning in every storm.

Manidoo Envoy

Ronin Ainoko Browne beat on my door at the Hotel Manidoo in Nogales, Arizona. There was no cause to answer because the sign in the lobby made it perfectly clear that the residents of the hotel were never at home to strangers or solicitors.

Ronin was persistent that morning. I watched him through the eyehole in the door. His moves were theatrical, a measured strut, and his manner cocksure. Open this door, he shouted.

Who are you?

Where is my father?

Not here.

Who are you?

Who is your father?

Sergeant Orion Browne.

Nightbreaker?

Ronin, at first sight, could have been mistaken for Toshiro Mifune. He bounded into the room as if he were on the set of the movie *Rashomon*. He looked around, gestured to the chairs and furniture. Then he turned toward me. My father lives here, he said, over an empty theatrical smile.

Ronin dressed for his father. He wore beaded moccasins, loose black trousers, a pleated shirt shrewdly decorated with puffy white chrysanthemums, and a dark blue cravat. Sadly, he was seven days too late.

Nightbreaker, my best friend, died in his wicker chair near the window. His last gesture was to the raucous ravens perched in the cottonwoods. Ravens inspire natural memories, he told me, and then continued his stories about the tricky imperial ravens in occupied Japan. Ravens create stories of survivance in our perfect memories.

Nightbreaker invited me to move into his room, one of the best in the hotel. We cared for each other as brothers and veterans. That awkward admission soon turned to humor and personal trust. Ronin told me he would stay with his father, late or not, for a few days.

Nightbreaker never mentioned a son, but he told many stories about his lover, Okichi. The name has a grievous history. Japanese authorities, more than a century ago, provided an adolescent by that name as a consort for Townsend Harris, the first consul of the United States. Some prostitutes now bear the same name.

Okichi was a boogie, or *bugi*, dancer. "Tokyo Bugi" was the most popular song in the early occupation. Nightbreaker said they first met at a rodeo sponsored by the military and later danced at the Ernie Pyle Canteen in Tokyo. They saw *No Regrets for Our Youth*, directed by Akira Kurosawa, one of the first Japanese films produced after the war. Okichi was not interested in heroic, political stories that were not celebrations of the emperor.

Nightbreaker told me she learned how to kiss in romantic movies and was infatuated by Humphrey Bogart in *Casablanca*. Her favorite song was "Sentimental Journey." Nightbreaker never knew she was pregnant. Okichi disappeared one night and never returned to their regular meeting place at the moat near the Imperial Palace in Tokyo.

Nightbreaker lost his war with cancer, the mortal wounds of his military service. He had been exposed several times to nuclear radiation. If only he had known about his son.

Ronin lived with me, and the memories of his father, for more than a month. The corner room on the second floor overlooked three giant cottonwood trees and the border between Mexico and the United States. He sat in silence for three days in the wicker chair and wrote notes to his father. Then he wore his father's dress uniform and signature cravat every night to dinner and imagined his moves. Ronin learned about the tender manner and sensibilities of his father from the many stories told by other native veterans at the hotel.

Nightbreaker wore the same blue cravat. Naturally, the flourish was familiar, and so was the story. Ronin told us, as his father had years earlier, that their ancestors in the fur trade wore blue to entice women, a practice learned from stories about the wise bower birds who decorate their elaborate nests with something blue. The color is an avian aphrodisiac. Fur traders sold blue cravats to natives, and the myth endures.

Handy Fairbanks founded the Hotel Manidoo some twenty years ago. He is native, a decorated veteran, and once a great hunter on the reservation. Handy lost both of his legs on a land mine, and then the last of his close relatives died in an automobile accident.

Handy created a hotel of perfect memories for wounded veterans. Nightbreaker, who earned his nickname for amorous adventures on the reservation, had lived in the hotel for the past nine years.

8

Many residents thought his distinctive nickname was connected to his military service at nuclear test sites.

Five nights a week we came together for dinner and to create our perfect memories. The marvelous, elusive tease of our many stories, and variations of stories, became concerted memories. Our tricky metaphors were woven together day by day into a consciousness of moral survivance. More than the commerce of reactive survivalists, mere liturgy, ideology, or the causative leverage of a sworn witness, survivance is a creative, concerted consciousness that does not arise from separation, dominance, or concession nightmares. Our stories create perfect memories of survivance.

Natives once named the storiers of the day on trade routes in the canoe country. At night, around a fire, by the signs of natural silence, chance, menace, tricksters, and endurance, the native provenance of stories, were given to perfect memories, and so the wounded veterans of the hotel named a storier of the day.

Nightbreaker was an original native storier, and the tease of his stories became our perfect memories. He touched by totems and metaphors the imagic animals and birds of our survivance. We were always in the bright light of his eternal fires of imagination.

Ronin became a storier, and he mailed his journal to me several years later with vague instructions to provide notes, the necessary descriptive references, and background information on his father and others. The original stories were first scrawled on scraps of paper and later handwritten in seven ledger notebooks.

My personal library, a considerable collection of books about the history, literature, and theater of Japan, aroused his interest in me as a trustee, and he wanted his stories to be associated with his father and the perfect memories of our survivance at the Hotel Manidoo.

Hiroshima Bugi was read out loud at dinner by the storiers named for the day. Ronin would be pleased to hear the creative counts that became part of his tricky stories, and, of course, my commentaries.

Handy, for instance, elaborated on the scenes about romantic movies. Okichi, he said, learned how to dance and tease from *Gone with the Wind*. A copy of the movie was confiscated by soldiers in the Philippines and shown before the end of the war and occupation of Japan. Mister Nightbreaker Butler, when did those nasty soldiers burn Atlanta? Why, Scarlett Okichi, you know it was the Civil War. The Japanese lost the war to the Union.

9

Handy was a marvelous storier that night, and we honored the perfect memories of Nightbreaker. Clearly, the tricky *renga*, connected scenes, ghost parades, the nuclear kabuki theater in Ronin's *Hiroshima Bugi*, and our imagic bits and riffs, are concerted stories of perfect memories at the Hotel Manidoo.

Oshima Island, or Izu Oshima, a volcanic island, was a prison for lepers near the Izu Peninsula on the Island Sea. Oshima was recently released from the island after sixty years of separation from society. The sentence and banishment for his disease was sanctioned by the Japanese Leprosy Prevention Law. Many families complied with the law and erased the names of their sons, daughters, and other relatives who were lepers. Oshima, a nickname, lost his real name, his sense of presence, cultural associations, and most of his close friends on the island.

The Atomic Bomb Dome, first protected as a historic site, with no intended irony, is now registered on the World Heritage List. The Sphinx in Egypt, the Great Wall of China, and Grand Canyon National Park, for instance, are also registered as sites of World Heritage.

The Atomic Bomb Dome, near the shore of the Motoyasu River, is the actual ruins of the Hiroshima Industrial Promotion Hall. The Dome, however, is not as real to many tourists as the simulated miniature dome constructed inside the Peace Memorial Museum.

Toyofumi Ogura described the Industrial Promotion Hall in *Letters from the End of the World*. "That old brick building, with its rather exotic dome, was well known in Hiroshima. Though the building was virtually destroyed, roof and floors both having caved in, the steel frame of the dome and the outer walls of the building are still standing. If you step over the rubble and into the remains of the building, you can look up and see the blue sky through the skeleton of the dome, making you feel as if you might be standing amid the ruins of Pompeii."

Ronin declared war on the simulations of peace when he saw, for the first time, the miniature dome over two stories of plaintive peace letters etched on metal plates. Hundreds of reduced metal letters were mounted around a pathetic peace column.

Tadatoshi Akiba, mayor of Hiroshima, for instance, wrote to President William Jefferson Clinton on December 15, 2000. "The United States should look objectively at the history of the 20th Century and realize that nuclear deterrence does not prevent war. Rather, it invites escalation and proliferation of nuclear weapons, thus placing the entire human race at risk of annihilation. Please listen to the international community's sincere desire to eliminate these weapons. Please immediately halt your subcritical nuclear testing, and take your proper place at the forefront of the effort to make the 21st Century free from nuclear weapons." The entire letter is etched on metal, reduced, and mounted on the column of peace. Nearby, there is a letter of protest to Jacques Chirac, president of the French Republic.

Ronin told me he summoned many spectators at the museum and read out loud to them, by shouts and roars, parts of several letters on the column. These letters do not represent peace, but the passive, pathetic apologies for the absence of nuclear weapons. Ronin said the audience rushed to the exits when he announced that the column should be incinerated at the annual peace ceremonies and the country should bear nuclear weapons.

"Peace is the order, however imperfect, that results from agreement between states, and can only be sustained by that agreement," wrote Michael Howard in *The Invention of Peace*. Peace is "not an order natural to mankind: it is artificial, intricate and highly volatile." Japan would reach a better agreement on peace if the military possessed nuclear weapons to protect the peace, said Ronin. Peace is not a column of mundane letters to heads of state. The peace museums and souvenir counters only weaken the stories of nuclear survivance.

Akutagawa Ryunosuke published the story "Rashomon" in 1915. *Rashomon* the movie was actually based on another story, "In a Grove," and directed by Akira Kurasawa. "Rashomon" the story is set in twelfth-century Kyoto.

"The Atomic Bomb Dome is my Rashomon," wrote Ronin. The allegory of the first line of his journal, the short story, and the film, starts in the rain. Akutagawa's story opens with the servant of a samurai and an old woman in the twelfth century. The servant becomes a thief and the old woman tears hair from corpses that are dumped at Rashomon Gate in Kyoto. Ronin's journal opens with an orphan and a leper in the Atomic Bomb Dome in Hiroshima.

Akutagawa and Ronin are poets of disasters. Ronin created a ceremonial circle with a rope of twisted reeds in the tradition of sumo and the kabuki theater. Misery and mischance are exorcised by enter-

11

ing the circle, and, as he reveals later, by stomping on a picture of the emperor. The many corpses at the gate in the twelfth-century story are the shadows and nuclear dead of today.

That metaphor, human horseweeds, is borrowed from stories told by the *hibakusha*, the survivors, of the first flowers to bloom after the nuclear destruction of Hiroshima.

Ronin creates dialogue in a kabuki theater style, short, direct, positional words and sentences. He never discussed the style of his scenes, shifts of pronoun, transformations, or metaphorical tease, but he was strongly influenced by kabuki and sumo theater. Ronin created from perfect visual memory a theatrical, literary style. The characters, as in the scene with the leper, could be transposed in a nuclear allegory.

"Kabuki has attained its own blend of reality and unreality. It has created its own flavor which derives from hovering in its own way between the two poles. It now remains only a matter for the spectator to draw delight from the result," wrote Faubion Bowers in *Japanese Theater*. "There are moments on the stage of complete and literal representation of reality, followed by such fancy as to border on the nonsensical. Sometimes through the vast art resources available to kabuki, a perfect illusion is created, independent either of reality or of methods of creating fiction. Often this illusion is deliberately broken by the insertion of passages which of necessity force the spectator back into an awareness of himself and reminds him that what he has been seeing is merely a stage performance. For example, often actors will refer to themselves or to other actors in the course of the play by their names."

The kabuki theater is a measured transcendence of the obvious. The sound of *hyoshigi*, clacker sticks, and the curtain opens on a trace of sumo wrestlers, the circles, and narrow approach to the arena and stage. "Not only is the stylization of gestures and the marking out of ceremonial space common to both sumo and kabuki, but both performances also feature ceremonial stamping," wrote Yamaguchi Masao in "Sumo in the Popular Culture of Contemporary Japan."

Ronin posed in his black trousers and chrysanthemum shirt, sounded the *hyoshigi*, he told me, and created a nuclear kabuki theater in the registered haven of cultural shame, The Atomic Bomb Dome. His theatrical tease was nuclear, not feudal, and by his tricky

12

moves the illusions of peace were converted into stories of survivance. He was a teaser, not an appeaser, of nuclear peace.

The Peace Memorial Museum created the simulations that dominate the international politics of nuclear peace, and by boosters, souvenirs, and ritual tours weaken the traditional art of war and creative nuclear survivance.

The Japanese would rather rebuild a shrine as a traditional ritual than preserve a shrine, so the preservation of nuclear ruins is an ironic gesture. The ruins are true, beyond ritual preservation. Ronin pointed this out and announced at the annual peace party that the possession of nuclear weapons is a ritual balance, a traditional renewal of peace. Japan rebuilds shrines, why not peace by nuclear weapons?

"Preserving material objects is not the only way to conserve a heritage," wrote David Lowenthal in *The Past Is a Foreign Country*. "The great Ise Shinto temple in Japan is dismantled every twenty years and replaced by a faithful replica built of similar materials exactly as before. Physical continuity signifies less to the Japanese than perpetuating the techniques and rituals of re-creation." The techniques of peace, then, are ritual power and persuasion, and an active peace is created by the possession and renewal of nuclear weapons, not by passive memorials. Ask any samurai warrior about peace, shouted Ronin.

Ronin, by his presence in the ruins, created a ritual, a nuclear kabuki theater that teased and defied the preservation of peace. The Peace Memorial Museum, at the same time, constructed a theme park miniature of the Atomic Bomb Dome.

The kabuki theater is a ritual trace of the feudal past, the rue and craze of loyalty. "Kabuki seems to me to have the perfect balance between the sensuality and ritual which are the two poles of Japanese culture," wrote Alex Kerr in *Lost Japan*. "At the same time, there is a tendency in Japan towards over-decoration, towards cheap sensuality too overt to be art. Recognizing this, the Japanese turn against the sensual. They polish, refine, slow down, trying to reduce art and life to its pure essentials. From this reaction were born the rituals of tea ceremony, Noh drama and Zen. In the history of Japanese art you can see these two tendencies warring against each other."

Ronin was at war with traditions and simulations of peace, and in a mighty theater pose he advanced the outrageous idea of more nuclear weapons for peace and called for a supranational soldiery to enforce a nuclear peace. He borrowed that general idea from Albert Einstein, who wrote that mankind "can only gain protection against the danger of unimaginable destruction and wanton annihilation if a supranational organization has alone the authority to produce or possess these weapons." Einstein prepared that obscure message for the Peace Congress of Intellectuals at Wroclav in 1948.

Ronin boldly declared that the Japanese must vote to amend their constitution so the government can possess nuclear weapons as a theatrical balance of crucial, reductive rituals and pleasures. The nuclear kabuki theater is a ghost parade and the aesthetic symmetry of erotic power. Ronin surely lost his audience with these comments about a nuclear-armed soldiery.

2 Ronin of the Imperial Moat

Ronin is my name, as you know, and he has no parents to bear his stories, no memorable contours, creases, or manner of silence at night. My name is wild, a nuclear orphan, a samurai warrior without a master to exact my loyalty.

My parents are shadows.

That me of creation is the face of the other, the virtual you by my absence, and now we come to the same aesthetic vengeance of pronoun closures. You never had a calendar of promises, or cultural service, nothing to remember by the sanguinary rights of way. My father, the touch of you is mythic, the tease of our nature is forever in my story.

My parents might have posed for me in that photograph, the only trace of their romance and my conception. My father is set in his uniform, a sergeant and interpreter for the occupation army. He could have been an actor in the kabuki theater. I hear him at night in that theatrical voice. My mother wears a print dress decorated with giant chrysanthemums. She has a shy, coy smile, the coquette of romantic movies, a fugitive of war in *Casablanca*. Nightbreaker was her Humphrey Bogart. I was conceived there, in the grassy background of that snapshot, on the banks of the moat outside the Imperial Palace.

My royal conception.

Ronin must be my name, an orphan of the ruins outside the imperial moat. My only association is a snapshot simulation, and the evidence of my conception is an emulsive document. No dates, no records, and no relatives to celebrate my first, sudden breath in the world. Yet, the animistic stories of my survivance are perfect memories.

Death is my vision in the faint morning light. The master said, We are separated from a sense of presence because of our fear of death. Consider the instance of nuclear wounds every morning and the fear of death vanishes. The samurai warrior is never shamed by the fear of death.

My first death was by chance, a high fever at the orphanage. Great ravens crashed through the windows in a burst of brilliant light.

Suddenly, my feathers, yes my feathers, turned black and we soared over paddy fields and circled Mount Fuji.

I could see the orphanage in the distance and blue shivers of waves on the bay. We soared over docks, bridges, ceremonies, and military camps in the ruins of great cities. Many kabuki actors posed at a distance in traditional costumes. Tokyo, to the north, was an expanse of shanties and mounds of ashes. The Oasis of Ginza and the Imperial Palace were standing alone in the ruins of war.

My father was there, an interpreter for the occupation army. We soared over the imperial moat and my father watched me circle and dive right past his shoulder. My mother, in the abundant reign of the emperor, leaned back under the course of raucous ravens, raised those puffy chrysanthemums, and conceived an ainoko boy, me, on the moist grassy bank of that moat.

My second death was staged seven years later. Those vivid scenes of ravens last night after night. I could not resist the wonder and lust of the ruins and ran away to Tokyo. Most of the shanties were gone and the streets were cleared. The new public buildings obstructed some views of Mount Fuji. I camped for three nights in the memory of my parents, as they had appeared to me in my death dream as a raven. Many soldiers and bugi dancers were on the moat that night.

I stood in the same place my father watched me soar over his shoulder. The imperial ravens circled overhead and teased me on that grassy mound near the moat, the actual site of my conception in the wicked reign of the emperor. The ravens strutted on the empire bridge, bounced and croaked in the secure trees. My tatari, raven vengeance, in a nuclear theater.

I am memory, the destroyer of peace.

I am time, the vengeance of fake peace.

I am the father, a perfect memory.

I am death, the apparition of peace.

The idea of peace is untrue by nature, a common counterfeit of nations, but the most treasonous peace is based on nuclear victimry. There is no more treacherous a peace than the nuclear commerce of the Peace Memorial Museum in Hiroshima.

I am dead, the one who shatters nuclear peace. Some of my deaths have been reported in obituaries around the world. Dead Amerika Indian, hafu peace boy out to sea, was the report of my second death at the orphanage. I am forever an orphan, a tatari of the ruins, and the curse of commerce in the name of nuclear peace. Okichi praised the emperor in her renunciation note to the orphanage. The emperor was the very cause of her deceptions of paradise. She could not protect or nurture an ainoko, a hafu, or halfbreed child, born of the erotic sensibilities of the occupation. She did not mention my father by name, only by occupation, a translator, and by simulation, Amerika Indian who worked with Faubion Bowers and General Douglas MacArthur.

My father was almost there, only seven days short of my awkward presence at the hotel and my movie rush to overbear the absence of a natural touch of paternity. I wore my chrysanthemum shirt to remind him of his lover, my mother, the bugi dancer in a lost empire. My stories create perfect memories of my father.

I am dead once more, my most memorable samurai signature. The person you see has become a raven, a bear, a sandhill crane of anishinaabe totems. The nuclear orphan is a ronin, out of time, and with no crisscross of ancestors to avow and avoid in the ordinary.

The nature of my conception is imagic, the lost art of romance by the occupation, bugi dancers, the miniature emperor, and motion pictures. My resistance is more to manners, hand towels, the cast of mean cultural burdens, and amenable bows than to fate. Chance is my perfect sovereignty. My samurai loyalty, as an ainoko ronin, is to those who are menaced and demeaned by the decorous, unbearable commerce of nuclear peace. My vengeance as a tatari is for those who shame the nuclear dead with souvenirs of peace.

The simulations of nuclear peace will be complete when the hibakusha, the atomic bomb survivors, wear souvenir tee shirts with messages such as, "Hiroshima Loves Peace," or the entreaty "No More Hiroshima, August 6, 1945, A Day to Remember, Atomic Bombing of Hiroshima," or the understated "Hiroshima, A-Bomb Dome," with letters turned awry, as if the last two words had been cutely bombed. Tourists wear these vacuous shibboleths in the Peace Memorial Museum.

I mocked the awry worded tee shirt once at the museum and promised autographs to every tourist. The shop sold twice as many shirts that day, and no one, not even the peacemongers, caught the cruel irony of my autograph. I signed the name Paul Tibbets on each white shirt in bold cursive letters.

I wore my favorite tee shirt only once in the museum. Printed on the front, sleeve to sleeve, was a famous question about the atomic bomb, Is it big enough? The museum security guards teased me because they thought it was a gesture to my penisu. I never wore it again in public.

> The Peace Memorial Museum is a pathetic romance, a precious token to honor the state memory of a culpable emperor, as my mother might have done, with a sensuous, passive, origami pose of occupation victimry. Peace is the tease of the nuclear war no one dares to declare.

The Atomic Bomb Dome might have been the death of my father. He was an army interpreter with the advance occupation forces at the end of the war and traveled with investigators and photographers to Hiroshima.

> Near here, in my nuclear kabuki theater of the ruins, he was exposed to nuclear radiation, and twenty years later he was diagnosed with cancer. Hiroshima he might have survived, had he not been ordered a few years later to witness nuclear tests at Yucca Flat in Nevada. He retired from the army, nursed his nuclear wounds, and built a cabin at the headwaters of the Mississippi River near the White Earth Reservation in Minnesota. He recovered by meditation, native medicine, and the annual stories of survivance at the headwaters. Later, after many years as a roamer, he moved south with two other wounded veterans to the Hotel Manidoo in Nogales, Arizona.

My samurai deaths are traced by chance, by the occupation, the tricks and ironies of romance, and by eternal solitude, that elusive disease of orphans. The ainoko orphans with the disease are seldom deceived by the politics and commerce in nuclear souvenirs at the Peace Memorial Museum.

> The courage of a samurai warrior is hidden, his loyalty a tease, untested, wasted in a culture of simulated peace. The new political masters are separated by manners and compromised by the commerce of peace and victimry.

Manidoo Envoy

Ronin is the invincible samurai of his marvelous stories, the eternal teaser with a vacant smile, a simulated death pose. By his account he has been dead and buried seventeen times in the past decade.

Mifune, his nickname at the orphanage, vanished once as a raven in a fever vision, as you know, and his second death was staged, a swimming accident at Oiso Long Beach on Sagami Bay. "Orphan of Destiny Drowns in the Bay," might have been a headline story, but a week later a teacher found him on the Ginza in Tokyo. Who, at the time, would not run away to the Ginza?

Mifune vanished by tricky maneuvers, a strategic death, and an imagic rise in another name and place. This was not an unusual practice because the Japanese do the same thing for economic reasons. The common ruse is known as a "midnight run," a change of identities arranged by a third party. Thousands of people "disappear each year," wrote Alex Kerr in *Dogs and Demons*. "They discard their homes, change their identities, and move to another city, all to hide from the enforcers of Japan's consumer loans."

Mifune was entranced by scenes of *Chushingura*, and later *Genji Monogatari*, at the Kabukiza Theatre in Tokyo. He had a perfect memory of the scenes, and on the way back to the orphanage he described in visual detail the music, costumes, gestures, hairstyles, and cosmetics of the actors. He tormented his teachers by beating the *hyoshigi*, or clacker sticks, to announce his orphan play.

I was stationed there at about the same time, in the late fifties, as a legal investigator for the Army. I might have been at the very same theater with the orphan Mifune.

Nightbreaker had been reassigned ten years earlier, but even so we shared many stories and created our perfect memories of Japan. We were both *anishinaabe*, but from different reservations. I am a member of the Leech Lake Reservation, and he lived to the west, on the White Earth Reservation. The *anishinaabe* were named the Ojibwe and Chippewa.

Nightbreaker was an interpreter for the first year or so of the occupation, and then, because of his experience with investigators

19

at Hiroshima, he was assigned to Camp Desert Rock, a nuclear test site in Nevada.

Reason Warehime had similar experiences in Nagasaki and at the Nevada Test Site. He and Nightbreaker participated in atomic test site maneuvers. Reason noticed "when you get out closer that a lot of the sand had kind of melted into a glaze, like a brown glass. Then we got sunburn, and the guys all started throwing up in the truck going back," he told Carole Gallagher in *American Ground Zero*. Nightbreaker, Reason, and many other men lost their teeth and hair after the test. "It started every time you put your comb through your hair, you come out with a big gob of hair," said Reason. "It would have been three years later when they finally had to pull every tooth in my mouth because they had all turned black and came real loose."

The Nevada Test Site was their Rashomon.

The Kabukiza Theatre was destroyed at the end of the war and rebuilt in 1951. Faubion Bowers was first moved by the artistic tradition and then obsessed with the eminence of the kabuki actors. The first production he saw was *Chushingura* at the Kabukiza Theatre a year before the attack on Pearl Harbor. When he returned five years later, and two weeks after the surrender, as an officer and interpreter with the advance forces of the occupation, he had kabuki theater on his mind. The Japanese newspaper reporters and nervous officials were surprised when Bowers asked them about a famous kabuki actor, "Is Uzaemon still alive?"

Ichimura Uzaemon XV, "the leading *kabuki* actor of his generation, had died of a sudden heart attack" three months earlier, wrote Shiro Okamoto in *The Man Who Saved Kabuki*. Bowers said Uzaemon was his favorite actor, "the kind of star who could stir people up about anything. He was a legendary *kabuki* actor." Uzaemon is one of the oldest and most traditional names in the theater.

Bowers intervened to protect the kabuki theater from closure by the occupation. Military censors had reduced the great kabuki tradition to a tincture of feudalism, a dangerous art. Bowers, by his advertence, aesthetic enterprise, and compassion saved kabuki. He even brought food to the hungry actors in the early months of the occupation. Japan "has maintained in a living form most of the traditions of her earlier theaters," Bowers wrote five years later in his first book, *Japanese Theater*.

"Amidst the prohibitions of the postwar period, it was Bowers who expanded the range of permissible actors and plays," observed Ichimura Uzaemon XVII. "His existence was crucial. It was especially crucial for *kabuki*."

Mifune, by chance, saw Ichimura Uzaemon XVII years later in a production of *Chushingura*, or *The Treasury of Loyal Retainers*. Kabuki stage names are either inherited or bestowed. Uzaemon, Bowers, Nightbreaker, Mifune, and this storier are connected by chance and the perfect memories of kabuki theater.

Mifune was never the same after first seeing *Chushingura*, and then *Genji Monogatari* at the Kabukiza Theatre. He told me that he had already decided to live by more than one name and that he staged his death to defy the obvious outcome of an *ainoko* orphan in Japan. The kabuki theater inspired him, as it had his father and me, and he created spectacular turns of chance, funerals, and created many new identities.

Okichi might have named her son Atomu, for "atomic," as no other name was revealed. There are no public records of his birth; however, he has created a record of death in various names. Atomu was a teaser name at the orphanage, but he was soon given the name of the actor, Mifune. The name was inspired by the actor's scruffy nature, empty smile, and the surly, confident gestures of a samurai warrior. Mifune the orphan would more than consummate the nickname.

Toshiro Mifune appeared in several movies at the time. He was a yakuza in *Drunken Angel*, and he played the role of a bandit in *Rashomon*, directed by Akira Kurosawa. "Mifune has no drive for perfection, he has a drive for virtue," wrote Donald Richie in *Public People, Private People*. Mifune, the runaway orphan, on the other hand, had no earthly drive for virtue, compared to the actor, but he had a mighty desire for perfect memories.

Ronin was the nickname he earned after his adoption on the White Earth Reservation. The tribal council conferred his surname in memory of his father, Orion Browne. Ronin, as you know, created a gutsy visionary presence and perfect memory of his father at the Hotel Manidoo.

Bowers and Nightbreaker first met in military language school at Camp Savage in Minnesota. Bowers was drawn to the language because of his prewar experiences in Japan. Nightbreaker learned about haiku poetry from a Benedictine monk at the mission school on the reservation. Later he studied Japanese on his own for several years because he was fascinated by the adventures of Ranald MacDonald,

21

who was a native and, ironically, the first teacher of English in Japan. Nightbreaker had prepared to make the very same journey, more than a century later, but instead he enlisted, at the start of the war, in the Army. He spoke *anishinaabe*, which was not of much value to the military, and to prove his basic competence in Japanese he recited by memory several haiku poems and scenes from "Rashomon," a story by Akutagawa Ryunosuke. Father and son were inspired by the same authors and by kabuki theater.

Ronin, the son of an interpreter, carried out his father's vision and traced the enterprise of MacDonald from Ainu communities in Hokkaido to Nagasaki. He created perfect memories of his father on the road of visions, and that was how he returned with his father, a visionary union, to Japan.

Ronin was determined to find his parents, but he had only a note and photograph to represent his family. These rather cryptic documents were attached to his clothes when he was abandoned, apparently by his mother, at the Elizabeth Saunders Home. He was about two years old at the time and had no memory of his mother.

Ronin created a new era calendar to name the year of his surrender, the tricky reign of the *ainoko* orphans. Atomu 3, on the atomic *gengo* calendar, marked the reign of nuclear peace, or the number of years since Little Boy, the first atomic bomb, destroyed Hiroshima. His system mocked the imperial reign of the emperors, Showa for Hirohito, Heisei for Akihito. "This marriage of calendar to sovereign is not a traditional way of counting time in Japan, but rather a highly modern way of engaging in symbolic politics," wrote John Dower in *Japan in War and Peace.*

Okichi wrote, "atomu ainoko, jugatsu 1946, amerika indian chichi worku by babinu bowu to macatu." She meant, of course, that her son was born a *hafu* in October 1946, his father was American Indian, and he worked with Major Faubion Bowers, the interpreter and assistant military secretary to General Douglas MacArthur, Supreme Commander of the Allied Powers. Nightbreaker was in the same occupation unit as Bowers. They were close friends from Camp Savage.

Mifune and thousands of *ainoko*, or *hafu* children, were the untouchables of war and peace in two countries. Japan would never embrace the progeny of the occupation, and his father had no idea that he existed. The United States, at the same time, enacted very restrictive immigration laws. Mifune was actually adopted by the tribal government at the White Earth Reservation.

"Getting permission for half-Japanese adopted children to enter the United States was extremely difficult because of the racial exclusion provision of the immigration laws," observed Yukiko Koshiro in *Trans-Pacific Racisms*. "The task facing Japan was to find a way to assimilate this 'inferior' racial group into society. The absence of their American fathers made their situation different from other minority groups."

Mifune was one of many "Orphans of Destiny" at the Elizabeth Saunders Home at Oiso, a town south of Kamakura on Sagami Bay. Miki Sawada established the orphanage about three years after the end of the war. She was related to the founder of Mitsubishi, and her husband, an ambassador before the war, was a representative to the United Nations.

Sawada "remained the foremost advocate of the separation policy, which she believed would protect the children's 'mental and physical handicaps' from the hostile outside world. Only in a shielded world would they learn to gain self-esteem and become strong and secure," wrote Yukiko Koshiro.

Mifune, and the other orphans, studied two languages to endure as *ainoko* in two cultures. Sawada taught the children to "serve as a future link of the two nations." Ronin would be more than a dubious, tractable connection of separatist nations. He would establish a nuclear kabuki theater in the ruins and forever haunt the obedient peacemongers.

The Japanese Ministry of Welfare declared that there were some five thousand mixed-blood children born during the first few years of the occupation of Japan. Others were convinced there were as many as two hundred thousand children fathered by occupation soldiers.

Mifune was fortunate that he was abandoned at the Elizabeth Saunders Home. The nurses and teachers were both sensitive and strong, but a generation later he would overturn the passive notions of peace that he had once been taught.

Sawada was a dedicated, honorable humanist, and persuasive in the world, but she could not overcome government resistance to more liberal adoption policies for orphans.

Military investigators finally identified the errant sergeant in the photograph and located his last residence. Nightbreaker had retired with a medical disability after fifteen years of active service. When the military assumed he had died of radiation disease the

23

orphanage negotiated with tribal leaders at the White Earth Reservation. Nightbreaker was highly respected for his sense of tradition, he was a native speaker of *anishinaabe*, a great storier, and was honored for his military service.

The White Earth Reservation petitioned federal officials to set aside immigration laws and allow a native child to return to his family. Mifune was an unusual adoption, as the tribal government had the support of the state delegation in Congress. Mifune Browne, as he was named in the petition, an *anishinaabe* and Japanese orphan, age fifteen, was adopted by special legislation and without a specific family. Congress was eager to please tribal officials because they wanted easy access to natural resources on the reservation.

Mifune, and then Ronin, is a citizen of Japan and the United States. His adoption was political, not familial, and so he remains a citizen by birth of Japan.

Japan was forever in his memories, a road of chance not to be taken twice, but then he learned of his father's vision, alas, too late to recover the touch of his humor, here at the Hotel Manidoo.

"I am memory, the destroyer of peace," wrote Ronin. Surely he mocked J. Robert Oppenheimer, the nuclear physicist and director of the Los Alamos Laboratory. Oppenheimer had studied scriptures in Sanskrit and remembered a verse from the Bhagavad-Gita, "I am become Death, the destroyer of worlds," after the first atomic bomb test at the Trinity site near Alamogordo, New Mexico. Ronin was aware of at least two translations of the Bhagavad-Gita. Kees Bolle translated the same verse, "I am Time who destroys man's world." Stephen Mitchell's version, "I am death, shatterer of worlds, annihilating all things," slightly alters the tone. Ronin wrote that he was time, memory, and death, the destroyer of the pretense of nuclear peace. He would destroy the nuclear peace simulations at the Peace Memorial Museum.

Colonel Paul Tibbets was the pilot of the *Enola Gay*, the plane that released Little Boy, the first atomic bomb, over Hiroshima. For that he received the Distinguished Service Cross on his return to the airbase at Tinian Island in the South Pacific.

Niels Bohr asked J. Robert Oppenheimer at Los Alamos, "Is it big enough?" Mary Palevsky commented on the context of that question in her book *Atomic Fragments*. Hans Bethe explained in a conversation on nuclear arms control that the question meant, is the bomb "big enough to make war impossible?"

Ronin borrowed the idea of peace as the "nuclear war no one dares to declare" from *The Invention of Peace* by Michael Howard. "It has often been said that between 1945 and 1989 peace was kept by a war that nobody dared to fight."

Ronin adapted the phrase "the abundant reign of the emperor" from the *norito*, the ancient traditions, rituals, and prayers of Shinto. The Hirano Festival contains the entreaty "All these various offerings do I place, raising them high like a long mountain range, and present. Receive, then, tranquilly, I pray, and these noble offerings; Bless the reign of the Emperor as eternal and unmoving, Prosper it as an abundant reign."

The *tatari* are spirits of retribution and vengeance, a curse of *kami*, a spirit of nature and ancestors. The "Japanese had feared the *tatari* of the dead, that is, the vengeance of people who had been killed, or killed themselves, after being falsely accused or unfairly treated," Maurice Pinguet wrote in *Voluntary Death in Japan*. "The vengeful could persecute its enemies, strike at the innocent in passing, and unleash all manner of scourges."

Donald Richie described the firebombed wasteland of Tokyo in 1947. Mount Fuji was visible, one winter day early in the occupation, from the Ginza. "Between me and Fuji was a burned wasteland, a vast and blackened plain where a city had once stood," he wrote in his journal, later published in *The Donald Richie Reader*. "Mount Fuji stood sharp on the horizon, growing purple, then indigo in the fading light," he observed. The Kabukiza Theatre and Mitsukoshi Department Store were in ruins, but the mountain was resplendent. "Fuji looked much as it must have for Hokusai and Hiroshige."

Mount Fuji, a mighty, natural spirit, remains the same, only the views have changed since the occupation. Mifune would have had a similar view of the mountain when he ran away from the orphanage. The Ginza today is a wild, postmodern, international trade center.

3 Ronin of Sagami Bay

The sword was mine, a natural, driftwood bounty shaped by steady ocean currents to fit my tiny hands. I raised that sword over my head, slowly turned about to my shadow, and practiced the cuts, thrusts, and blocks of a seven-year-old hafu ronin on the beach, the serious, solitary, ingenuous pantomime of a samurai warrior.

My wooden sword, a natural contour, had washed ashore near the orphanage at Oiso Long Beach on Sagami Bay. I was roused by a sense of tradition and secret power, and at first touch that sword cast a mighty shadow on the beach.

The ocean gave me another chance to create a lasting presence in the world. My heart beat with the waves as the bony clouds raced out to sea. Nearby, four ravens strutted on the beach and teased me with garrulous croaks. The sun warmed the sand, my hands, and drew me into a natural pocket of solace stories.

Suddenly, a strange animal, a mongrel with soft webbed feet, stole my sword right out of my hand. He ran down the beach and into the trees. There, the mongrel changed from a sandy coat to shades of pale green and then vanished in the luscious blues and hues of the forest.

I heard hushed voices, but my vision was blurred by the bright leaves and mighty trees. I must have lost consciousness. Sometime later a tribe of water tricksters, curious, moist, miniature humans, surrounded me in the green. They were nude, bluish at the creases, and comely armed with wooden swords, but not one of them meant to threaten me. I pointed my finger at the outlaw mongrel who stole my sword.

Who is that mongrel?
Kaisoku, the pirate.
Who are you?
The mighty nanazu.
What name?
Bay water nanazu.
Right here?
Twice by humor.
No, how so?

Free, naturally.

No school?

Only a trickster academy.

The nanazu turned around, a wobbly pirouette, and burst into hardy laughter. Then, with every gust and flurry of sound, they raised swords and bounced from one foot to the other, a natural dance of miniature tricksters.

Chaimu, a healer, caressed my cheeks with her moist, webbed hands, and several other nanazu peered into my mouth, ears, and other places and parts. Their touch was soft, warm, and dewy.

The nanazu were born miniature, and mature. There were no obvious children, no scent of suckers, primal cries, or baby cargo. They never mentioned age in their creation stories, and they never used the words, toshi totta, elderly, or toshi o toru, to grow old.

The nanazu were curious about my navel and tiny penis. I was shied by their moist webbed hands, as you can imagine, and when my penisu arose they shouted the word, kyojin, kyojin, kyojin, over and over, and danced around me with swords raised high over their heads. The word kyojin means a giant person, a natural nanazu tease.

Nori, the poet of the nanazu, leaned closer and told me stories about trickster creation, the vast empire of water and stones. They were vigilant, miniature warriors, and they watched my penisu rise and wane by the sound of their words. Swords were raised to words of ascent, and downcast by other words. Nori said the nanazu were engendered by the natural tease of words, and that words created me in a tricky, visionary story.

What is your word?

My name?

No, your promise.

Mifune.

Not your name.

My word?

Your mighty words.

Atomu hafu.

Nori and the other nanazu raised their swords, leaped into the nearest trees, and perched on the wide boughs, a natural, wild sway. Overhead the lean blues melted into the greens, and the nanazu shouted, Atomu hafu, over and over, Atomu hafu arise with our swords near the shore.

Kaisoku, the mongrel pirate, returned with my sword and turned sandy again when he sat beside me. I could hear crickets and many frogs in the green, ravens on the wings, and the rush of ocean waves in the distance.

Nori told me to shout out three natural words to create a poem, a new world of perfect memory. The nanazu bounced out of the trees and circled me once more in the blue shadows. They waited in silence to hear the sound of my precise words.

> Natural words?
> Three words.
> Samurai sword.
> Two words.
> Yes, one more.
> Who gave you that sword?
> My ocean bounty.
> No, the mighty nanazu.
> This is your gift?

Nori said my wooden sword was a gift of the nanazu, the tricksters of rivers and ocean waves. I was shied again, and rescued at the same time when he shouted three words into the crotch of a tree. Minutes later the trees seemed to consider the words and then, at a great distance, a voice repeated three scenes of an imagistic haiku poem.

> ancient pond
> the nanazu leap
> sound of water

Nori told me to throw fresh, small cucumbers into rivers and the ocean whenever my words seem to wander, weaken, and escape unheard into the mushy curse of crowds. Throw cucumbers into the water when your visions and dance of words are about to vanish in the undertow of a crowd. The water is our perfect memory.

> The water holds our names, words, and stories, but not our souls, said Nori. Our souls have no words or memory. The spirit of the nanazu is a grant, and a bounty. Your soul is a story only when you give it away.

The teachers were worried about my absence. I could hear their urgent voices in the distance. They searched the grounds and found me asleep on the beach that afternoon. Nairon, one of the teachers, told me she never believed for a minute my stories of the nanazu water tricksters. Firumu, the lean, frail, almost transparent nurse, revealed that the mongrel in my story was similar to the dog that changed colors in a short story by Ryunosuke Akutagawa.

> Shiro is his name.
> Whose name?
> That dog in the story.
> Kaisoku is his name.
> Pirate dog?
> Yes, a water mongrel.
> Nickname?
> Kaisoku.
> Really?
> Call me Shiro.
> Maybe inu Mifune.
> Take my soul.

Sumo, the head of the school, confiscated my samurai sword later that afternoon. I was overcome by an unbearable sense of betrayal, and evermore that memory has turned on a solitary word, confiscation, the outright theft of my wooden weapon of survivance. I was seven years old that autumn, and that wooden sword was my secret, my samurai treasure, a great and memorable grant of the water tricksters. Sumo discovered my secret, but she would not listen to my nanazu stories. She banned weapons and any toys of war at the school.

> My sword, my sword.
> No weapons of war.
> My sword is wooden.
> Driftwood war?
> The nanazu are tiny.
> No war toys.
> Samurai tradition.
> No weapons.
> Please, my bounty.
> No war toys.
> My sword is a story.
> Alas, not a story here.
> Take my soul.

Sumo confiscated my sword and because of my strong and lasting protests over a natural driftwood weapon, a grant of the nanazu, she promised to return it to me in the future.

What future?

When you are adopted.

No, never, never.

Weapons are not our future.

Take my soul.

Sumo warned the students that swords and warrior traditions were forbidden by the occupation. Tricky vengeance was on my mind. I disrupted a convocation several years later with an ironic, impulsive performance. I shouted, My skin is hafu, but my heart is mine, not an orphan heart. I was encouraged by a story about the great entertainer Josephine Baker, a friend of Sumo. "You have white skins but black hearts," she told the other dancers and then walked out of a racist theater. "I have a black skin but I have a white heart." She was a hafu of another world.

Sumo was silent, dispirited, worried about my commitment to retaliation, and yet she honored my persistence and curiosity, and taught me the values of bushido, the way, discipline, moral code, and loyalty of samurai survivance. She encouraged the talents and interests of every orphan at the school. Sammy had polio and learned how to walk. Matsuo learned to play the organ. Ikuo was a court jester. Eunice was pure, beautiful, and she was a real Indian. Her father was a soldier from the Punjab.

I moved on to other visions as a samurai warrior and forgot about my wooden sword. Naturally, the nanazu water tricksters are forever in my stories of the ocean. Many years later the memory of that sword became my literary thrust, my signature of bushido, and my eternal loyalty as an orphan raised and educated at the Elizabeth Saunders Home.

The emperor renounced his divine power, the occupation created a constitutional monarchy, hafu children were abandoned by the thousands, and she gave me a home. Sumo was an honorable warrior, true to her word as a secret ronin in the samurai tradition. Several months after my adoption she returned that wooden sword to me at the White Earth Reservation.

Sumo admired my imagination, and, at the same time, she teased me about my stories of the nanazu tricksters. She was never convinced that water tricksters honored me with a driftwood sword. She was educated, determined, and overcame the burdens of war to protect hafu orphans, but she never met the miniatures with moist, webbed hands and wooden swords. She would agree, though, that our hafu souls are a great bounty.

Manidoo Envoy

Sumo is a nickname for Miki Sawada, the resolute founder of the Elizabeth Saunders Home. Mifune gave her that name because of the way she rescued orphans and raised money. She was clever, prudent, and steadfast in that sacred ring of tradition, mission, and corporate philanthropy. Pearl Buck, the vainglorious author of *The Good Earth*, once falsely accused her of taking financial advantage of sponsors.

Sumo wrestlers throw salt into the ring, and the children at the orphanage told stories about how she tossed salt around the world to win support for orphans. Sumo Sawada was their salty protector and diplomat.

The *nanazu* mongrel, a visionary trickster that changes colors, hints at moral lessons of devotion and conversions in "The Dog, Shiro," a short story by Ryunosuke Akutagawa. Shiro is a loyal dog, but because of one mistake he must earn back his color and the recognition of his home and family.

The Kappa are comparable to the *nanazu* water tricksters by cultural traces and scenes of perky miniatures. Ronin told me the *nanazu*, a name that evokes *naanabozho*, the *anishinaabe* trickster, are real, and are masters of the *bokken*, or wooden sword. At the time of his experience, almost fifty years ago, he had never heard about the river monsters in "The Kappa" by Akutagawa.

The Kappa are short, devious, and fishy. The *nanazu* are short, ironic, and dewy. The only direct comparable connection is that both miniature tricksters are webbed and watery. The stories contain the ancillary advice to throw cucumbers into the water to divert the attention of water demons and envious tricksters.

Ronin praised his spirit as a grant of the dewy *nanazu*, and later, when he lived on the reservation, that notion of a giveaway soul became a mythic wishbone, a tricky *naanabozho* pledge of security. The *nanazu*, he reasoned, were not bound by linear time, economic ventures, or market value, so a generous grant of spirit was almost frivolous. He perceived that his giveaway gestures were not taken seriously, so he decided to pawn his soul, and the covenant, the real treasure of his soul, was promissory.

Nori interposes a "*nanazu* leap" in the second line of a famous haiku poem by Matsuo Basho. A frog leaps in the original. The turn of the haiku scene, frog to *nanazu*, is a double irony. A Kappa, not the frog, leaps in "The Kappa," the story by Akutagawa. Tokk, the spirit of a poet in the story, is questioned by a member of the Spiritualist Research Society. The poem "An ancient pond, a frog leaps, sound of water" is recited, but no one can remember the name of Basho. "Do you believe it to be a masterpiece?" Tokk, the spirit, answered, "I think it's really not bad at all. Only, if he had selected a Kappa instead of a frog, it would have been still more dazzlingly brilliant."

Ronin said the *nanazu* are real and insisted that he has never read "The Kappa." Basho is my spirit poet, he said, and then recited several haiku poems. Ronin told me that he traveled with the spirit of the master poet and his father on the roads north to Matsushima Bay.

Ronin was inspired by stories of Ikkyu Sojun, the fifteenth-century eccentric monk and poet who wore a wooden sword. That comic pose became a wily tease of mortality. Ronin raised his sword in the same tradition of trickster signatures, and by the adoption of ancient stories, the *nanazu* gift of a wooden sword, and the *bokken* tradition, he matured as a warrior of survivance.

The finest *bokken* were carved from white oak and ebony. Ronin carried a driftwood *bokken*, downed in the mountains and then shaped by the ocean currents.

Dave Lowry, a traditional swordsman, pointed out in *Bokken: Art of the Japanese Sword* that many "wooden swords are now made in Taiwan." The wood is light with a wide grain, and has a "poorly balanced feel." The *bokken* "should always be thought of as a real weapon," he wrote. "This attitude encourages the seriousness of purpose that will set the practitioner on the correct path toward mastery."

Mifune was roused by any chance.

Ronin is a master of many poses.

Nori, the wise *nanazu* poet, earned the word for edible seaweed as a nickname. Chaimu, the healer, is a name that means "chime," and she created that sound, *chaimu no oto*, the sound of chimes, by her moist touch. The word *kyojin* means "giant," an ironic notice of a seven-year-old *penisu* on the rise, and *inu* means "dog."

Nairon, the teacher, earned that nickname because she wore nylon stockings in Tokyo. Firumu, the frail, undernourished nurse who barely survived the war, appeared almost transparent in the bright summer light. She was like an exposed negative film, and so the nickname.

Ronin created many nicknames, sometimes more than one, for the teachers and nurses at the Elizabeth Saunders Home. Mifune was his first nickname, and that verifies a nickname practice at the time, but who created nicknames for teachers and nurses is not certain. Ronin may have created some nicknames later for the tone of his stories. Sumo, for instance, is not mentioned as a nickname in *The Last of These: Miki Sawada and Her Children* by Elizabeth Anne Hemphill. Ronin, his current nickname, as you know, was earned at the White Earth Reservation.

Miki Sawada first met Josephine Baker in the nineteen-thirties in Paris. Renzo Sawada, her husband, was the acting chief of the Japanese Mission. Baker was a *hafu* of two cultures, a Spanish father and an African American mother. A sensational dancer and entertainer, she was discovered in La Revue Nègre at the Théâtre des Champs Elysées.

Sawada and Baker renewed their friendship in New York City. The Ziegfeld Follies, a theatrical review, contracted Baker to be in the cast. Rehearsals were underway when she overheard a racialist comment by a chorus girl: "We should wear masks so that our boyfriends don't see us dancing with a Negro." Baker turned and said, "You want to wear a mask because of your poor dancing." The rehearsals were strained, and then the other chorus girls "refused to appear in the grand finale with Josephine Baker," wrote Hemphill. Baker shouted, "You have white skin and black hearts—I have a black skin, but I have a white heart." She "strode down the aisle" and out of the theater. "Miki thought her dramatic exit worthy of the Kabuki theater."

Baker performed in several concerts to benefit the Elizabeth Saunders Home in Japan. Mifune was eight years old, and evermore entranced by the elegant and stately chanteuse. He was inspired by the story of her exit lines at the Ziegfeld Follies. "My skin is *hafu*, but my heart is mine, not an orphan heart," he said in her honor. "The more the *hafu* parts, the greater the story," he told me. "Two halves are a mighty entity."

The Code of Warriors is bushido, the ethics, or way, of the samurai. The *Hagakure*, an evocative narrative by a samurai, declares that bushido, "or the way of the samurai, means death. Whenever you confront a choice between two options, simply choose the one that takes you more directly to death."

Eiko Ikegami observed in *The Taming of the Samurai* that the unusual power of the *Hagakure* "derives from its fundamental tone, which evokes and stimulates the most dangerous part of the samurai ethos: a fusion of class honor and personal self-esteem in the crucible." Ikegama argued that to "live as a samurai was to confront death, if only imaginatively, every day. The message of this behavioral ideal is eccentric but spiritual."

Ronin is a storier of death, and by the evocation of bushido, his many deaths are imagic, an eternal end and tricky resurrection by another name, in another character and presence. Death is his kabuki theater, his native giveaway spirit.

Ronin creates words, names, and turns combinations of words, some native words, to intimate desire and the critical thrust of new ideas. "Survivance," for instance, is not merely a variation of "survival," the act, reaction, or custom of a survivalist. By "survivance" he means a vision and vital condition to endure, to outwit evil and dominance, and to deny victimry. Ronin told me that survivance is wit, natural reason, and "perfect memory." Dominance, he said, is inherited, "a dead voice pursued by trickster stories." Tragic wisdom is heard in stories of survivance, not dominance.

Dominance, he declared, honors victimry.

Natural reason is an active sense of presence, the tease of the natural world in native stories. Ronin said that natural reason is the use of nature, animals, birds, water, and any transformation of the natural world as direct references and signifiers in language.

Perfect memories arise from natural reason, communal wit, experience, and native trickster stories. Ronin told me that the *nanazu* are created and teased by natural reason. His idea of perfect memory evokes the comparative ideas of collective memory and "exact imagination."

Theodor Adorno argued by theory, logic, and aesthetics his own fate and traces of experience as "exact imagination." His focus of imagination is configurational, or the compact of elements and episodes, rather than creative. The exact details and arrangement are endorsed by imagination, the actual configuration of material and experience that reveals the inseparable and yet tricky connection of objective and subjective activity. Possibly, the course of experience is synecdochic.

36

"The more the observer contributes, the greater the energy with which he penetrates into the work of art, and he gains access to objectivity," wrote Adorno in *Aesthetic Theory*. "He participates in objectivity where his energies, including the energy of his deviant subjective 'projections,' are extinguished in the work of art. The subjective digression may completely miss the work of art, but without it no objectivity becomes visible."

Shierry Weber Nicholsen observed in *Exact Imagination, Late Work: On Adorno's Aesthetics* that "undisciplined subjectivity," as natural reason and perfect memory might imply, seems to be the "opposite of exact imagination" but is rather the "means to objective understanding." Ronin has not read Adorno, or anyone else on the subject, but he might agree that his idea of natural reason is an objective experience that arises in subjective, creative references to nature.

"Subjectivity and objectivity in aesthetic experience, then, are completely interdependent," wrote Nicholsen. "On the one hand, it is through subjectivity that objectivity is attained. On the other hand, if the subject's experience imitates the dynamics crystallized in the artwork, then subjective aesthetic experience is very much like the work of art itself."

4 Ronin of the Peace Park

Atomu 57 on my calendar of fake peace. This is my promissory time, eight fifteen, my gate of giveaway souls, and my rites of passage in the ruins of the Atomic Bomb Dome. Remember the abundant reign of the emperor in the era of nuclear peace. The ghost parade is my tricky empire of Rashomon Gate.

I poured gasoline on the Pond of Peace at the Peace Memorial Museum. Thin, elusive ribbons caught the morning light and spread across the water in magical hues. The phantom plumes reached out from the Cenotaph and almost touched the Flame of Peace.

I counted the seconds and threw a lighted match into the water at eight fifteen of the hour, the start of the ghost parade. The fire burst, tumbled, and roared over the pond. That moment was a tribute to natural reason and perfect memories.

The fire wavered, curved higher, bounced downwind, and never once licked back at my hand. The flames that seared the fake peace that morning last forever. Shadows, faint traces of a ghost parade, were burned on the concrete containment walls around the pond. The mighty ravens croaked at a great distance.

A fire engine arrived a few minutes later, and then the police searched the area. I waited near the ruins, on the stone stairs to the river, and cast fresh cucumbers into the dark water to tease and appease the nanazu tricksters. The police questioned the roamers who were camped on the other side of the river. I shouted my hafu nickname and waved at the police. They stared back at me and then bowed slightly. The roamers were amused and waved wildly.

I became a sandhill crane, and bounced with my wings trimmed close to the side, and danced down the stones to the riverside. My forehead turned reddish, and my dance turns were erotic and crazy.

Oshima was touched by my dance, but he warned me to be cautious, more discrete around the police. They shame by turns of sympathy, he told me, and they have too much authority. You have none, ainoko of the ruins, and the roamers watched you light the sacred pond this morning.

Little Boy souvenirs.

Not a wise story.
Roamers are storiers.
Yes, and twicers.
Who would listen?
The police.
Not by stories.
Always by story.
What stories?
The leper story.
Empire evidence.
No, fear by story.
So many, many versions.

Several roamers on the other side of the river leaned out and pointed in our direction. I shouted my hafu nickname once more and danced at the riverside. The police radioed for assistance and then hurried across the Aioi Bridge. The ravens soared over the river, circled the police, and then perched on the skeleton beams in the ruins.

The police discovered the ghostly shadows on the wall around the Pond of Peace. They sighed for shame, public shame, and then copied each shadow into a notebook. There was no other evidence of a fire or trace of the cause. The stories of the fire were elusive.

Suddenly, several police cars were on the scene. They asked our names, our residences, and continued, respectfully, with the usual manner of an interrogation. Oshima refused to speak because of his memories of betrayal. The last time he dared to trust the police he was removed from his world, his family, and with no medical or legal consideration sentenced to a leprosarium for sixty years.

The police might have shouted to threaten his silence, but instead avoided him when they discovered his blunt fingers and the sores on his face. They shunned the leper, secured their white gloves, and surrounded me. I resisted by shouting my nicknames, and refused to speak Japanese.

You namae.
No, no.
No namae.
Yes, name.
You namae.
Atomu Ainoko.

You adana.
Mifune.
No adana.
Ronin Browne.
No adana.
Take my soul.

Oshima was ordered to leave the area and never return. He boldly refused to move, and sat in silence on the stone stairs to the river. Tosuto, the mongrel, and three ravens waited nearby. I was detained at last in the back of a police car.

Kitsutsuki, that surly veteran with a wooden leg, and several other roamers rushed over the bridge and tried to intervene, but the police would not listen to their stories. They were very worried about us, and they told me that the police had abused their generosity and distorted their gestures and stories. Kitsutsuki executed a mighty frown, and he was famous for his frowns. He told the police that we might know, but not as perpetrators, who was responsible for the fire on the Pond of Peace.

I was taken to a koban, a police post a few blocks away near the river, but was never arrested. The koban was surrounded by giant sunflowers, and on the inside, every windowsill and counter was decorated with potted plants. The post had a strong scent of mold, probably from the soil in hundreds of pots. Out back in a shed there were bicycles, a piano, a golf bag, giant ceramic pots, many lost or abandoned objects, and several wooden legs.

Osaka, a former catch girl, told me later that she has favored the local koban for several years. By favor she meant tea and flowers. She was grateful to the police for their discrete protection at a time when yakuza creditors were in pursuit. She moved from another city, a midnight run, to avoid high interest debts. The debt was paid in time, and since then she has dutifully served teas and decorated the tiny post with flowers. Surely she would have done something else if the senior officer had not been secretly in love with flowers, or as many neighbors might say, covertly in love with the bearer of the flowers.

I was directed to sit in a sturdy, straight, and narrow wooden chair, stationed in the center of the room and in front of a shiny metal desk. The light shimmered through the windows. I removed my coat, and the police pointed at the words on my tee shirt.

What mean?

Bomb, big enough?

What bomb?

Atomu bakudan.

I raised my hands, puffed my cheeks, traced the shape of a mushroom cloud in the air, and then pointed to the words on my chest, Is it big enough?

> The police stared at me, lighted cigarettes, and then turned away in silence. They were gentle and friendly at first, and then apologetic for the delay. An interpreter had been summoned from the central police station.

The real fun started when the police interpreter arrived in a huge van, a mobile koban. The van wheezed to the curb, the doors cracked open, and a tiny woman leaped out. Tonase was dressed to the nines in a blue uniform. The short black visor of her peaked hat rode low and almost covered her eyes. The gold star on the peak of her hat shined in the morning light.

> She pointed at the words, one by one, on my tee shirt, looked to the side, blushed, and then said something about the size of my penisu in Japanese. The other police were stunned by her comment, and then they burst into laughter.

The police misunderstand the message, but it was too late to explain the history. I laughed only to rescue my sense of presence and pointed at her socks as she crossed her legs behind the desk. The bright white socks were trimmed with bloated cartoon images of cats and chickens. She wagged one foot and stared at me.

> Please, your names.
>
> Your names?
>
> Yes, your names.
>
> Ainoko Mifune Ronin Browne.
>
> Japanese citizen?
>
> Big laugh.
>
> Amerika name?
>
> Nickname, adana.
>
> Yes, adana?
>
> Mifune.
>
> Clan name?
>
> Big laugh.
>
> You citizen?

Born ainoko, an orphan.
Please, you ages.
You ages?
Yes, you ages.
Atomu fifty six.
What time?
Fifty six in the ruins.

Mister Browne, we know you are ainoko, and we respect you, but you left many years ago, a hafu adopted by Amerika Indians in United States. You stay, never return to Japan.

Japan is my country.
How you return?
By Ainu.
By who?
Ainu in Hokkaido.
Ainu shaman.
No Ainu.
Ainu boaters.
You joke me.
Yes, yes, but truly.

The cats and chickens vanished as she uncrossed her legs. She leaned to the side and told the others about the minority boaters in Japanese. The police looked at each other, then at me, and laughed politely.

You joke everyone.
Yes, by irony.
Ainu gone.
Not the bears.
Now, where you live?
Rashomon Gate.
Please, no jokes.
I live with a leper in the ruins.
What leper?
Oshima, the kabuki leper.
What ruins?
Atomic Bomb Dome.
You joke me again.
Big enough?
No jodan, joke.

You hear my tease.
Amerika tease?
Tease of interrogatory.
Who are you?
Samurai warrior.
No, no sense.
Bushido survivance.
No jodan.
Buy my soul.
What soul?
Samurai soul.
No buy.
Take my soul.

The courage and loyalty of a samurai warrior remains hidden, never tasted, the savor wasted in a time of sentimental, simulated peace and victimry.

Suddenly, the show of courtesy had ended in the koban. She raised her right hand, pointed, and shouted at me. The sympathetic manner of initial police interrogations had turned to verbal abuse, but the pitch of her voice was not convincing. My resistance was by tease and irony, not by deceptive tactics and practices. The police, as usual, would never believe that my ironic confessions and stories were true. So, my best defense was a tricky style of sincerity.

Now, where you sleep?
National treasure.
On street?
Nuclear ruins.
Where?
Ground zero.
Why wooden sword?
Honor my nanazu.
What name?
The nanazu water tricksters.
You crazy.
Take my soul.

She stood firmly behind the desk and shouted at me over and over, kyoki, kyoki, lunacy, lunacy. Where do you sleep around, around, around in the park? The other police were amused and turned away. I stood, and then turned away, but she order me to sit back down in the chair.

> Who mother?
> Okichi.
> Your mother?
> Okichi.
> No, no.
> Yes, yes.
> No, no, no.
> Take my soul.

The police burst into laughter, doubled over, and staggered out of the room. She tried to hold back the derisive laughter, but she could not control the humor over that teaser name. She removed her hat, laughed loudly, and pounded her hands on the desk. Then she recovered and started over.

> Who are you?
> Ronin Browne.
> No, honto ni nai, not truly.
> Atomu ainoko.
> Yes, ainoko of the ruins.
> Where did you buy those socks.
> What socks?
> The bloated chickens.
> My daughter.
> Okichi, my mother.
> You, you, crazy.
> Yes, me, me ronin.
> You, police maniac.

The interrogation ended with counterteases. The interpreter boarded the mobile koban. I walked out of the koban on my hands. The police cheered and then drove me back to the river, the scene of the crime. They opened the car door for me, bowed slightly, and waved me out. I heard them say, Police maniac, police maniac. They laughed, bowed, and drove away.

Oshima and several roamers waited for me in the ruins. We cooked rice and vegetables and told stories about the police. The mongrels, feral cats, and other creatures of the ruins were there in time to eat. Tofu, a calico cat, and Tosuto, a wirehaired, crispy mongrel, were always together at the park, the only wild tofu eaters in the ruins. Tosuto, shied by the envy of the other roamer mongrels, was a savage over a photograph of Hirohito.

Why the emperor?

Poetic justice.

By photographs?

Savaged in the ruins.

By a mongrel?

Yes, Tosuto.

Mongrel justice.

Tosuto, for some obscure reason barked, pounced, and stomped the picture of the emperor every time he crossed the circle. Maybe he lost relatives in the war, eaten by soldiers or abused by empire pedigrees. Hirohito was dismembered in the ruins by a ferocious mongrel.

Kitsutsuki once devoured the beaten, photographic remains of the emperor. Hirohito and the militarists aroused the lower pick of officers to abuse their soldiers. The emperor, by his divine, remote manner, deserted the hibakusha of Hiroshima. The empire was a wicked curse that haunted my mother.

Samurai traditions were obscure, the old masters were muted, and the emperor incited the cruelties of the war in his name. Rightly, you see, the emperor on his white horse is always underfoot in the ruins of the Atomic Bomb Dome.

Later that night we created another tricky kabuki version of Rashomon. Kitsutsuki hobbled out of the rain and told horrific war stories. He raised a shadow weapon, fired seventeen times, and counted the prisoners, nurses, and soldiers dead. Crack, crack on his wooden leg, and bodies moldered in his memories of war.

Banka Island.

Listen, crack, crack, crack.

Dead on the beach.

Nurses bear the cross.

Soldiers by number.

Dead again at the gate.

Oshima played the part of a leper who stole hair from bodies abandoned at the gate. Some of the roamers were distraught by the mastery of his kabuki execution, and no doubt they worried that some leper might snatch their hair one night in the peace park.

Naturally, the roamers understood that any pretence of peace was risky, but they were worried about the tatari, the curse and vengeance of those who were incinerated and those burned raw who rushed into the river. The roamers avoided the ghost parade, but now they were constrained by the nuclear kabuki theater.

I assured the roamers that we were evermore secure in the nuclear ruins, and more so because the police named me a maniac. The police would never believe my confessions, stories, or perfect memories in the ruins.

Ronin created these stories in Atomu 57. He established an original measure of time in the ruins, an ingenious calendar to count the years since the first simulated nuclear peace, August 6, 1945. The Atomu calendar is based on a standard solar year that starts with the nuclear destruction of Hiroshima.

By "simulated peace" he means the fake, sentimental, passive peace of museums and monuments. Japan, he declares, should build a nuclear arsenal, and he argues that nuclear weapons should be monitored by a supranational soldiery.

The Flame of Peace burns perpetually at the end of the Pond of Peace. The flame is set to burn to the end of nuclear weapons in the world. The Cenotaph for victims of the atomic bomb is at the other end of the memorial, where it seems to float in the pond. Ronin set a fire that rushed between the monuments.

Ronin told me he first met Kenzaburo Oe, the distinguished novelist, at the Peace Memorial Museum. He memorized sections of *Hiroshima Notes* in preparation for the chance encounter in the gift shop. Ronin smiled, waved his hand at the tacky tee shirts on display over the counter, and recited these actual words by the author.

"In Hiroshima, I met people who refused to surrender to the worst despair or to incurable madness. I heard the story of a gentle girl, born after the war, who devoted her life to a youth caught in an irredeemably cruel destiny. And in places where no particular hope for living could be found, I heard the voices of people, sane and steady people, who moved ahead slowly but with genuine resolve."

Ronin praised the author, and, at the same time, derided the slogans on the tee shirts. He posed his ridicule as natural reason, the practice of native storiers. Ronin told me that he pointed out the window toward the Flame of Peace and shouted that the flame is a habit not an honor or protest. The flame is a passive promise of nuclear peace, no more than a sentimental flicker of victimry.

Ronin poured gasoline in the pond at the opposite end of the Flame of Peace. Surprisingly, the perpetual flame did not ignite the gasoline. The traces of the blaze were haunting images of the atomic explosion when shadows of incinerated humans were cast on the stone and concrete in Hiroshima. The police made these associations and bowed in shame to the memory of the thousands of dead at the peace memorial.

The Aioi Bridge near the Atomic Bomb Dome was the actual target site. The bridge was repaired after the explosion and used until a new one was constructed in Atomu 38.

Ronin celebrates the roamers as storiers. They are the actual natives of the peace park, the last *ronin* of a great samurai tradition. The police, who were trained to be sympathetic but not romantic about stories, recounted the roamers as street people, and more and more of them gathered every year in the peace park. The police gently rousted them by day when the peace tourists were about and then avoided them at night.

Ronin and Oshima invited certain roamers to eat with them in the nuclear ruins of the Atomic Bomb Dome. After dinner they created kabuki versions of the "Rashomon" story by Akutagawa. Oshima was a lightning chancer, and his kabuki poses were always better in a thunderstorm.

The *kobans* are police posts in urban areas. There are more than six thousand of them around the country. The police *kobans* are an active part of governance in the community. They are familiar with the commerce, crime, and situations of the residents. The police are formal, sympathetic listeners, day and night always on patrol in the community. The *koban* is a service center. Children even come by for candy.

Osaka, a former catch woman, once solicited men for private striptease shows, but now she serves tea to the police and decorates the *koban* with bright flowers. Obviously, her nickname was a disguise. Ronin was truly touched by her coy smile and gestures. Osaka was always ready to tease and be teased in public.

Ronin was detained for interrogation by a special police interpreter at the *koban*, but he was never arrested. The police have the discretion to interview and release anyone, or remove a suspect for arrest at a police station.

Tonase, the police interpreter, was annoyed by his evasive responses and demanded to know his name. Ronin answered, "The courage and loyalty of a samurai warrior remains hidden, untasted, a savor wasted." His response was paraphrased from the first act of the puppet play *Chushingura*, translated by Donald Keene. The poetic phrase "savor wasted" and the notion of being untasted is quoted by the narrator of the play. "The sweetest food, if left untasted, remains unknown, its savor wasted" is from the Chinese. "The same holds true of a country at peace: the loyalty and courage of its fine soldiers remain hidden, but the stars, though invisible by day, at night reveal themselves, scattered over the firmament. Here we shall describe such an instance, a chronicle told in simple language of an age when the land was at peace."

Ronin probably read *Chushingura* when he stayed with me at the Hotel Manidoo. He borrowed many books from my library at the time, including studies of religion and the samurai tradition, and marked two stories, "The Kappa," and "Shiro, The Dog," in *Exotic Japanese Stories* by Akutagawa.

I watched him one morning as he leaned back in his father's chair at the window and browsed through a stack of my books at his side. He lightly touched each paragraph with his fingers until he found an idea or scene of interest, a creative, untested, and liberated reader with a rightful memory.

Ronin mentioned the showy socks the interpreter wore at the *koban*. Several weeks later a newspaper published a story about the roamers, a kabuki leper, and an *ainoko* peace buster. The reporter, a sympathetic young man, caught the interpreter on duty in her wild chicken socks and included that picture in the feature story.

The police wear blue uniforms, and every stitch and fold is regulated, but there is no policy on socks. Singularity is measured by the socks. "Only socks have escaped standardization, and when policemen cross their legs a wide assortment of lengths and colors are displayed," wrote David Bayley in *Forces of Order*.

Faubion Bowers told Ronin that his mother might have been Ainu from Hokkaido. Nightbreaker was the source of that elusive notice, but there is no evidence, not even a name. Ronin, of course, has always been eager to bear that association in memory of his father.

The Ainu are the indigenous natives of the islands of northern Japan. Nightbreaker first learned about the Ainu in a narrative by Ranald MacDonald, a native who taught English in Japan before the arrival of the naval officer and diplomat Commodore Matthew Perry in 1854. The Ainu and the *anishinaabe* told similar stories about natural reason, their creation, animal totems, and survivance.

"Ainu culture is based upon a world view which presumes that everything in nature, be it tree, plant, animal, bird, stone, wind, or mountain, has a life of its own and can interact with humanity," noted Yoshio Sugimoto in *An Introduction to Japanese Society*.

Ronin actually carried out the vision of his father and traveled the same course as Ranald MacDonald. The Ainu would unwittingly engender a presence of his father. Ronin, by his father's unrealized journey, created a union of perfect memories with a native teacher and the Ainu.

Ainu Moshiri is their homeland, a new nation, and a sense of native presence. Nightbreaker might have been part of those stories of revival and survivance at the time, but, in a sense, he was wise to leave that to chance, the miseries of war, and the visionary journey of an unrealized son.

Kitsutsuki is a nickname that means "woodpecker" in Japanese. He earned that obvious name for his many carved and decorated wooden legs. His war stories and death count in the kabuki version of *Rashomon* are similar to the stories told by soldiers and nurses who survived a massacre on Banka Island near Sumatra.

Kitsutsuki was a lieutenant in the same division stationed on the island, but he was never indicted as a war criminal. Ronin learned that he was aware of many details of the massacre, but there were few survivors and no direct evidence that Kitsutsuki was involved in any atrocity.

"At the time of the massacre all nurses were in the uniform of the Australian Military Nursing Service and wearing Red Cross armbands," Yuki Tanaka wrote in *Hidden Horrors*. The nurses reached Radjik Beach on Banka Island and "raised the Red Cross flag, thus clearly indicating they were noncombatants."

Vivian Bullwinkel was the only nurse to survive the massacre on the island. Japanese soldiers shot nurses and bayoneted other prisoners of war, according to war crimes investigations. "All my colleagues had been swept away and there were no Japs on the beach. There was nothing. Just me. I got up, crossed the beach and went into the jungle," wrote Bullwinkel.

Ronin was not aware that the wounded lieutenant had been a suspected war criminal. Kitsutsuki could have been present when the nurses and solders, unarmed prisoners, were assassinated at Banka Island.

Hirohito was never honored in the ruins of the Atomic Bomb Dome. Ronin heard stories about the persecution of the *kakure*, or "hidden

Christians," when he lived at the Elizabeth Saunders Home. He convinced me that his practice of stomping on pictures of the mighty emperor was an original, specific resistance to the consecration of dominance.

Miki Sawada was moved by the many stories of the *kakure* who were ordered to walk over pictures of Mary and Jesus. The "trampling ceremonies" started in nineteenth-century Japan. Each person was "forced to stomp on a picture of Jesus or Mary as a sign of contempt and renunciation," wrote Elizabeth Anne Hemphill in *The Least of These*. "Some converts waited until the picture was dirty and obscured, and performed the ceremony with a clear conscience."

Ronin pointed out that the police would never believe his stories, and by that strategy of tease and irony he could attack peace fakery with impunity. Remarkably, he reported his acts and thoughts in the dialogue book in the Peace Memorial Museum. Ronin declared that tourists seldom, if ever, take peace messages seriously.

Yesterday, for instance, he wrote in the dialogue book about the actual fire he set on the Pond of Peace. There, in his own cursive words, he reported his actions against the simulations of peace.

Ronin's confession was written under this plaintive note, one of hundreds in the dialogue book: "My name is Anna and I am visiting from U.S.A. I am Japanese but was born in the U.S.A. After the exhibit, I feel very angry and ashamed at my own country. I pray for the world to come to peace. I also pray for this occurrence to never ever happen again anywhere in the world."

5 Ronin of the Inu Shrine

Virga was at the peace fires last week, but she never came near me. I watched her circle the pond, an elusive shadow near the monuments. Later, she waited for me at the shrine near the koban, always at escape distance, and then followed me in the police car back to the ruins. She has short mottled ears, as you know, and curious dark circles on her chest and belly.

Virga is my virtual shadow.

The Children's Peace Monument is her regular haunt, and she teased me there yesterday. She rolled over near the tower, pushed her wet nose into the origami peace cranes, and then sneezed three times. Many tiny cranes burst into flight and crashed on the stones. Some of the children pushed their faces into the peace cranes and tried to imitate the tricky mongrel.

Virga is a pure roamer, an elusive wisp of rain, always a teaser at escape distance. She has been wary of me at every turn. She trusts the children in the peace park and honors their eager attention, a hand to mouth affinity. Last week she carried several chains of red and blue paper cranes around her neck, and lingered near the monument to eat with the children.

Virga is forever on park duty.

She waited on the children, nosed their hands, and so wisely waited for their cues, cautious not to tease the clumsy overtures. She never missed the tiny morsels, and celebrated every tasty bite, every puffy grain of rice with a raised paw and a hafu smile for the clumsy peace progeny.

Virga is my shadow.

The Atomic Bomb Dome has become her new home at night. Oshima and the roamers feed the ravens, feral cats, and mongrels of the ruins. Virga, though, is the most loyal mongrel, the only one there in the morning. She stands alone on the creased picture of the emperor, abides the sacred circle, and awaits the rise of the mighty ghost parade at eight fifteen.

Virga is my eternal shadow, a tricky trace of my motion and natural reason. She could be my mother, always at a distance, but never an escape. I reached out many times to touch her, to heal the secret wounds of slight and separation, and once circled back to catch my shadow by chance, but she constantly evaded me. She is a bear at dusk, my shadow hafu, and always the same mongrel in the morning.

Virga stole my wooden sword, but she is not a nanazu pirate. She crossed the circle, took the blade in her mouth, and carried it across the river. Loyal roamers chased her through the park and around the paper cranes several times. Strategically she abandoned the sword at the base of the Peace Bell. Naturally, the roamers raised the sword and posed as samurai warriors. One by one they advanced and struck the great bell with the blade of my sword. The wooden beat was muted, a puny sound of peace.

Kitsutsuki, the wounded lieutenant, raised his hand, shouted a command, and the other roamers paused under the dome, a moment of silence at the aesthetic center of peace in the universe. Oshima told me that the peace park roamers always obey that surly veteran with the woodpecker nickname.

Kitsutsuki returned my sword minutes later. The warrior bowed his head and presented the sword in his open hands. Then, when he saw the creased picture of the emperor at the center of the ruins, he hissed, as usual, a predatory sound, and enacted a great kabuki grimace. He had an imitation blue eye that turned inward, out of balance. His silence was ominous as he raised my sword and struck Hirohito. The emperor lost his head.

I learned later that he lost his right leg and one eye on a land mine on the same day that his wife and son were incinerated by the atomic bomb over Hiroshima. He has been a roamer in the peace park for almost a decade, a natural leader who inspects his motley soldiers every morning.

Kitsutsuki has seven wooden legs, each one intricately carved and painted for service. He stores them in a shed behind the nearby koban, an informal arrangement that started by confiscation. The police removed his legs from various locations in the park and stored them at the koban.

Kitsutsuki carved the faces of the nuclear dead on his wooden legs. Twisted faces, airy bodies, chinked bones, the haunting pouts and frowns of death undone forever. One leg is covered with wild, uncertain eyes, the jumpy eyes of terror, and on another leg he carved a flock of scorched, disunited birds with huge eyes, puny feet, and feathers turned under, melted away at the stump.

Sir, your sword.
Virga teases.
Stole my leg once.
Trickster spirit.
Much too heavy.
Swords lighter.
Hand carved wounds.
My nanazu sword.
Where is that country?
Sagami Bay.
My Banka Island.
So many years ago.

Kitsutsuki told stories of the war over dinner in the ruins of the Atomic Bomb Dome. He never mentioned the emperor in his stories, but he frowned, cracked his teeth, and turned his boot many times on the decapitated picture of Hirohito.

He moved his wooden legs one by one from the koban to the sacred ruins. Once a week he disunited a leg, hopped and hobbled to the koban near the river and returned to the ruins on another leg. He would rather hobble to the koban than be seen carrying a wooden leg. The wounds of war were his cues of vanity. Two months later his seven legs were upright in the center of the ruins, a proper gate for the phantoms of the city.

Virga is no nanazu, but she runs in the tradition of the tanuki and water tricksters. Kaisoku, the bay pirate, was the first mongrel to steal my wooden sword. Surely he would run with the mongrels in the peace park, change colors, and bark at the sound of the bell, but the nanazu are moist miniatures, as you know, and they live by the natural cover of the lush forests on Sagami Bay.

Osaka crossed the river last night in my dream. She ducked the wind and told me a story about forty-seven hafu samurai, peace mongrels, and how she has cared for them at the shrine near the koban. I was a casual doubter, even in my dream, but she was specific, the actual number was forty-seven mongrels, the same as in the puppet play *Chushingura*.

What mongels?
Virga, to be sure.
Virga?
Yes, yes.

The hafu roamer?

Yes, an outcast samurai.

My shadow ronin.

Yes, yes.

An eternal warrior.

The hafu seppuku.

She stole my sword.

Virga borrows.

She steals.

What, driftwood?

Kaisoku was the first.

One of the forty-seven.

The nanazu pirate?

Yes, yes, the moist one.

Osaka recited the awesome story of the forty-seven ronin, and by the sound of her voice the same number of mongrels appeared on stage in my dream. Great billowy clouds moved across a painted landscape, and simulated trees waved at the back of the stage. The Inu Shinto Shrine, a memorial for mongrels, was located near the river, south of the koban. The hyoshigi sounded as the hafu samurai rinsed their paws and entered the shrine. The stage was at the back of the shrine.

Mishima, Shinji, Reiko, Kaisoku, Virga, Kenka, Yubi and forty other hafu samurai with no masters turned and posed by name on stage. They moved in an ethereal light. Three mongrels posed as ravens, a noisy air, and bounced across the stage. Kaisoku carried a wooden sword. Kenka, a hafu toy terrier, was an odori shaman, an acrobatic warrior who taunted any pose of royalty. Several other roamers wore feathers, two were ecstatic lepers who covered their twisted paws with miniature white tabi, and together with the other hafu samurai became a mighty chorus of tatari vengeance.

Osaka told me that she created the *Chushingura Inu, The Loyal Dog Retainers*, or the forty-seven hafu ronin, a play staged for the very first time in my dream. The shrine had become a kabuki theater, a perfect vision of my own death.

Princess Asagao, a wispy, white, hafu borzoi with black teeth, minced under the torii and floated down the walkway. She was a ghost, almost invisible, and the train of her hoary kimono created a romantic murmur on stage. The hyoshigi sounded as she entered, and then the tsuke beat faster, clack, clack, clack, clack, a dramatic sound to enhance her magical motion.

Mishima, the hafu samurai master, an akita, whippet, and lurcher by shares, chased the princess down the walkway and caught her train at center stage. The airy material vanished in his mighty paws. Only a shimmer of light lingered, a trace of thin, transparent bones, and the princess vanished in a wave of clouds.

Mishima licked his crotch on stage.

Lord Nox, an avowed royal hafu Shih Tzu, was insulted by the crude manners and obscene pursuit of Princess Asagao. He peevishly insisted that his proud ancestors were loyal to Murasaki Shikibu, the author of *The Tale of Genji*, and, with that dubious story of royal authority, he ordered the hafu samurai to commit suicide by seppuku at the Inu Shrine.

Kenka bounded on stage, circled, wheeled, and leaped over the royal poser, an acrobatic tease, and then he performed backward somersaults. The tsuke sounded, clack, clack, clack, clack. Lord Nox, flustered by the kabuki ridicule, ordered the odori shaman to leave the stage. Kenka continued to somersault down the walkway.

The princess is a ghost.
Royalty endures.
Masks are not princely.
Mongrels have no tradition.
Rightly so.
Your lechery is over.
Never, the samurai endures.
Only by loyalty.
By honor, and my death.
But no noble cause.
This is my hafu shrine.
River roamers.
Your torment of liberty?
The hafu have no masters.
My honor is ichibun.
Then seppuku is your honor.

Mishima kneeled on a thick white cloth spread out in the center of the stage. The scene was silent, not a breath was heard, and even the clouds were unmoved on the kabuki landscape. Only the faint murmur of the river teased the silence.

Mishima raised the dagger, turned the blade inward, and pressed the point on the side of his stomach. A tiny bead of blood formed at the point of the dagger. The tsuke sounded once, twice, and then silence.

Mishima thrust the blade into his hafu stomach and pushed across, under his navel. The sound, clack, clack, clack, clack, clack, increased over his screams of mortal agony. Blood spurted on the white cloth, and then his intestines burst over his thighs, hot and steamy. Still alive, he raised the dagger a second time, unstable, and by the last motion of his honor as a hafu samurai cut the jugular vein on his neck. Clack, clack, clack, clack, clack, clack, clack.

The Loyal Dog Retainers were revolted by the gruesome scene on stage at the Inu Shrine. Osaka said the hafu ronin would avenge the death of their master. She moved closer to the stage.

Yubi, a stocky hafu bull terrier with a huge head and heavy dewlaps, was related to the original kabuki outcasts. He was a river roamer, and the tattoos on his massive chest and shoulders, the black scenes of the kabuki mono, actors who wore wicker hats, revealed his criminal fraternity.

Yubi lost one paw in a test of loyalty, but only a distinctive limp belied his cunning and power as a hafu samurai warrior. Osaka told me that he would avenge the death of his master. Yubi waited in the shadows on the walkway. Clack, clack, clack, and the other hafu ronin moved out of sight.

Lord Nox was heard in the distance.

Yubi limped out of the shadows down the walkway toward the stage. He was pushed aside and overtaken by the sovereign party. Lord Nox appeared at center stage. He announced with a royal wave and wince his disgust over the mere presence of the wounded mongrel. Lord Nox was protected by his many cautious sycophants. They imitated his severe manner. Yubi mocked his cast and teased the fake monarch.

Remove that beast.
So disgusting.
Wait, consider your fate.
Remove that creature.
Cripples alike.
Royalty has no lament.
None but you.

Envy of the lame.
Nox, a catch of consorts.
Royalty bears no slight.
None by destiny.

Yubi raised his severed paw as a guise, turned to the best side, drew his sword and, in a flash of light, beheaded Lord Nox. The head landed in center stage, bounced once, and came to rest upside down, mouth twisted with contempt. Blood shot out of his neck and stained the royal party. Several sycophants lost their arms, hands, and other body parts as they reached for their swords.

> The hafu ronin returned to celebrate their revenge on stage, but that was not the end of the kabuki story. Osaka said Yubi, Shinji, Reiko, Kaisoku, and Kenka would commit suicide by seppuku to honor their master. Virga would run across the stage with my wooden sword and close the play.

Shinji was a lieutenant in a transport battalion, a loyal officer who committed suicide by seppuku at home. He had dishonored the uniform by an association with mutineers. "Long live the Imperial Forces," he wrote in a note. Reiko, his wife, cut her own throat with a dagger and died with her husband. She wore a white silk kimono.

> The Inu Shrine has been a sanctuary for river roamers. Shinji was re-born a hafu spitz in Hiroshima. Reiko, his loyal wife, returned to his side as a white hafu spaniel. Proudly, they committed seppuku a second time in the tradition of honorable warriors.

One by one the other hafu ronin disemboweled themselves in gruesome scenes. The stage became a sea of blood, organs, and in-testines. The great clouds were bloody.

> Virga was the last to position the point of a sword on her stomach, a final ceremonial seppuku on stage, but instead she raised her head, caught my eyes, and turned a tricky smile in my dream. Clack, clack, clack, clack. The last scene was a kabuki tease of loyalty and hafu mortality.

Osaka caught me in my own vision, a kabuki play by dogs. The Inu Shrine must have been animated by stories in *The Animal Court*, a fable by Ando Shoeki. Osaka avoided my comment and directed my attention once again to the stage. I persisted and asked if she had read *The Animal Court*?

> What animal court?
> The Inu Court.

Shoeki was an animal poser.
Animal philosopher.
Satirical scientist.
Champion of animal rights.
By twos and fours.
Yes, the creature dualist.
Mutual shares.
By cultivation rights.
Dogs and cats.
Emperors and menials.
Animal stages.
Shoeki was a hafu spaniel.
Mutual mongrels.

Osaka teased me as a hafu airedale and corgi in her exotic ronin stories. I was there first as a dreamer, and then again as a shadow with an elusive sense of inu presence, but with no substance, no heartbeat, no real body.

I raised my hand to wave, a pocket gesture to my friends, but only my shadow was present on stage. My pose was an absence. No one could see my moves in the dream.

I was there in perfect memories, by my interior sound, sense, and motion, but lost in a shadow that existed outside of time, and with no obvious source of natural light. The motion of my hands was a shadow gesture, a tricky pose, and my sense of presence was the actual absence of my body.

I am a hafu ronin, dead once again.

Manidoo Envoy

Shinto is a native persuasion and an active animistic religion.
The participants celebrate nature, honor their ancestors, and, for a
time, surrendered to a fascistic emperor. The *kami*, or the spirits of
a vast, eternal nature, are venerated at many shrines. The *kami* are
honored at shrines and courted as unworldly visitors. There are no
monotheistic creators, no grave founders, no sacred scriptures, no
authoritarian doctrines, and no sincere notions of almighty dominance.

The raison d'être of the shrines "is to promote, through ritual
activities referencing transcendent powers, a sense of continuity,
stability, and the management of uncertainty," John Nelson wrote
in *Enduring Identities: The Guise of Shinto in Contemporary Japan.*

Ronin is a master of uncertainties and survivance. He revels in
the stories of the *kami*, the spirits and shrines, and savors the sensibilities of a religion that has no missionaries, but he spurns the
divine descent of the emperor. Royalty, he told me, is a depraved
convention of cruel separatism and mannered dominance.

The Shinto movement in the nineteenth century centered on the
"reverence of the emperor," and the "cult of the imperial ancestors" became "more nationalistic and eventually came to seek a new
unity under symbolic imperial rule," wrote Edwin O. Reischauer in
The Japanese.

Shinto honors the *kami*, the mountains, animals, rivers, stones,
and more. The *kami* spirits are ancient and superior. "These numinous
presences have been the principal objects of worship" for centuries,
wrote Carmen Blacker in *The Catalpa Bow: A Study of Shamanistic
Practices in Japan.* "They are difficult to describe, because they are
elusive, enigmatic, heterogeneous." The *kami* "are best understood
perhaps as hierophanies, manifestations of sacred power in the
human world."

Ronin creates personal connections to nature in his stories, and,
at the same time, he could be seen as "unclean" because he associates
with lepers, and teases the memory of blood as a presence. Shinto
notions of pollution include the avoidance of blood and death. People considered unclean were once "prohibited from participating in

religious rituals, mixing with other people, and even returning home from a funeral without being purified," wrote Susan Hanley in *Everyday Things in Premodern Japan*. "Salt, water, and fire are all considered purifying agents and used both in religious ritual and to clean and purify."

Ronin told me that animals talk to him in dreams, and the way of the *kami* has a real presence in his stories. Animals, birds, and nature are not separate creations in his tricky metaphors and view of the world. He was native by dreams long before he learned about his father.

The White Earth Reservation elders were aware that he was in touch with animal spirits, and that convinced them he was native, the *anishinaabe* son of Nightbreaker. Ronin was rightly embraced by many families partly because he told animal stories on the very first day he arrived at the reservation. Many natives remember his *nanazu* stories.

"The Shino kami and the anishinaabe manidoo are common ancestors in my dreams," he told me. He is certainly not a religious scholar, or even a student of comparative cultures, but his stories are wise, heartfelt, and inclusive of the natural world. He is a mongrel, a roamer, and his stories are a worthy tease of nature, culture, and empire dominance.

Ronin is a dreamer, and his creative memories of *hafu* samurai are no surprise to those who know him and who have heard his wild, passionate stories. Animals and birds are the primary source of his visions. He imagines and presents the sentiments of humans, animals, and birds in the same sense of moral reality.

Ronin strongly resists any association with cults or the mythic concoctions of animal tenancy. Animals do not haunt him, or by guile penetrate his body. Clearly, his creative, perceptive powers are innate, similar to the poses of an ascetic or shaman, and his tricky visions are not imitations or derived from others. He is the animal of his mind, a spirit by stories not by the possession of sorcerers. He is a unique and ironic healer, a trickster by stories, not by character simulations. "I am hafu, a ronin trickster by chance of my conception," he told a journalist, and explained that his presence is not secured by a pure originary moment. His native stories evade closure and victimry.

The Japanese traditional theater is "living theater," wrote Karen Brazell in *Traditional Japanese Theater*. The "kabuki dance," or *odori*, ecstatic dance, was first performed some four centuries ago in Kyoto. The word "kabuki" literally means "to tilt" or "to slant," a reference to the "outlandish behavior and dress." Early kabuki was based on puppet plays. Kabuki, *kyogen*, a play of wild words, Noh, and the puppet theater "share the same historical background" and are "continuous performance traditions."

Kabuki and puppet theater evolved in the seventeenth century, "struggled to cope with strict government regulations and financial and social restraints, and competed for the same urban audiences," observed Brazell. The "initial subject matter" of kabuki was "daily life in the pleasure quarters."

Ronin used two words to describe the clack, clack sounds of a wooden clacker and clapper. The first, *hyoshigi*, is a clacker that announces the "opening of the curtain" in the kabuki and puppet theater. The second word, *tsuke*, is the "art of striking two shorter wooden rectangles or clappers on a flat board placed on the floor," noted Brazell. "The beating of these clappers emphasizes entrances, exits, running, striking, falling, or fighting, and they also intensify the movements of actors during poses."

The Children's Peace statue is dedicated to the memory of Sadako Sasaki, who died of leukemia caused by radiation exposure, the black rain from the atomic bomb. She was twelve years old at the time of her death, October 25, 1955, Atomu 10.

Ten thousand children attended the dedication of the memorial three years after her death, on May 5, 1958. "Sadako would be remembered forever," wrote Takayuki Ishii in *One Thousand Paper Cranes*. "On the very top of the statue was the figure of a girl holding a large crane as she looked skyward."

"Every year, thousands of visitors make pilgrimages to the memorial to honor the memory of the children who died as a result of the atomic bomb and its aftermath," wrote Ishii. "In silence, people place colorful paper cranes at the foot of the memorial statue."

Ronin is haunted by the dead children every morning in the ghost parade at the ruins of the Atomic Bomb Dome. Exactly at eight-fifteen in the morning the children float in his memories, an eternal motion of moral silence. Commonly, the children are summoned as consorts by the bounty of origami cranes, and the image of the crane has been associated with the voice of the emperor. Ronin told me that many children lost their names that morning, but the memory of their gentle touch is an ethereal presence over Hiroshima.

Virga courts the children at the same memorial, an unabashed roamer for a share of lunch. She celebrates the children over the tiny morsels of their lunch. The other park roamers shun the innocence at the memorial statue. And the dead children must forever count the paper cranes in search of a name, an ancestor.

Sadako told her parents that she would fold a thousand paper cranes, and then her wish would come true as in the story. "I believe that my wish to be healthy again will come true." In two months she folded about fifteen hundred cranes and then died in the hospital.

Daily, thousands of ephemeral paper cranes are sent from around the world to decorate the statue. These words, in memory of those children who died, are engraved on the granite base of the statue.

This is our cry

This is our prayer:

To create peace in the world.

Ronin is not easily influenced by the metaphors of innocence, peace, or patent sincerity. He observes irony, as you know, because literal, reductive stories are always sincere simulations. Yet his heart is with the spirit of the children. He declares that the virtue of their death, innocence, absence, and silence, is not in a statue, memorial stones, or in the sincere origami cranes, but in the "eternal visionary ghost parades of the nuclear dead in Hiroshima."

"An easygoing conscience," wrote Kenzaburo Oe in *Hiroshima Notes*, "cannot remain untroubled, except by intentionally refusing to listen to the stories that come out of Hiroshima."

Ronin treads on a photograph of the emperor at least once a day in the ruins. His original practice, as you know, was similar to the "tramping ceremonies" of nineteenth-century feudal Japan. Christians were ordered to "stomp on a picture of Jesus or Mary as a sign of contempt and renunciation."

Ronin forsakes the emperor in the memory of those who died in the dubious name of a divine, militaristic monarchy. Kitsutsuki, the lieutenant with a wounded heart and seven carved wooden legs, is more determined to erase the actual historical image of Hirohito.

Japan was decorated with pictures of the emperor during the war. Children were taught to fear Hirohito. "The photograph of the emperor is in the elementary and other schools and has been a revered object more important than life itself," wrote Kiyosawa Kiyoshi in his wartime diary, *A Diary of Darkness*. "Because of this, great numbers have lost their lives."

66

"The lone *kamikaze* pilot," for instance, "assumed a task 'beyond the limits of human might,' a task that common sense can only judge as being absurd, even insane," wrote Ivan Morris in *The Nobility of Failure*. "*Harakure*, the most influential of all samurai treatises ever written, combines the characters" for "dying" and "going mad" into a "single word, *shinigurui*," or "death frenzy." Morris noted that in many descriptions of suicide attacks "the pilot's last words refer to the Emperor, who, despite his somewhat lacklustre personality, was the supreme father figure." Ronin said the "death frenzy" of the kamikaze pilot was his absolute service to the mythical, fascist, divine emperor.

Hirohito was born on April 29, 1901. He was the firstborn son of Crown Prince Yoshihito and Princess Sadako. Hirohito matured as the nation became a great imperial power, only two generations after the military imposition of Commodore Perry.

Emperor Meiji died in 1912. Crown Prince Yoshihito became Emperor Taisho. He was "totally devoid of the qualities needed to be an emperor," wrote Leonard Mosley in *Hirohito: Emperor of Japan*. Taisho's "whole life had been little more than a cipher, a shadow Emperor manipulated by the men behind the throne, not only mad but helpless." These were the same men who resisted a constitutional monarchy because it "meant democracy, and democracy was a condition they least wished to see." Men who were rightly suspicious that their military power and adventure would be diminished in a democracy.

Emperor Taisho died in view of Mount Fuji on December 25, 1926. Hirohito named his reign Showa, "Enlightened Peace," an ironic inscription that would only inspire imperial expansion and military cruelties. His empire ended in the atomic incineration of two cities, the occupation of the nation, and abatement of the monarchy.

Koichi Kido, Lord Keeper of the Privy Seal, noted that Emperor Hirohito was very troubled and in a highly emotional state when he was told that an atomic bomb had incinerated Hiroshima. "He was overwhelmed with grief for the innocent civilians who were its victims." Kido was naturally overwhelmed, but his revisionist memories of a sympathetic imperial voice are very practiced.

Hirohito responded, according to Kido, that "we must bow to the inevitable. No matter what happens to my personal safety, we must put an end to this war as speedily as possible." Mosley noted that the survivors "picking their way out of the scorched plain where a city had been" pleaded for help "from those with no idea of what sort of help to give." The *hibakusha*, the survivors of the atomic bombs, were shunned by their own government.

Hirohito announced the surrender in a broadcast, and when his voice was heard for the first time in public people bowed to radios and loudspeakers across the country. The once divine emperor was evasive about the "general trends in the world," and the "actual conditions" of the empire. "We have decided to effect a settlement of the present situation by resorting to an extraordinary measure." The horrors of the war were reduced to the "present situation." Mosley pointed out that Hirohito was nervous and "seemed to stumble" over "phrases such as 'the war situation has developed not necessarily to our advantage' and 'the general trends of the world have all turned against'" Japan.

Kenzaburo Oe was deprived of his innocence on August 15, 1945, when the emperor announced the end of the war. Hirohito, at that moment, waived his deity by hesitant deceptions and became a "mortal man." Until that day of surrender, "like all Japanese school-children, he had been taught to fear the Emperor as a living god," wrote John Nathan in his introduction to *Teach Us to Outgrow Our Madness* by Oe.

Hirohito had spoken in a human voice, wrote Oe. *"The adults sat around their radios and cried. The children gathered outside in the dusty road and whispered their bewilderment."* One of his friends cleverly imitated the emperor. *"We surrounded him, a twelve-year-old in grimy shorts who spoke in the Emperor's voice, and laughed. Our laughter echoed in the summer morning stillness and disappeared into the clear, high sky. An instant later, anxiety tumbled out of the heavens and seized us impious children."* They looked at each other in silence. *"How could we believe that an august presence of such awful power had become an ordinary human being on a designated summer day?"*

Ronin told me that he had read sections of *Reminiscences* by Douglas MacArthur. "Hirohito was honored when he should have been arrested as a war criminal," said Ronin. He cited comments that General MacArthur made after his first meeting with Hirohito. "I come to you, General MacArthur, to offer myself to the judgment of the powers you represent as the one to bear sole responsibility for every

68

political and military decision made and action take by my people in the conduct of war."

Lord Nox bears a name that means "sound," and he boasts that his ancestors are in a novel, *The Tale of Genji*, by Murasaki Shikibu. Mishima, a *hafu* samurai, is the ironic trace of the celebrated author Yukio Mishima. Nox, the dubious *sound* of royalty, orders the lusty samurai master to perform *seppuku* for chasing an apparition, and the entire scene is a kabuki play of mongrel warriors.

Ronin is a dreamer, a mind roamer, a teaser of peace, and a master of irony. Those who admire his sensibilities understand that there is never a separation of imagic consciousness from substantive notice, or reality, in his marvelous, ironic stories of survivance. The perception of the real must be sincere, yet the sense is ironic, never actual, he told me, and then continued his theoretical chant. Chance and tricky metaphors are the traces, the actual connections, and not a separation of the authentic.

Princess Asagao is a royal character in *The Tale of Genji*. Her name is descriptive and means "morning glory." When her father died she retired from her position as high priestess and moved away. Genji, a suitor, was adrift, and, eager to be remembered, "sent frequent inquiries about her health." Her answers were formal, "determined never again to be the subject of rumors."

Genji was not pleased, but persisted with earnest entreaties. She held her distance and seemed "less disposed to welcome gallantry." The royal politics of gallantry was more than any one person could understand or contain at the time.

"You turned me away in shame and humiliation, and the thought of how the rout must have pleased you is not comfortable," he wrote. "I do not forget the morning glory I saw. Will the years, I wonder, have taken it past its bloom?"

The letter was short and civil by metaphors, "which it would be wrong to ignore." An inkstone was prepared. "The morning glory, wholly changed by autumn," wrote Asagao, "is lost in the tangle of the dew-drenched hedge." She closed in this way, "Your most apt simile brings tears." This translation of *The Tale of Genji* is by Edward Seidensticker.

Murasaki Shikibu lived at a time when "the most powerful aristocratic families competed to marry their daughters to the emperor, for it was by maternal control of the throne that power was ultimately obtained," wrote Haruo Shirane in *The Bridge of Dreams*.

Genji, like the *hafu* samurai in Ronin's kabuki dream, had lost his aristocratic rank, a severe penalty at the time. "Though Genji claims to be innocent of the public charges brought against him," notes Shirane, "he privately associates his loss of office and present difficulties with that 'one deed,' his illicit affair with his father's consort." Asagao raises the narrative tension of "social status and marriage," an ethereal sentiment at the Inu Shrine.

Osaka created the Inu Shrine in a dream story about dubious royalty, a sense of presence, and the cultural status of mongrels. The word *inu* means "dog," as in *akita inu*, a large dog, and in *Chushingura Inu, The Loyal Dog Retainers*. Mishima, the *hafu* samarai master, pursues a lusty vision and is dead by suicide.

"The victim arches his body, giving a lonely, piteous shriek, and there is a spasm in the muscles around the wound. The knife has been buried in the rippling flesh as calmly as though being inserted in a scabbard," wrote Yukio Mishima in *Confessions of a Mask*. "The pleasure you experience at this moment is a genuine human feeling." The excitement is "entirely normal," and your "mind quivers under the rush of primitive, mysterious excitement. The deep joy of a savage is reborn in your breast," and you "glitter with debauched loneliness."

Mishima was born on January 4, 1925, in Tokyo. He married Yoko Sugiyama on May 30, 1958, and twelve years later committed *sepukku* in the uniform of his fascistic Shield Society on November 25, 1970. *Confessions of a Mask* was published in 1949, *The Temple of the Golden Pavilion* in 1956, *The Sailor Who Fell from Grace with the Sea* in 1963, and *The Decay of the Angel*, his last novel, in 1970.

Mishima was obsessed with death, the "death frenzy" of the samurai warrior. He wrote about death in *Confessions of a Mask*, in the tragic story, "Patriotism," in *Death in Midsummer*, and in a kabuki play, *The Moon Like a Drawn Bow*. He ended his own life in a spectacular act of *sepukku* and was ritually beheaded in a "glitter" of blood at the headquarters of the Japanese Self Defense Force.

"Dress my body in a Shield Society uniform, give me white gloves and a soldier's sword in my hand, and then do me the favor of taking a photograph" he wrote in a final letter. "My family may object, but I want evidence that I died not as a literary man but as a warrior." Yoko, his wife, "placed his fountain pen" and manuscript paper in the coffin with his body. The novelist became a warrior by death, the "debauched loneliness" of a character in a story.

Ronin is a warrior, a shaman of other worlds, but he is not obsessed with the savage, literary glitter of death. He is a visionary, an aesthetic warrior of eternal survivance, a *hafu* samurai, but never a fanatical romancer of nationalism or the emperor.

Mishima "exhorted" eight hundred soldiers of the Self Defense Forces "to rise up with him against a postwar democracy that had deprived Japan of her army and her soul," wrote John Nathan in *Mishima.*

Mishima would reverse the constitution created by occupation forces and restore nationalism, military traditions, and the divine emperor. Ronin declared the constitution must be amended to allow the development of nuclear weapons as a balance of peace, and he would establish an international armed soldiery.

Mishima was bored with his nation, a wasteland of honor and traditions, and he lived by many contradictions. He was "fascinated by the unselfish idealism of the men who gladly laid down their lives for the emperor," observed Donald Keene in *Dawn to the West: Japanese Literature in the Modern Era.* "Before long the emperor came to mean Japan itself for Mishima, and by the mid-1960s he was publicly expressing views that were interpreted by some as fascistic or, at any rate, of the far right, though Mishima often seemed to say no more than that Japan's unique traditions must be preserved."

"To really shake people up, he had to resort to something very extreme," asserted Ian Buruma in *The Missionary and the Libertine.* The world was truly shocked by his suicide. "But I do think most Japanese are right in regarding Mishima's *seppuku* as little more than the pathetic act of a very gifted buffoon."

Mishima created Lieutenant Shinji Takeyama in his novella "Patriotism." Shinji was loyal, but associated with mutineers, and, after dinner and sex with his wife, committed ceremonial *seppuku* at his "private residence." Reiko watched from across the bloody mats, and then she stabbed herself to death. That story was first published nine years before Mishima committed sensational *sepukku* at a military headquarters.

Shinji wrote, "Long live the Imperial Forces." Then, with "only his right hand on the sword the lieutenant began to cut sideways across the stomach. But as the blade became entangled with the entrails it was pushed constantly outwards by their soft resilience," wrote Mishima. "He pulled the blade across. It did not cut as

71

easily as he had expected." Reiko "gathered her strength and plunged the point of the blade deep into her throat."

Ronin heard their names in his dream, and their names became metaphorical connections in his stories. Mishima, Shinji, and Reiko, three *hafu* samurai mongrels of diverse breeds, became *ronin inu* in a kabuki version of *Chushingura*. Osaka, as you know, created the Inu Shrine nightmare, *Chushingura Inu, The Loyal Dog Retainers.*

Chushingura, The Treasury of Loyal Retainers, the original tragic story, was created by several playwrights in the eighteenth century. "The historical event behind the play occurred on January 30, 1703." The "former retainers of the late Lord Asano burst into the mansion of Lord Kira Yoshinaka in Edo and killed him to avenge the death of their master almost two years earlier," wrote Donald Keene in *Traditional Japanese Theater,* edited by Karen Brazell. "Asano, an inexperienced country lord who had not offered the expected bribe to Kira, was goaded by him into drawing his sword in the shogunal palace. For this drastic breach of decorum, Asano had been ordered to commit ritual suicide. Although people of every class cheered the boldness of the retainers' retaliation, the government ruled, after some debate, that it was not a 'legal' vendetta and condemned forty-six retainers to ritual suicide less than two months after their deed."

Yubi, the *hafu* samurai, is a nickname derived from *yubitsume,* a word that means the practice of finger cutting in the world of the *yakuza,* a criminal organization. The first joint of the little finger is severed as a mark of devotion or apology to the *oyabun,* or *yakuza* father. Yubi lost part of one paw, and he wears tattoos, as do many *yakuza* members.

"The movies glorified yakuza" as heroes at the bottom of society, and "as the embodiment of the samurai code of behavior," wrote Mamoru Iga in *The Thorn in the Chrysanthemum.* The *yakuza* "use intimidation tactics or even kill people when they are asked to by persons in high positions."

The Animal Court is a translation of the eighteenth century political fable *Hosei Monogatari* by Ando Shoeki. Ronin and Osaka created by turns a short kabuki satire on the philosophies of Shoeki. His stories are creature satires of religious doctrines and cultural notions, and he uses birds, beasts, and others as court philosophers to critique human sensibilities of the time.

Shoeki critiqued native religions, observed Jeffrey Hunter in the introduction to *The Animal Court*, "but since Shinto has always been a rather informal, unorganized amalgam of animistic beliefs and rituals, it isn't as easy a target as Confucianism or Buddhism."

The beasts gather at a seminar to discuss the state of human world law. Many beasts raise questions about human dominion. We are "born of the energy of the pots and pans of human homes. We eat leftover scraps of human food and uneaten rice. We help our masters by barking at suspicious shadows and thieves," but we are dominated, said a dog.

"But barking at shadows is actually the task of dogs," said a dog. "The teachings of Confucianism, the preachings of the Buddha, the writings of Laozi and Zhuangzi, the medical treatises, the Shinto texts, and in addition all poetry and literature are nothing more than the yapping of a dog at an insubstantial shadow."

Shoeki was a dualist, as he imposed a structure of pairs that share "mutual natures" in the world. Hunter noted that Shoeki believes animals "know themselves better than we do, and as such they not only deserve far better treatment than they get at the hands of humans, but our profound and humble respect as well. Their eloquent pleas to have their inherent rights respected are quite moving even today, but in Shoeki's time and culture they were positively revolutionary."

Kenga, the *hafu* samurai, bears a nickname that means "fight," or "fighter." Virga is a metaphor name educed from the word that describes those wisps of rain that evaporate in the air between the clouds and the earth.

6 Ronin of the Black Rain

That radiant woman orders an almond kuchen dessert and a pot of green tea every morning. She sits at the same small table near the window, cuts the cake into precise pieces, raises the china teacup with both hands, and looks out the window at the rush of people in the arcade. The way she puckers her lips to cool the tea arouses me.

I write on a tiny bakery napkin, day after day, and note her every move, the reach of her fingers, bank of her shoulders, and the sensuous rise of her thighs in loose hakama trousers. A blue heat emanates from her sleeves, from every tone and summer heave of her body.

My hands are blue in the rainy light.

The arcade is crowded with shoppers.

The older clerk faults the weather.

The radiant woman caught my eye twice last week. Once she smiled, and then turned away, shied no doubt by my rather eager gestures. This morning, however, by chance of the weather and a loyal mongrel we sat at the same table near the window.

Virga, who tracks me at a distance, as you know, unwittingly brought us together. Caught in an early thunderstorm, cold and bedraggled, she roamed around the bakery, moaned at the counter, circled, and then shivered under the table.

What name?

Virga.

Funny name.

Strange mongrel.

What means?

Fake rain.

Why fake rain?

False, phony.

Not nice name.

Maybe not.

Virga was soaked to the skin by the heavy rain. The strong scent of wet hair saturated our corner of the bakery. The story of this tricky mongrel could have been mine, the hafu orphan at the head table, but not this morning. The park children were at school, so she was content to have a new friend at the bakery.

Miko moves with a natural radiance, an erotic trace. The turn of her hand is ethereal, the way a treasure, or a memory, is savored, or the tease and easy smile of an image in a poem. My hands were rough, a blue favor of my time outside.

> What your name?
> Ronin.
> No, not really.
> Yes, Ronin Browne.
> Funny name.
> Your name?
> Amerika?
> Very funny name.
> No, no, not my name.
> What then?
> Miko.
> Lovely name.
> Thank you.
> What does it mean?
> Shaman.
> Bakery shaman?
> Shaman of the ruins.

Virga moves closer to her tiny feet. Miko reaches down to touch her on the head. She seems to be aroused by the scent of a wet mongrel. Miko crosses her legs, and teases one shoe on her toes, a natural, sensuous balance. The blue, thin leather shoe moves to the side, at a slight pitch, and reveals the perfect curve of her moist arch.

Miko told me she is an artist. She paints watercolor scenes of children in the park. Virga, she said, is always with the children, and in some of her paintings. She is a teaser and waits on any morsel of food in the hand of a child or shaman. Now she poses for the almond kuchen at breakfast.

> What do you write?
> The turn of your hand.
> Amerika man.
> My last stories on a napkin.

I reached across the table and touched her hand, and then her tiny wrist. She turned her eyes away, and at the same time moved closer to my hand. Then she raised my hand to her cheek. She was warm, moist, and generous to an old hafu roamer. Her radiance touched me at the heart.

Miko lost the balance of her shoe, and her naked toes reached out to be touched. Virga groaned, pushed the shoe to the side with her nose, and licked her toes. I was aroused by the faint sound of slobber under the table.

> Miko, the shrine maiden.
> What shrine?
> Shinto inu shrine.
> Dog shaman?
> Yes, an inu roamer.
> Virga the roamer.
> My friends are roamers.
> Where you live?
> Atomic Bomb Dome.

The Andersen Bakery is located in a restored bank building near the ruins at the Hondori Shopping Arcade. The modern building survived the atomic bomb. An arcane bronze mermaid is mounted at the entrance to the bakery. Fresh baked brioche de raisin, maple and almond kuchen, many custard cakes, and other singular breakfast desserts, are served every morning. My favorite is the raisin brioche.

Virga licked the arch of her foot, and watched me with one eye. I was distracted by a lazy lick that reached from her toes to slender, polished ankle. That mongrel once stole my wooden sword, and now by tongue and touch she stole my fascination over a shrine maiden. I gave her pieces of almond kuchen under the table, but that mongrel was determined to torment me.

> Miko blushed, a bright rosy hue spread over her cheeks, neck, and then moved by sudden waves under her loose blouse, but she did not move her foot away. She pinched her nose over the strong scent of a wet mongrel at her feet. Virga, she said, gently licks the tiny feet of the children.
> Just like yours.
> No, big feet.
> Virga slobbers.
> What?
> Your tiny feet.

No, not slobber.

Miko ate the last piece of my brioche, sipped her tea, and then turned toward the window and arcade. Virga sensed the moment, the turn of manners, and moved to the door. We walked slowly down the arcade, past the many stores, to the main street. Virga always ran ahead, received and licked the hands and feet of eager children, but she was never out of sight. She looked back only to torment me.

Miko opened a bright red umbrella at the end of the arcade. The rain was heavy, warm, and noisy on the main street. Cars crashed through the standing water at the intersection. Our cheeks touched under the small umbrella. The heat was magical, and her breath was sweetened by bakery dough, and with a trace of overnight garlic. The rain, the black, poison rain, no one can ever be sure of the rain.

Why not sure?

Children in the black rain.

Yes, turned their faces.

We moved closer, arms entwined, and the rain soaked our backs, shoulders, and shoes. The rain hissed around us on the sidewalk. Miko perspired in the storm, and her thighs, so close to mine, moved in a kabuki cloudbank. Virga ran ahead, but much closer to us in the heavy rain.

The black rain exposed thousands of people to radiation. The natural fear of thunder, and that pure pleasure of the rain, was lost forever on that ghastly morning of the atomic bomb. Hiroshima was incinerated by a nuclear thunderstorm, and the hibakusha were poisoned by the rain. The dead were resurrected in museums, in the wretched name of peace. Listen, you can hear the undertone, the hints of their sudden, lost breath in the rain.

Children without names.

Death stories.

Thunder, so distant.

Nuclear ghosts in the rain.

The lonesome souls.

Miko works as a hosutesu, a hostess at the Tea and Cocktail Lounge in the Ana Hotel Hiroshima. When we arrived there, wet, heated, and mussed, she told me to wait in the lobby while she changed her clothes. Just then, the hotel manager warned me that animals were not permitted in the hotel or lobby. Virga pushed against his legs with her head and shoulder and stained his trousers. The puny man raised his hands in disgust. He was overly worried about his appearance.

> Stains of black rain.
> No dogs.
> Not my dog.
> Dog with you.
> Not mine.
> No dogs hoteru.

> Virga shivered at his ankles, but the manager was not moved by the hafu spectacle. He smiled and pointed with both hands toward the door. Virga walked slowly, with a slight limp, out the door, turned, and pressed the side of her mottled face on the glass. The manager retreated to brush his wet trousers.

Miko emerged from the back room, transformed in a lounge habit. She wore a golden silk blouse that revealed a trace of her erect nipples, and black hakama trousers. The sound of silk was shamanic as she walked toward me. I reached out to touch her moist cheek, but she turned away. Virga groaned and shivered against the glass at the hotel entrance.

> Miko said she wanted to see me soon again for breakfast at the bakery, and then, without a pause, she directed me to a gallery show of her watercolor paintings. I was more direct and asked how late she worked that night. She smiled, counted with her fingers to eight, and then rushed away to the lounge. I was aroused by her distant moves, the sway of her thin waist, rise of her buttocks, her perfect tendons, and the erotic tone and billow of silk on her bare breasts.

Miko painted watercolor scenes of children at the peace park. The awesome images were in magic flight. The Karasu Gallery prominently mounted seventeen watercolor paintings near the entrance. The paintings were large, at least two feet square, and a placard was attached to describe each of the scenes. The children were expressionistic, painted with enormous, almost transparent, asymmetrical heads, with huge faces and embryonic eyes, twice the proportion of their bodies. Faces were painted in many bright, primitive colors, as bold as those horses created by Franz Marc. One blue child, for instance, was soaring over the peace pond with a white pigeon on her shoulder, and a singular shadow of the same bird, burned and bloody, was reflected in the pond. Morning glories and the flames of peace were faintly seen in the head of a child, as if the slight, obscure traces were thoughts or visions of horrific transmutations.

> The placard attached to the painting explained that the wounded white pigeon, once at liberty with humans, crashed in the pond. The image of the pigeon was based on scenes in the novel *Black Rain* by Masuji Ibuse.

The mighty heads of children are faintly awash with scenes from stories of the atomu ruins. There was a miniature, watercolor mirror in every painting, and at least one real, but broken mirror. The shards were mounted in distinct patterns on the canvas. My image was fractured, distorted, and never the same at any pose.

> The painted mirrors were gruesome miniatures, obscure cameos that reflected images and scenes of horrific nuclear death. The scenes were shadowy, broken and twisted bones, transparent organs, eyes, fingers, worried smiles turned under, and human traces, shadows burned forever into the stone.

Miko is my great mystery.

> This was the perfect day, in memory of the children who were caught in the black rain, to erase that column of fake peace letters at the Peace Memorial Museum.

There are hundreds of miniature letters etched on metal and mounted as a permanent exhibit on a huge column in the museum, a prominent pillar under the new simulated dome. The scale model plaster dome is a stagy, contemptible memorial of atomic destruction. The greedy scheme might have eliminated the real, the actual ruins of the dome by erecting an imitation in the new addition to the museum.

> Many people were critical of the real dome because of the land values, a constant reminder of the war and hibakusha, the survivors of the atomic bomb. The detractors conspired to raze the real to save the faux as a museum catchword, but proxy politics did not prevail. The Atomic Bomb Dome was recognized as an international historic site and registered, along with the Great Wall of China, on the World Heritage List.

I live with roamers in the real dome, in the ruins of the atomu bomb, and despise the models. The museum is a cynical theme park of human misery, and the miniature letters are a testament to the arrogance and deceptions of political peacemongers. Hundreds of presidents, prime ministers, pacifists, and worldly mediators write promissory letters that are read by tourists, a column of pretense and duplicity. Come with me, you materialists, and bear a kabuki ghost parade in the ruins.

> I described in the museum dialogue book my destruction of the metal peace letters on the column. The ghost parades, the fire on the pond, my tattoos, the roamers, and my home in the ruins have been described in the book, but no one reads my stories.

Mary Rose, in one of the entries ahead of mine, wrote that her favorite uncle had died of cancer caused by exposure to radiation in the military. She was uncertain of the actual place because her uncle was secretive about his service. My father, as you know, died in the same way.

> Mary Rose introduced herself as a teacher and started her comments with an apology. "I am sorry to say that the museum is empty compared to the stories of the survivors," she wrote, "and in that way too, my comments are empty." At first she was impressed with the column of letters, but then, as she read more, she wondered about the "worth of so many words of peace by so many great and powerful men when the world continues to be at risk of nuclear war. The same men who wrote these letters also ordered my uncle into harm's way to test nuclear weapons. I wish he were here now to help me understand the real meaning of this museum."

My concise entry in the museum dialogue book that afternoon was written a few minutes before my actual attack on the column of peace letters. My action should come as no surprise to those readers who have doubts about a column of peace promises. Some letters seem to be sincere, but the ideology of peace makes bad poetry. These letters are the worst of the occasional politics of peace and victimry. The museum elevates the peace letters, the government solicits a free ride on the passive road to peace, and, at the same time, there are tricky moves to contract nuclear weapons in the country.

> I prepared a corrosive chemical in three small steel containers. My moves were contrived and chancy. The museum guards greeted me at the entrance, as usual, and then waved me through the gate. They teased me about the style of my protective goggles, but said

nothing about my rubber gloves. The guards usually mocked my museum nickname, hafu atomu, the atomic mongrel, but that afternoon they were busy with a tour of dignitaries from the People's Republic of China.

I walked through the old museum, past the dioramas of atomu destruction, the twisted tricycle, curious manikins with molten arms, a miserable course into the new museum. American bombers soared forever in a circle of television monitors. The simulated dome is at the end of the tour. The pathetic peace letters are etched on metal plates, as you know, and mounted in rows on a tower of pretense under the dome. I shouted sections of some letters and by the wild tone of my voice turned the fake sincerity into irony. An eager crowd gathered around the column, including the party of cautious Chinese. The translator, no doubt, misconstrued my irony, because they applauded my performance. The other tourists frowned at me, protected their children, and moved away.

One tourist, a talky man in wrinkled clothes, burst into noisy laughter. He shouted and mocked my reading with a practiced accent, embellished the content of the peace letters, and created an instant, ephemeral letter about sex and peace from Queen Elizabeth of England. By then, of course, the tourists had abandoned the simulated dome.

> Who are you?
> The liberty queen.
> Who?
> The last queen.
> Where?
> Out of England.
> Last queen?
> The very last empire.
> Nice floral shirt.

Margarito Real said he was a visiting professor from a remote college in England. That much was obvious by his voice and his penny loafers, but the wild, ironic wit caught me at my own tricky game. I was on a mission to destroy the letters, and he was about the column with creative mockery and curious duplicity. Real teased the voice of former president Clinton at one turn, and then on the other side of the column he became the prime minister of India in a lusty chat about the raj with Queen Elizabeth.

Nice goggles.

Thank you.

Prescription?

Naturally.

Rubber gloves?

My mission.

Real was overly concerned about my rubber gloves and suggested that we meet at another time. He told me his mother wore similar gloves when she beheaded chickens. He turned to leave, and then invited me to dinner that night at the Ana Hotel Hiroshima.

My chance of perfect memories.

The last wave of tourists circled the dome, the column of peace letters, and then made their way to the museum gift shop. The perfect moment had arrived for my mission. I slipped into rubber gloves, opened the three containers and, one by one, pitched the corrosive chemical on the sides of the column. The watery substance dribbled down the metal letters. The peace promises spumed, seethed, hissed, and then rightly vanished forever in a wispy cloud of silence. I resealed the containers, removed my gloves, and calmly walked away.

The museum gift shop was crowded with raucous students in blue uniforms. They stared at me, mocked my baggy black clothes, and then laughed at my goggles. I waved my yellow rubber gloves at them and turned to the wide windows.

Hundreds of tourists marched on the promenade to the pond, the eternal flame, the origami cranes, and other precious sites in the peace park. I waited to hear a shout, some gesture of panic over the chemical ruins of the letters, or at least an announcement, but not a word was broadcast. The museum director might have decided to say nothing. Maybe no one really reads the letters. Noisy students and two waves of tourists wandered through the museum before the guards were told that most of the letters on the peace column had been erased. At last the alarm was sounded, and visitors were ordered to leave the museum. The guards waved to me on the way out.

Virga waited for me at the gate.

I walked with the tourists for a short time, and then sat on a park bench near the peace bell. Oshima heard the emergency alarm and rightly assumed it had something to do with me. He sat next to me in silence.

Police cars and fire engines rushed to the museum. Soon the police escorted a band of students around the park. Suddenly, the students surrounded the bench and pointed at my clothes, goggles and rubber gloves. The police listened to their stories, and then laughed at me. I was recognized as a nuisance, a park roamer, and a police maniac, but not a criminal. The students were unnerved by the humorous response to their accusation. They were meekly apologetic.

I was a warrior, a hafu ronin of the atomu ruins, and my pose as a buffoon was a perfect disguise. Oshima raised his twisted hand in silence. Virga circled the monuments, hurried over the bridge, and returned to the ruins. The storm clouds had passed, but the air was humid, unmoved, and the haze shrouded the sun. I soaked my feet in the dark, slow river, and then rested in the corner of the ruins.

Manidoo Envoy

Ronin is the tricky master of the ruins, the baseborn, *hafu ronin* of an empire war, the occupation, nuclear memories, and the eternal ghost parades in Hiroshima.

He rants about the rain, black rain, the emperor, and fake peace, but never the erotic brush with that shaman of the bakery. Miko is the exception to his rave, but not the weather. Evermore he hounds the mongers of peace museums and wily sponsors of *atomu* victimry. The park roamers, as you know, are not serious, but they are loyal to his cause, curious courage, and his sense of survivance.

Ronin never revealed how he obtained the corrosive chemicals that he poured on the simulated peace letters. He told me about his contacts with subversive nationalists, and that is the likely source of untraceable explosives, poisons, and other chemicals. The letters, as you know, were mounted on a pillar in the new addition to the museum. Ronin said it was an "empire column of fake peace" and that it was located near the simulated atomic dome. He is determined to destroy the fake dome, but that would require a timed explosion after hours to avoid injuries to tourists or employees, and he is not yet ready.

Ronin told me that he posed as a tour guide and lectured to a group of tourists from the People's Republic of China. The Japanese government was eager to show the Chinese that they were victims of the Americans. Only a few untitled photographs in the museum represent the atrocities of the Japanese military in Shanghai and other cities in China.

Ronin told me he craved that mysterious, radiant woman at the Andersen Bakery. Miko was a shaman, and by coy poses over a cup of tea, she apparently teased and plucked his *hafu* nature for pleasure. Ronin would never resist her coy disguise, but maybe she pursued him from the ruins to the bakery, hotel to gallery, peace park, and then back to the Atomic Bomb Dome.

The Shinto *miko* is the name of a shrine maiden, a diviner and shaman, an ecstatic, erotic dancer who enchanted the *kami*, or the spirits of nature, and so honored the ancestors. The modern bakery *miko* no doubt honored the *hafu* ancestors of the occupation and the shadows that haunt the stories of Rashomon. Miko is an *atomu bugi* dancer.

"It seems that originally the *miko* were supposed to be virgins, who would abandon their practice when they married," wrote Benito Ortolani in *The Japanese Theater*. The *aruki miko*, or wandering *miko*, "act as mediums conjuring the souls of the living and the dead, pronounce divine oracles, and pray for the faithful. A relatively high percentage of these wandering *miko* were blind. A number of *miko* became professional entertainers and prostitutes."

Ronin is a diviner and dreamer too, a teaser of *kami* spirits, but that morning he was truly enraptured by a bakery *miko*, a shaman of almond kuchen in a silky disguise. I read his notes on that scene and the description of her bright, moist feet, the touch of their thighs under an umbrella in a hard, warm rain, aroused me. I was there by his literary touch, seduced by a shrine dancer, and then, wet and aroused, we were directed to an art gallery.

"Shrine *miko* are usually dressed in red *hakama* and white blouse, or in pure white for special occasions," noted Brian Bocking in *A Popular Dictionary of Shinto*. The duties of the shrine maiden "include taking care of visitors, helping the priest with ceremonies and performing" the *kagura*, the sacred music and dance of *kami* spirits.

The word *kami* means a sacred spirit in nature, or "for all beings which possess extraordinary quality, and which are awesome and worthy of reverence, including good as well as evil beings," wrote Joseph Kitagawa in *On Understanding Japanese Religion*. "With the gradual emergence of professional priests, the role of women was reduced to that of being a *miko*," a shaman or diviner possessed by *kami* spirits.

Shinto is a sense of presence and the real, "a religion of the relative," wrote Ueda Kenji in *Religion in Japanese Culture*, edited by Noriyoshi Tamaru and David Reid. "In their origin, human beings and nature are, as it were, blood relatives, common offspring of the *kami* who brought Japan into existence."

Miko created the aesthetic, watercolor ghosts of children in the peace park. The contorted images were ethereal by common accounts, and the distorted, dismembered children were twice revealed in the painted mirrors. My eyes, hands, and the slant of blue light would have been cracked in the actual mirrors embedded in the canvas.

"The mirror is the most frequently found *kami* symbol," wrote Ueda Kenji. "According to the ancient myth of Japan's creation, Amaterasu, the *kami* who founded the imperial line, bestowed upon her descendants a mirror representing herself." The sacred mirror shows the presence of the *kami*, and for centuries the mirror has been regarded as "a symbol of authority." The *kagami*, or mirror, in fact, is a *kami* spirit catcher.

The *yata no kagami*, mirror of creation, is bronze and shaped like a flower with eight petals. This ancestral mirror is one of the "three treasures of the imperial dignity," wrote Louis Frédéric in *Japan Encyclopedia*. The sacred mirror is a symbol of the sun, and "purity of spirit."

Miko painted the *obake*, the ghosts of children, in simulated mirrors, and the real mirrors embodied in the canvas were broken. The images of the *kami* are "forever fragmentary, a nuclear aesthetic," wrote an art historian for the *New York Times*.

Ronin asked me to acquire at least one watercolor painting of children in the peace park, and to be certain it had an embedded mirror. He did not explain why. Several paintings were available at auction, but the international art dealer reported to me that the provenance was deceptive, unclear, undone, only sketchy. Miko never signed her paintings, and there were serious doubts that she was the actual artist. The Karasu Gallery would not, for any reason, reveal the name of the painter. The word *karasu* means "raven" or "crow" in Japanese.

Ronin assured me that Miko was a shaman of the *kami*, and her presence as an artist does not need a signature. He rescued a watercolor she had discarded to decorate the cover of manuscript notes that became this book. The publisher, however, would not consider the mutant images as cover art for *Hiroshima Bugi*.

Ronin suggested a broken mirror as a cover but cost was a factor. The book designer considered an elusive conversion of a human and a raven. Miko learned of my search and sent me two haunting watercolor paintings of nuclear children in the peace park. The bent faces of the children in the painted mirrors are folded as origami cranes. Ronin vanished, once again, and does not know about the art or the publication of his book. I try but never find my face in the actual, broken mirrors of the paintings.

The Mitsui Bank was one of the few structures that survived, in part, near the hypocenter of the nuclear explosion in Hiroshima. The

Andersen Bakery is located in that restored historical bank building. The Hondori Shopping Arcade is a popular covered street market area a few blocks from the peace park and the Atomic Bomb Dome.

Toyofumi Ogura observed a shadow on the stone at the entrance of the Sumitomo Bank. "Just before the explosion, someone was sitting on one of the lower steps, taking a rest, apparently with an elbow propped on his knee and his chin lowered onto his cupped hand," he wrote in *Letters from the End of the World*. "Then came the blinding flash, followed by intense heat. No doubt the person was killed instantly, as he was just four or five hundred meters from the hypocenter. But an indelible shadowlike image was formed on the part of the stone steps that was shielded from the flash by his body."

Hiroshima was a castle town built more than four centuries ago. Gokason, one of the first names given to the island villages, became an important trade center. Hiroshima is partitioned by seven rivers that flow into the Inland Sea.

The Genbaku Dome, or Atomic Bomb Dome, once the Hiroshima Prefectural Industrial Promotion Hall, is located, as you know, near the hypocenter and the Aioi Bridge.

The Atomic Bomb Dome is one of the buildings that survived the explosion. The Hiroshima Prefectural Hall, a wooden structure several blocks from ground zero, was destroyed. The Hiroshima City Hall, close to a mile away, burned but the concrete structure survived.

The Gokoku Shrine, located less than a block from the hypocenter, was incinerated, but the *torii* gate "was still standing amid the burned ruins, as if nothing had happened," wrote Ogura. "The blast came directly from above in this part of the city, and perhaps slender objects like these, whose tops presented a small area to it, were not blown over unless they had been structurally weak in the first place."

The Zuisen Temple, about two miles from the center, survived the explosion, but the traditional thatched roof was ignited by radiant heat and burned to the ground.

"Throughout the war, we could not be true to our own selves," wrote Ota Yoko in *City of Corpses*. "We lamented the fact that we could not say what we wanted to say; but we also had to say and do things we didn't want to say and do. That was very painful. We who revered a rational peace, liberty, and democratic politics nevertheless were forced to turn our backs on the world of those fine ideals and commit our souls to the grave. We had to play dead." Ota, an author and *hibakusha*, survived the nuclear incineration of Hiroshima. She wrote her stories on scraps of paper in about four months. *City of Corpses* would have been the first critical book published by a witness of the destruction, but the occupation authorities censored the manuscript. Richard Minear, the editor and translator, pointed out that the "first edition appeared in November 1948."

The Ana Hotel Hiroshima is located a few blocks from the peace park. Miko was employed as a *hosutesu*, a hostess or cocktail waitress, in the spacious, cushioned lounge at the far end of the lobby. She is one of the new *atomu* shrine maidens, an erotic *hosutesu* who arouses the *kami* spirits of hostelry.

The salary of a *hoteru hosutesu*, hotel hostess, is minimal, and there is no custom of public gratuity. The means of a *hoteru miko* are modest, modern, and the ends are forever the *kami* spirits and the ancestors. Why else would anyone wait on corporate patrons in a cocktail lounge?

7 Ronin of the Origami Cranes

Margarito Real and two other men were seated at a table near the window of the restaurant at the Ana Hotel Hiroshima. Real, a feral storier, waved and turned his hands, an oral punctuation and diversion, and with each gesture he bounced in his penny loafers. He leaped out of his seat to shake my hand, and then with his head cocked to the side, he examined my face, ears, and clothes. His hand was moist, sticky, and withered by contact. Real must be a hafu terrier in disguise.

> No goggles?
>
> Mission over.
>
> Where?
>
> Peace museum.
>
> Big news.
>
> What?
>
> Dead letters.

Real abruptly introduced me to the others at the table, and then he asked me about the rubber gloves. I was distracted by his sudden query, but anticipated his fascination and pulled the yellow gloves out of my shirt. He puckered his lips and slowly, in total concentration, slithered his hands into the gloves. I told him that rubber gloves make the man, and he was taken by the gift. Real admired each floppy finger, and then raised his gloved hands and waved to the hotel manager, the same man who had evicted Virga.

> My leprosy gloves.
>
> No, really?
>
> Yes, yes almost.
>
> You order now?

Derek Decisis said he was a retired justice on vacation from California. Stare, his legal nickname, has dark eyes, white hair, a great smile, and from time to time he recites poetic lines from country and western popular music. He ordered the pork medallion platter with fresh asparagus.

> No vegetables.
>
> Why not?

Touch of poison.

Real ordered a whole fish, any fish, and a bottle of red wine, any wine, and then expounded on the vintage and year. His showy toast was a seductive but evasive invitation to visit his wine cellar in a secret place that he promised to reveal later.

Petros Komuso, the other man at the table, was a culture and language teacher at the university. Later he told me in a secretive tone of voice that he was a covert secret agent.

What sort of agent?

Corporate spy.

Covert?

Yes, furtive.

For what?

Fiscal policy.

Why?

The future.

Petros wore a huge straw hat that covered most of his face. His smile was furtive, hidden in the shadow of the wide straw brim. He ordered a tofu sampler, a wide selection of sushi, and taruzake, a golden sake that has been aged in cypress casks. Later, he ordered nigori, a sweet, cloudy dessert sake.

Mine was salmon, rice, and seaweed.

Real devoured the fish, most of the wine, and turned every nonce, notice, and conversation into irony. He gestured with those yellow rubber gloves over a second bottle of wine. The synthetic rubber fingers squeaked on the glass.

Stare carefully severed the heads of asparagus and pushed the tender tips aside on his plate. He ate each cut of stalk with tiny medallions of pork. Hiroshima women, he boldly announced, as he sliced the asparagus, have very thin waists. Petros sipped sake, smiled under his hat, and slithered lower and lower into his chair.

Miko on my mind.

Look, atomu waists.

Wispy genes.

Mutant generations.

Real told the others about our meeting at the museum earlier that day, and they surely heard the news about the dead letters. One by one they offered me peculiar and indirect advice. Stare borrowed words, lines, diction, and reason from several blues and country

—

western songs to construct his stories of native resistance and survivance.

Johnny Cash, for instance, created a boy named Sue. The line was
lost on me at first, but then he described the scene. This is a nasty,
rough world, and you must be tough or die, and so the sentiment
of a father who named his boy a girl. Stare was indirect, to say the
least, but he probably meant to say that a hafu is a rough name,
and to survive you must fight. Likewise, rough peace might be the
allegory. The world of peacemongers is severe, and one must resist
the fakery. Finally he pushed his plate of asparagus heads aside
and recited variations of a song about an egg sucking dog. I
counted seven severed heads and asked him why?

Slight and fleshy.

No the heads.

Loose ends.

Puny favorites.

Petros invited me, by a generous grant of sake, to teach a course at
his university, but my mind was on asparagus, not an academic
summons. He waited for me to eat the last head and then resumed
his invitation. He suggested a seminar on the languages and metaphors of peace and liberty.

Fakers of peace.

Yes, of course.

Minutes later, he posed as a spy and told me that many corporate
executives are curious about the images that associate peace,
amity, and serenity with various commercial products. Many studies, he noted, indicate that economies are more advanced by force,
aesthetic coercion, and the sentiments of violence than by the
promises and pleasures of passive peace. He implied that my sortie
on the miniature peace letters would be good for corporations and
the global economy. Petros smiled once again under his hat and
slowly slipped away under the table and out of sight.

Sake spy.

Where?

Doctor Komuso.

Real counted out the cost of each dinner and collected the money.
He paid for the wine and sake, a generous pose, as we had only
met for a few minutes that day under the simulated dome in the
museum. He was enchanted by the rubber gloves, and clumsily

counted out the exact amount of the total dinner check, down to the last coin. The manager was very nervous, actually flustered, and refused to touch the money. Instead, he ordered a waitress to move the check. Real, we learned later, had craftily overestimated the cost of each meal, a sleight of hand in rubber gloves. We bought his meal and paid for the wine.

> Miko worked on the other side of the hotel lobby in the Tea and Cocktail Lounge. The asparagus heads, sake, spy comments on peace economics, and resistance music were very intense, but it was time to leave the burdens of rubber gloves and restaurant irony.

Miko was in the service area to prepare an order for a party of corporate executives. The manager was at the reservation podium. I asked to be seated at a table for two, and ordered the same green tea that she drank at the bakery.

> Miko returned from the service area with an order of wine. She heard my voice and brushed past me without a notice. She was radiant, always clean, blushed, moist, and my heart raced over a vision of her naked body. Surely that blush moves across her breasts, over her slight stomach, and thighs. She avoided me, and directed another hostess to serve my table. Miko changed clothes in the back room, and then, without a word or gesture, she walked right past me and out of the hotel.

Later, as we walked toward the peace park, she explained that the manager does not allow a cocktail waitress to sit with anyone in the hotel. I mentioned his weird reaction to the rubber gloves. She gasped, laughed nervously, and then told me he has a morbid fear of leprosy. The manager saw the hands of a leper under those rubber gloves.

> Leper manager?
> No, big hotel family.
> No leprosy.
> No, no.
> Do you worry?
> Leprosy?
> Yes, the curse.
> No, maybe.
> Oshima bears the curse.
> Who, regrets?

Oshima of the ruins.
Virga away?
Peace park duty.
Virga duty?

The night air was perfect, a slight, warm, moist wind from the river, and the luscious scent of flowers from the peace park reached us a block away. Miko danced on the sidewalk and bounced ahead of me as we reached the plaza at the museum. She wore a beige pleated skirt that billowed with her spirited moves, and her legs flashed in the faint light.

Several couples strolled nearby. Only hushed tones were heard in the peace park at night. The light of the peace flame shimmered on the pond. Miko moved around me in a slow, sensual dance. I gently reached out for her hand, but she turned and suddenly pulled away. She circled the peace flame on the concrete rim of the pond, the very site of my morning peace fire.

Miko paused at the edge of the pond, and then she pretended to push me into the shallow water, an erotic tease. I caught my balance, and at that moment saw her radiant face reflected on the water. I might have fallen into her image. She was a natural spirit, almost transparent as the children in her watercolor paintings. Her hands were warm, silky. She turned in a dance and my bare arm touched her breasts. She moved closer, teased me, and raised my hand to her breasts. I pushed her to the side, moved behind, and touched the rise of her stomach. She blushed and the heat rushed across my hands. Slowly, a blue aura surrounded her body and enclosed me, contained me in a shimmer of heat and natural motion. The sexual excitement was surreal, and the heat ethereal, a shadow. A slight breeze broke her image in the pond.

Suddenly the aura waned, a slight shimmer, and then she became a shadow dancer in the distance. I shouted, laughed, and crashed into the pond. The trace of her aura is in my stories.

Miko is a shaman, a trickster and visionary, disguised as a cocktail waitress and watercolor painter. She was possessed by the erotic kami of the peace park. Who would she become in our kabuki ghost plays?

Once again we came together on the promenade near the giant mounds of origami cranes. I reached for her hand, an ordinary motion. She touched me, a warm glance, and then danced around the monument dedicated to Sadako Sasaki.

You fear me?

Not yet.

My children?

Maybe so?

Children in the mirrors.

Yes, atomu ghosts.

Eyes and hands.

Sadako Sasaki counts cranes.

Caught in black rain.

I was much too eager, lusty, and always behind in her tricky games. My moves were too slow, and she outwitted me by erotic shamanic poses. So, it was time to pose my own native resistance. The park ravens heard me and circled the statue.

I picked several paper cranes from the many mounds at the monument. I had no idea how they were actually made, and tried to reverse the origami folds to understand the practice. Miko danced out of sight, but she was curious about my concentration on the paper cranes. She danced closer, circled me, and pushed her breasts against my back.

Faces on the cranes.

No, you tease.

Faces of atomu children.

Many, many faces.

Soaked in the black rain.

Torn, unfolded.

Politics of peace.

No politics.

Kabuki crane dancers.

Yes, where?

The ruins.

What ruins?

The Dome is my Rashomon.

Miko danced at my side and listened to stories of the ghost parade at the ruins. I told her the origami cranes forever tease the nuclear dead, and thousands of children are tricked at every fold by the emperor.

Miko moved behind me, pressed her thighs close to mine, and with both hands she touched my stomach, and then unbuckled my belt. At the same time she pushed me down the path to a shrouded bench near the peace bell. We were alone, no one could be heard or seen, not even Virga.

> Buy my soul.
> How muchie?
> Promises.
> Samurai promise?
> Maybe so.

> She opened my trousers, raised her skirt, and mounted me face to face. My penisu, aroused by her touch and heave, ducked into her wet, swollen, fleshy lips. She sighed, we moaned, and then she pushed hard against my thighs. She raised her body and pounded against me, over and over. Our thighs smacked and the erotic sound lasted in the moist night air.

I opened her blouse, licked her neck and breasts, and teased her hard nipples with my tongue. Miko bounced and shivered on my thighs. She shouted my name, and the wild, mighty rush on that park bench breached the silence of the peace park. Her sudden, persistent moans reached across the river.

> Oshima heard the animal sounds, and his leprous bones were awakened. He was aroused by uncertain memories and shouted back, but his voice was too weak to be heard past the ruins. Virga raised her head, turned her ears to the sound, and ran across the bridge and into the peace park.

Miko shuddered, bounced, and thrust once, twice, three more times. She almost choked me to death on the rise of her fierce orgasm. The final erotic moans lingered in the dark trees and peace monuments.

> I was overcome by my own orgasm seconds later and shouted into the trees overhead. The spasms lingered and we soared over the river and atomu ruins.

Miko leaned back, sighed, and shivered, praised the hearty kami spirits, and noticed the pale waxen marks on the rosy glow of my body. She tore open my shirt and revealed the mienai irezumi, invisible tattoos, on my chest.

> What happen?
> My mienai pose.
> What irezumi?
> Ainu invisible tattoos.

Atomu One, Eight Fifteen, what does that mean? She traced the unseen outline of the tattoos and then curiously scratched the marks with her fingers. Suddenly, she turned her right shoulder to show me her tattoo, and at that moment the peace bell sounded. At each solid stroke of the bell my penisu arose in her swollen cunt. She squeezed me by the beat and sound and sucked on my neck. My tattoos were visible once again.

Oshima and the park roamers were aroused by our erotic moans and wild, native shouts. They sounded the peace bell to celebrate our lusty moment on the bench. The park ravens croaked their consent from the trees and monuments.

Miko heard their voices, the croak of the ravens, and moved to the side of the bench, buttoned her blouse, smoothed out her dress, leaned back, and crossed her legs, but her innocent pose could not hide the traces of our passion. The radiance of her body lighted the bench, a shamanic kami lure on a dark path in the peace park.

Manidoo Envoy

Miko is an artist, a *kami* street shaman, but not a storier. She is a
brilliant visionary watercolor painter, as you know, but her stories
are lame and mundane.

Ronin was so aroused by the tease of this erotic *kami* of the bakery that he lost his sense of irony. Fortuitously he recovered the
lusty might of his *hafu* pose on a wooden bench in the peace park,
at the very moment she uncovered his *mienai irezumi*, or invisible
tattoos.

Miko was fascinated by his invisible tattoos and insisted that he
decorate her body in the same way. The word *irezumi* means "tattoo,"
or design on the skin, and the word *mienai* combines two words that
mean the negative of an appearance, pose, or invisible.

The word *irebokuro* was used to describe the first tattoos in
seventeenth-century Japan. The word *ire* or *ireru* means "to insert,"
and combined with *bokuro* or *hokuro*, a mole on the skin, it means a
beauty mark or tattoo. The picture tattoos based on traditional art
and *sumie* ink paintings came much later.

Ronin was forever haunted by the *obake*, the ghost children in
her watercolors, and he mocked her erotic dance in the ruins, but he
remembered only one of her stories. So, as a tease, he told many original variations of that same story. The story, as she first told it,
brought together many silent mongrels with a deaf monk in the
early *kami* history of Japan.

The mongrels became monks.

The Japanese *hafu inu*, or mongrels, were more secure at that time
in monasteries. Mongrels were hearty meals outside the monastic community. Sakasu, one of the senior monks, taught the mongrels how to
dance and bark in a *kami inu* circus. Sakasu is a nickname that means
"circus."

Sakasu was deaf, but he could hear very loud sounds, the heavy
crack of timbers and beat of a hammer on stone, thunder, and the raucous bark and bay of dogs. He was a prescient monk and could hear or
sense earthly vibrations, the presence of others, even at a distance.
He commiserated with the mongrels and taught them erotic *kami*
dances and how to bark a circus musical at the monastery. His *kami*

inu circus brought much attention and feudal favor to the monastic community.

Sakasu and the mongrels shared an *inu* circus patois, and in this way they created a new consciousness of politics. Some of the monks, those who had not spoken a word for years, were roused by the circus and mongrel patois. They burst into barks to tease creation. The pitch of their barks, however, was not as mature as the mongrels. That monastic *inu* circus was the start of the mongrel bark that has forever circled the earth and has become an eternal remembrance of the circus.

The mongrels acquired a taste for tofu cuisine and sake by the bowl. Once considered a meal the mongrels became connoisseurs of monastic fare. Sakasu was content that nothing brought the silent monks more pleasure than to watch his mongrels drink sake over dinner and then totter and bark through the stone garden at dusk. These monastic mongrels of the *inu* circus were at the verge of a giant leap in evolution, a critical moment of canine transcendence. The *kami inu* became monks, and that originary monastic bark and bay is heard in succession around the world.

William Shakespeare wrote about the bark and bay of dogs at about the same time as the *inu* circus. Doubtless he considered the eternal circle and evolution of the global bay. "I had rather be a dog and bay the moon," said Brutus in *The Tragedy of Julius Caesar*.

Miko told me much later that the reason she rushed out of the hotel that night was because the manager was jealous of Ronin. The ironies of evolution are constant, that a man of an undiluted caste and ancestry worries about a *hafu* mongrel on the run. Liberty is heard in trusty stories not by the insecure simulations of culture and race.

The hotel manager was actually jealous of any man who even looked at Miko. Naturally, every man who ordered tea, wine, or sake watched her sensuous moves across the cocktail lounge. The manager was a nervous voyeur constantly aroused by his desires and doubts about women at the hotel. Miko said she was obliged to have sex with the manager in a service closet at least once a day. She had sex with the manager that very day she met Ronin at the Andersen Bakery.

The hotel manager was paranoid about animals and diseases, and his fear increased by the mere sight of a canker and by every rumor of blight, contagion, and chance malady. He could not even bear to hear stories of poor health or disability. A mongrel, a slight cough, dirty sheets, cocktail napkins, or a stranger's hand caused him such concern about disease that he showered several times a day with a disinfectant soap. Leprosy, however, was a train of absolute terror that he could not cover or bathe away. The sound of the word caused him to shun, shiver, and weaken at the bone. He lived in morbid fear of a leper's touch.

Margarito Real was an awkward comic in rubber gloves that night at the restaurant. The hotel manager was not amused by his gestures. He saw a leper under those yellow gloves, and the fear of the disease enervated his caste, manner, and erotic tease as a voyeur. Ronin told me the manager backed away from the table, refused to touch the money, and covered his mouth with his sleeve. He would not breath the same air as Real, Decisis, Komuso, and Ronin. Leprosy was his eternal curse.

Real was solicitous only because he thought the *hafu* native was curious enough to write a book on his peace adventures. Ronin was justly prepared and outwitted him at every turn with a courtly tease and tricky stories. The grant of rubber gloves was an evasive gesture, a patent dinner game, and, as it turned out, rather unsavory. Ronin and the others, however, were cheated and outsmarted by a treacherous sleight of hand over the dinner check.

Petros Komuso pretended to be a corporate spy, but, as we learned later, he actually was an academic informant for several international corporations. He provided obscure analogies and political notions that were considered in product promotion.

Petros insinuated the obvious, that corporate executives were concerned about the economic outcome of the military occupation and were cautiously envious of the high productivity in Japan. General Douglas MacArthur, he announced at a conference on robotics, is the man to read on international economic theory.

Petros was persuasive only because he was elusive. The turn of his information was rumor, overheard, and then asserted in the pose of corporate espionage. By that manner he convinced the cagey corporate sponsors that a "new economic aggression," once based on the notion of cheap labor and products, would now arise from counterpeace movements. The war on peace was good for business.

Ronin of the *atomu* ruins and new calendar, he said, by a perverse, futuristic analogy, is the Douglas MacArthur of the occupation of

Japan. Miko listened to this, a summary of his covert report to corporations, and then she pushed his hat back to reveal his wide, nervous smile.

Ronin, as you know, undermined the simulations of peace to remember the ghosts of *atomu* children and *hibakusha* survivance. MacArthur, by analogy, ordered that labor unions be established as a way to increase wages and production costs to avert economic aggression in the new markets of Asia.

MacArthur told a Swiss diplomat, "The only remaining danger with Japan was its potential export competence," reported the *Japan Times*. "MacArthur worried that Japan, supported by 'a salary of famine (cheap wages),' would dominate Asian markets with 'junk' products."

Petros admired the occupation general even more in the *atomu* world of peace fakery. He strained to compare the occupation of a defeated country to the ghost parade in the ruins.

Miko learned that he started his covert career with the United States Embassy in Japan. Petros, an eccentric academic, was in a perfect position to observe hundreds of scholars, writers, and musicians who were on official lecture and performance tours in Japan. He participated in seminars and mundane conversations on the economies of peace, attended dinner parties, and collected critical information about the political interests of many visitors.

Petros is cautious not to favor any analogies as a spy. Saul Bellow, for instance, he brashly compared to Douglas MacArthur. The correspondence was arrogance, not economics. Bellow was terse in his public lectures and curt in his responses to academics. The faculty favored the general over the novelist in matters of economics and literature.

Petros was stimulated by his pose as a spy, but the information he provided was a confidence game, hardly more than anyone might gather in a casual conversation. Ronin told him the precise details of how he erased the peace letters, the same notice he entered in the dialogue book. Petros listened under his hat but wanted to know more about his schemes and motivation than his actions. Miko heard him say the *atomu* stories were the bluster of a police maniac.

Derek Decisis chanted and ranted the precious metaphors of Johnny Cash. Ronin was convinced that there is a word, phrase, or title from one of his songs that rights every emotion, match, loss and irony. Stare was a man of humor, not obsessions or victimry, but he was tormented by the wasp waists of young women in the city. He was aroused, irresistibly serious, and convinced that thin, erotic waists were a mutation only in Hiroshima. Ronin named it the *atomu hosoi* waist. The word *hosoi* means "thin" or "slender."

Ronin wore invisible tattoos, as you know, on his chest and back. Atomu One, Eight Fifteen, printed on his chest, is the time and date of the nuclear destruction of Hiroshima. Atomu One is a new solar calendar that starts with *hibakusha* pain, torment, and misery. Ronin measures his time and memory by this new *atomu* calendar.

There are four principal calendars used in the world today. The first, and the most widely used, is the Gregorian, introduced in the sixteenth century as a correction of the Julian calendar. The Jewish calendar serves a religious community. The Islamic calendar is based on lunar time. The Atomu calendar is solar, a true measure and touch-stone of *hibakusha* survivance in the nuclear world.

Japan has a rich and distinct tradition of tattoos. The history of early *irebokuro*, or beauty marks, and the more modern *irezumi*, or skin design, is obscure, but evidence of facial tattoos are found on the *haniwa*, ancient clay figures.

The practice of tattoos "remains obscure," wrote Donald Richie in *The Japanese Tattoo*. "Since there is no direct connection between either the Ainu tattoo or the early punishment tattoo and the later pictorial tattoo worn as embellishment, this late flowering of the Japanese tattoo as we now know it is sometimes seen as a spontaneous artistic happening, a sudden and inexplicable aesthetic event. Actually, however, the process was slow and apparently steady."

The early tattoos were beauty stains, pledges, names, and marks of association, but not yet pictorial. The mark of a pledge or promise was personal and social. Ronin has a pledge tattoo on his chest, Atomu One, Eight Fifteen. The tattoos on his back are floral, pictorial. His tattoos, however, are not directly connected to the history and practice of tattoos in Japan.

The Ainu of Hokkaido created the invisible tattoos on his body. Ronin told me they might have used a secret concoction of beeswax, cedar pollen, salmon marrow, and ghost pumice, but he was not certain. He could not describe the source of the pumice.

Tattoos were once used as marks of punishment. Criminals wore tattoos on their arms, and others who committed several crimes wore the character for *inu*, or "dog," a character with three strokes on their foreheads.

"The tattooed criminals were ostracized by society throughout their whole lives," wrote Mieko Yamada in "Japanese Tattooing from the Past to the Present." Criminals were marked forever, and many could live only by crime. The practice was carried out for more than a century. "Consequently, the penal system formed a solitary minority group, called *eta* class, the social outcasts. For this reason, ordinary people became afraid of tattooed people."

Donald Richie argued that the tattoo masters are traditional artists who no longer have disciples, "so it seems that the art of the tattoo is doomed to extinction."

Western tattoos are mostly a mark of individuality. The Japanese, however, do not set themselves apart from others by tattoos. "The tattooed man is not an individual exercising his right to be different but a man who wants to join a group," wrote Richie. "Thus, in modern Japan, those who get tattooed are rarely loners. They are, rather, looking for some kind of membership," or "display of candidacy."

Ronin wears invisible tattoos as marks of singularity, and yet the message on his chest is a promise, a remembrance of the ghosts of *atomu* children, as invisible as his tattoos, and to honor *hibakusha* survivance.

8 Ronin of the Invisible Tattoos

Miko wore a tattoo on the back of her shoulder, a muted morning glory. The choice blue blossom was almost closed, captured late in the day. She turned to show me that tattoo on the park bench, but we were interrupted, as you know, by the roamers.

She stayed with me last night in the ruins, and bared her only tattoo in the shadows of the firelight. By morning she heard the children in the kabuki ghost parade.

Miko counted out the minutes to eight fifteen ante meridiem in the ruins. The overnight memories, worries, and dares of children, their faces, teases, secrets, and precious treasures, were incinerated in motion. Not one child had the time to fear the emperor. The carp swam over seared, black bodies in the river. Birds burned to ashes on the wing, and the soft shadows of withered hands mark the concrete sidewalks. The children became dust, eternal atomu cries at that moment in the ghost parade.

Miko gave me a mirror with a rough wooden handle that was out of balance and turned in my hand. I could not find my face in the mirror. The images were uncertain, distorted, unstable, but she was always there on the curve with a lusty smile. My face was lost in the mirror. She told me not to worry, my true image would emerge one day.

Miko distracted me with her tease, and then turned to a wicker basket in the corner of the ruins. She picked out several scraps of my notes and read sections out loud. She was moved by the story of my mother, a bugi dancer, and my spirited encounter with the nanazu over a wooden sword at Sagami Bay.

Kappa story.

No, nanazu tricksters.

Same story.

My manuscript was written on scraps of paper, on post cards, the back of tickets, napkins, broadsides, remnants of paper the roamers gathered for me in the peace park. Ota Yoko inspired me to write my stories in this way. She was hibakusha and wrote the *City of Corpses* on shoji and scraps of paper in one month of extreme misery after the atomu bomb destroyed the city. Manuscript paper could not be found at the time.

My stories are remnants.

Oshima walked to the river to wash his face and hands, a morning ritual after the parade. The stench of dead carp and putrid weeds lingered on the shore. Miko saw his twisted hands and blunt fingers for the first time as he removed his shirt. She was touched by his misery, but not worried, and with no hesitation she lathered his arms and hands. Then she rinsed away the soap and gently dried his hard, scaly skin.

Oshima looked away at first, but then turned to admire her perfect hands and the wild blush on her face. I could see he was shied by her attention, but, at the same time, he could not turn away. She asked if he wanted to see her tattoo. Tears came to his eyes as she opened her white silk blouse. She revealed one breast and the tattoo on her shoulder. He reached out to touch the morning glory, and only then she shivered slightly, but did not move away. He traced the outline of the choice blossom with his hard, blunt fingers. Oshima praised her as a healer, a miko of the silky shadows.

Shinto shaman.

Miko of the shrines.

Natural healer.

Oshima was roused by her touch and moved with a clumsy bounce, a modern kami dance on the way to the Andersen Bakery in the Hondori Shopping Arcade. The scent of fresh breads and cakes reached almost to the ruins. Oshima was on the rise, an easy promise denied for sixty years as a leper. He turned and posed as a kagura dancer on the street. The sun was muted in the humid morning haze, and the rash of light created a luminous, natural hue on our faces as we walked to the bakery.

We were kami dancers.

Wild shadows of tradition.

Virga ran ahead of us, as usual, and licked the bare feet of many children. That mongrel was a healer in the black rain. She was a dancer at creation, and we heard the sudden laughter of children in the distance.

Miko ordered her usual breakfast of maple kuchen and a pot of green tea. Oshima looked in the windows many times but he never dared to enter the bakery. He was at peace, heartened by the touch of a beautiful shaman, and the sense of a perfect, almost forgotten touch of human compassion. The memory of that erotic moment at the river, however, did not survive in the bakery.

Miko was his breakfast guide, so he ordered the same, a maple kuchen and green tea, but the older clerk turned away and refused to serve a leper. Miko smiled and moved her chair closer to Oshima. She leaned on his hunched shoulder and boldly reached for his hidden hands. The clerk was horrified by the sight of a young woman holding hands with a leper in the bakery. She removed her apron, retreated to the back room, and called the police.

Virga sensed a moment of human cruelty. She growled and then barked at the woman behind the door. The clerk peered out the oval window. The curved glass distorted her face, twisted her mouth. The other clerk, a shy young woman, delivered our orders to the table. She bowed, blushed, and whispered an apology to Oshima. He might have touched her perfect, tiny hands in gratitude, but instead he raised his crippled, blunt fingers and praised her courage.

Oshima told the young clerk that his hands were deformed, almost dead by a curse of the emperor, and his heart was worried, but because of her favor and decency he was for the first time in sixty years a free man in a bakery. The clerk turned away to hide her tears.

Miko had eaten only half of her kuchen when the police arrived by car. The two young officers entered the bakery, looked around, smiled, bowed to the patrons, slightly to me, and asked the clerk at the counter what was the trouble. She said there was no trouble, but at that moment the evil, older clerk rushed out of the back room and insisted that the leper be removed from the bakery.

What leper?

There, that one.

Where?

Leper at the window.

Who, inu man?

The police looked around the bakery, studied each patron, and reported no evidence of a leper, and no trouble, no kuro, no trouble but the mongrel. They seemed to be amused by the fear and panic of the nasty woman. The clerk pointed at me, partly because my hands were hidden, a coy deception. I turned my fingers in a crick to appear leprous, and then raised my hands.

One of the officers recognized me as a police maniac, the one who walked out of the koban on my hands, a signature maneuver. He told his partner of my position as a park roamer, and laughed over the name of my mother, Okichi. The police assured the older clerk there was no need to worry. She hissed and retreated to the oval window when the police bowed and left the bakery.

Kitsutsuki, the wounded lieutenant, arrived at that very moment. He had just returned from a visit with his sister, a medical doctor at a shrine hospital near Nara. The police bowed, held the door open, and then teased him about the carved atomu figures on his wooden leg. Kitsutsuki returned the tease and presented the police with charms woven by the old monks in the hospital.

What charms?

Big earthquake.

Miko told me she wanted an invisible tattoo on her back, but she could not decide on an image or scene. She had seen only the tangle of shadows on my back, chrysanthemums, morning glories, and wild lettuce, or horseweed, by firelight in the ruins, so that very afternoon we went to a sento at the hotel near the railroad station in Hiroshima. Most of the hot baths were reserved for private parties at the hotel. Trover, once a park roamer, was an attendant at the sento and he always favored my parties.

Stare and Petros were on their way to buy train tickets so we invited them to come with us to the hotel. Miko was on their mind, of course, and they would never waive a chance to see her naked, thin waist. Oshima covered his head with a hood and wore white gloves, disguised as a taxicab driver, when he entered the hot bath. There were separate lockerrooms, a common shower area, a sauna, and an enormous communal hot bath pool.

I was the first in the sauna and climbed to the highest of the three benches. I covered my back and shoulders with a towel and waited for my body to overheat, turn rosy, and reveal the invisible tattoos on my chest and back.

Petros followed me, but he sat at the lower level of the sauna. He wore his straw hat down to hide his eyes, once the practice of the outcast samurai. He probably sleeps in that hat. Stare was alone in the pool. He waded in circles and crooned a familiar country tune. Oshima carefully washed his body and treated his skin with olive oil. He was ecstatic to be at the hotel sento with friends. Most of his life he has been denied these ordinary pleasures.

Kitsutsuki hobbled down the hallway to the side of the pool and slowly lowered his phantom leg into the hot water. The wilted stump wagged on the edge and blushed by memory, a spirited presence of the heat. I suggested later that he allow me to create an invisible tattoo of two stout, flying legs on his stump, a tribute to the blush of ghost limbs.

Miko covered her breasts with a hand towel, and the rest of her body was bare. A great ravel of black hair covered her crotch, an erotic crest. She sat close to me on the high bench in the sauna. Some time later, when the men were more at ease with her nudity, she lowered the towel and touched her breasts. Her nipples were huge, bloated by the heat.

Miko watched the atomu date and time emanate on my hot, red chest. The invisible tattoos that arise on the blush were the first she had ever seen. I turned sideways on the bench, removed the towel, and uncovered the invisible, floral tattoos on my back.

Chrysanthemums?

My mother.

Morning glories?

Nuclear survivance.

Wild lettuce?

Yes, fare of the ruins.

The chrysanthemums are to tease my mother who wore a print dress with giant showy flowers at the time she conceived me near the imperial moat, and because she was obedient to the emperor. She truly honored the chrysanthemum crown and abandoned me for a racist war criminal, the emperor. My tattoos abide the ironies of a hafu native fugitive.

The wild lettuce, or horseweed, is a tribune to those who survived on that fare. Horses once ate the tender stems, narrow leaves, and ray florets. I wear this invisible tattoo to remember the horseweed dumplings that were made of the first wild flower to grow in the nuclear ruins of the city.

Stare crooned several tunes, country miseries and sentimental gospel, as he soaked in the hot pool. He waded by chance into a cove of electrical stimulation and his voice wavered. He danced at the edge of the therapeutic rush of current in the water and quavered a few lines from "He's Got the Whole World in His Hands." Stare was never without a few words of a song.

Oshima floated in the pool. He was at peace in an absolute paradise of heat. Only his face and hands were above the water. Petros, shrouded as usual under his straw hat, moved around him like a serpent and toward the cove of electricity.

"Take My Hand Precious Lord."

Please, not in a sento.

Take my towel, precious.

Take my phantom leg.

Miko traced the outlines of every flower on my back, marked the time and date on my chest, and then tried to scratch another date on my shoulder with he fingernail, but my savage body could not be marked. She was hot, and we were alone in the sauna.

She touched my testicles and wrote a tattoo on my penisu, the word pesu, or peace. I was aroused, naturally, by her touch and the heat. She moved to face me on the bench, her nipples pressed on my chest, right above the atomu date. She slowly mounted me and then bounced on my thighs. She moaned, shouted, and laughed in turns, and pounded me on the bench. Her orgasm was slow on the rise, and then steady in the heat of the sauna. Our heavy sweat stained the wooden bench. Later, we showered and my tattoos vanished in the cold water. She pinched the last trace of the flowers and pleaded for an invisible tattoo. She wanted me to create a giant, invisible chrysanthemum on her back.

No, you tease.

Really.

Funeral flower?

Yes, an irony.

But why?

Beautiful Oshima.

Oshima told her the story about the giant chrysanthemums that he and the other imprisoned lepers nurtured over the years on the island. The flowers of their great love and courage were sold for only a few weeks in a nearby town. The buyers discovered the source and they refused to touch the flowers of lepers. The director of the leprosarium sterilized the chrysanthemums with harsh chemicals to reassure the buyers. The growers were deeply depressed that the bright, hardy blooms were poisoned for the fear of leprosy. They abandoned their gardens, and many lepers died that year of extreme loneliness.

Oshima was truly touched by her request, and he was eager to learn a new kata, the art of the invisible tattoo. He studied the floral tattoos on my back, and then assisted me a few days later near the river, across from the peace park.

Miko undressed in the ruins. She wore a summer yukata and nothing more. I was aroused by her moves, the turn of her neck, the reach of her back muscles, the rise of her breasts, and that great mound of black hair. My lusty thoughts that morning inspired an original tattoo, a chrysanthemum in the hands of a leper. The site of the consecration was an enormous stone on the shore of the river. The atomu stone was at the center of the ruins.

The early morning clouds retreated from the ruins and statues in the peace park. Only thin, dreary ribbons of haze lingered on the river, once choked with the bodies of children. Gray carp nosed the surface, lost in the shadows of memory. The sun chased the last clouds over the stones, under the bridge, and a golden slant of sunlight burst and bounced on the river.

Miko spread a thick towel on the smooth, warm stone, untied the yukata, and stretched out on her stomach. Her shoulders and back shimmered, a natural radiance in the sunlight. I touched a giant floral outline, the broad petals of a giant chrysanthemum, kneaded her back with witch hazel, and then spread a rich olive oil. The sun burst in every pore on her back.

I used three blunt needles that were tied together and heated over a fire, glowing hot. The Ainu warriors taught me how to create invisible tattoos, and they gave me a small container of their invisible tattoo infusion, a secret concoction of pollen, beeswax, and pumice.

The sun glowed in every bead of blood on her shoulder. My hand held to the sensuous rise of her muscles and bones. Oshima leaned closer and spread the bright blood over the puncture traces of the chrysanthemum. He moaned and licked the blood on his blunt fingers.

The hot needles, punctures, and infusion created tiny scars and the invisible tattoo. The waxen scars are shadows that resist any blush, and when the body is heated the outline of the tattoo remains muted, only the natural color of the skin. My moves were swift and intense, a visionary creation of a giant chrysanthemum held in the blunt hand of a leper. The memory of that pain and the hues of my passion became the invisible tattoos on her back and shoulders. Horiatomu of the Ruins, my signature, in the tradition of a new master of invisible tattoos, was the last incision on her body. I wrote my name on the rise of her buttocks. The passion of my signature was an unseen tattoo near the hand of Oshima.

Manidoo Envoy

Ronin is the tattoo teaser of his own stories, the crucial native creator of aesthetic, erotic pain in the *atomu* ruins. Horiatomu, his signature as a tattooer, incised a giant, invisible chrysanthemum on the back of a *miko* shaman of the bakery.

Miko showed me the tattoo the first time we met some months later at the Hotel Manidoo. Ronin had vanished once more, another one of his eternal samurai suicides. She visited me first and then contacted other natives at the White Earth Reservation. She heard many stories about his cagey character, tricky shifts, rebuts, and fade away, but no one ever worried about his absence. Contrary to his peace moves in the ruins, on the reservation his presence was animated more by stories.

Miko lowered her silk blouse and turned to show me her shoulder, but only a faint trace, a mere shadow, of the floral tattoo was visible. Ronin teased me with descriptions of her lusty body moves. I was ready, naturally, and excited by the stories he wrote about her, and even more, of course, by the presence of her bare breasts, but her pose at the window was courteous, not erotic. She presented a work of art on her back, a tease but not a carnal show of her body. I was the trusty of the stories.

I was determined to see the hand of the leper, so she removed her blouse and invited me to massage her back. I was aroused, as you can imagine, and doubly by the sight of her huge nipples and the wild scent of her body. The natural heat of her soft, strong skin surrounded my rough hands. I was bound to the heat, and slowly the trace of an invisible chrysanthemum emerged by my touch. Then a marvelous, waxen, leprous hand moved when she turned her head and tightened the muscles on her back.

Ronin created forever a slight minatory motion on her back, an invisible trace and erotic memory of the leper in the *atomu* ruins, the Rashomon of the Atomic Bomb Dome. The motion of that hand on her back was a gift of a chrysanthemum story. Oshima cried, she said, when he saw the trace of his hand move on her back. He had never been so aroused or honored. Miko had sex with that lucky man twice on the bench in the peace park. She told me the second time he almost died by orgasm as he watched his three hands move on her back.

Ronin never mentioned Seikichi in "The Tattooer," by Junichiro Tanizaki, but he surely read that short story in *Seven Japanese Tales* when he visited me at the Hotel Manidoo. His father had read the same story, and the book was stacked at the side of his wicker chair near the window. Ronin shared the aesthetic practice and singular, literary pain of *irezumi*, or *horimono*, long before he was marked by invisible tattoos.

Donald Richie pointed out in *The Japanese Tattoo* that the tattoo master used the word *horimono*, "to dig things," but never the "rather common term, *irezumi*, for his craft." Once the tattoo is completed, the "master is ready to sign his work. He has left space, usually an oblong box under the arm or along the thigh. Into this he puts his name." The master uses the character for *horu*, "to dig," in his name. Horisada, for instance, is the name of a tattooer. Ronin, as you know, signed his name as Horiatomu of the Ruins.

Ronin borrowed the sense of an expression, the "hues of my passion," from "The Tattooer." Tanizaki wrote, "He saw in his pigments the hues of his own passions." Seikichi, the tattooer in the story, was "famous for the unrivaled boldness and sensual charm of his art." He "cherished the desire to create a masterpiece on the skin of a beautiful woman."

Seikichi promised a geisha that he would make her "a real beauty." He created overnight a huge spider with black ink and cinnabar, and in the morning the "weird, malevolent creature had stretched its eight legs to embrace the whole of that girl's back."

Seikichi was a tricky, master tattooer. Ronin must have been inspired by the story of that spider on the back of a geisha. "To make you truly beautiful I have poured my soul into this tattoo," said Seikichi. "Today there is no woman in Japan to compare with you. Your old fears are gone. All men will be your victims." Ronin might have said as much about the invisible chrysanthemum tattoo.

The geisha "slipped the kimono off her shoulders," Tanizaki wrote at the end of the story. "Just then her resplendently tattooed back caught a ray of sunlight and the spider was wreathed in flames." Likewise, the hand of a leper moved on the back of a *miko* shaman.

Ken Ito pointed out in *Visions of Desire* that Tanizaki was an "expert at using the past to give life to a sensibility that belonged to the present." Tanizaki created an aesthetic presence in his stories, and the sensibilities of color, hues of light, shadows, and traditions of beauty. Not "beauty in a natural state," he explained, as theater is a world of simulations, but simulations in the shadows of tradition. The new world is brighter and haunted by technologies. "A senseless and extravagant use of lights, I thought, has destroyed the beauty of Kabuki." The Bunraku puppet theater, he observed, is "far more richly suggestive" by lamplight than modern electricity.

"Our ancestors cut off the brightness on the land from above and created a world of shadows, and far in the depths of it they placed woman, marking her the whitest of beings," Tanizaki wrote in *In Praise of Shadows*. "If whiteness was to be indispensable to supreme beauty, then for us there was no other way, nor do I find this objectionable." He noted the "ghostly beauty" of older women, the blackened teeth and shaved eyebrows as a way to whiten the face. "I know of nothing whiter than the face of a young girl in the wavering shadow of a lantern."

Tanizaki revealed an aesthetic pleasure in the nuance of light, as in the "magic of shadows" in an alcove. "Were the shadows to be banished from its corners, the alcove would in that instant revert to mere void." These traces of the unseen, the shadows of presence, are the sensibilities of the invisible tattoo.

The *kagura* is the sacred *kami*, or spirit, of music and dance. The *miko*, or shrine maidens, performed the *kagura* to entertain and to entice the *kami* spirits of the shrine. Brian Bocking pointed out in *A Popular Dictionary of Shinto* that a *miko* is dressed in red *hakama*, a divided skirt or trouser, and a white blouse. There are many regional styles and types of *kagura*, both dance and trance performances.

The Japanese celebrate dance in the stories of their creation. Dance and music are magical powers in their culture. "The term *kagura* (or *kami no kura*, meaning the 'seat of *kami*') indicates that this type of religious dance, performed by female shamanic-diviners, has always been an important element in religious rituals from early days onward," wrote Joseph Kitagawa in *On Understanding Japanese Religion*.

Louis Frédéric noted in *Japan Encyclopedia* that *kagura* "dances are performed for various reasons, either to invoke the *kami* and thank them for their kindness, or to ask them for good health and a long life during a ritual of Chinese origin called *chinkon*."

Tanizaki wrote in *Childhood Years* that he observed a *kagura* more than a century ago and noted that the musical instruments were "rather simple and limited in range. By contrast, the masks and costumes were quite splendid." The *kagura*, he pointed out, had "absolutely no dialogue, the actors expressing themselves entirely through gesture and dance. Since there was no explanation provided of the title or contents, most of the audience would not have known just what incident from what period was being shown; we simply watched the actors and listened to the musicians without understanding much of the meaning. Later, when I began to read books of history and folklore, I would often come across something that made me realize for the first time just what it was I had been watching."

Tanizaki observed a production of the *Chushingura* at the Kabukiza Theatre in Tokyo. Ronin, some fifty years later, was entranced by scenes from the same kabuki play, *The Treasury of Loyal Retainers*, at the Kabukiza. The famous theater was first built in 1889, and it was rebuilt after the war. "Nearby were some eleven teahouses affiliated with the theater, and these displayed bright flowered hangings on their second floors," wrote Tanizaki.

The Japanese *kagami*, or mirror, is a symbolic *kami*, the spirit of the creation stories. The ceremonial mirror revealed the shadows of spirits. The shrine mirror "hides nothing," wrote Chikafusa Kitabatake in *Jinno Shotoki*. "The mirror is the source of honesty because it has the virtue of responding according to the shape of objects." The teacher and historian made his observations in the fourteenth century.

Miko gave Ronin a magic mirror, one that would not hold his image. He turned the mirror in every direction but never found his face. Miko, on the other hand, was always reflected on the curve of the rim.

Frédéric pointed out that magic mirrors "were made in Japan with a polished surface that reveals various designs under indirect light or when fogged." The designs or images in these mirrors change by the nature of the material. The *oni kagami*, magic or demon mirrors, are "relatively rare."

The Shinto *kagami* "is the sacred symbol of the Grand Shrine of Ise as well as many other shrines," wrote Sokyo Ono in *Shinto: The Kami Way*. "The mirror that stands before the inner sanctuary at Yasukuni Shrine in Tokyo is an ornament," a gift from Emperor Meiji.

Ronin once presented his magic mirror to a *miko* shaman at the Yasukuni Shrine. Only there, rightly dressed in his father's military uniform, did he find his face reflected in the mirror. Miko was

116

right to say he would find his image one day. The mirror was a tease of stature and diffusion, but his presence at the shrine was a profound confrontation, a desecration of the memorial.

The Shinto Yasukuni Jinja, or shrine, was founded in 1868, the same year that the United States government established the White Earth Reservation in Minnesota. The shrine is now dedicated to the memory of those who died in a century of wars.

Ronin wrote about an electrical cove in the hotel *sento*, or public bathhouse. Some hot baths have sections that were charged with electricity. The slight shock was thought to be a healthy stimulation. Stare, the justice, teased the border of the shock.

The word *kata* means a form, posture, or style, as in martial arts and other artistic practices. Karate, for instance, has ten *kata*, and judo six. Oshima would learn a new *kata* of the invisible tattoo. The word is also used to teach movements in traditional theater.

Miko wore a *yukata*, a summer bathrobe or kimono, when she was marked with invisible tattoos. She borrowed the *yukata* from the Ana Hotel Hiroshima.

Ota Yoko was *hibakusha*, as you know, a miserable survivor of the atomic explosion over Hiroshima. "I wrote *City of Corpses* between August 1945 and the end of November 1945. I was living at the time on a razor's edge between death and life, never knowing from moment to moment when death would drag me over to its side," she wrote in the introduction. She lost everything and moved to the country.

"I hadn't even a single sheet of paper, not one pencil, let alone pens and manuscript paper. At the time there wasn't a single store selling these items," wrote Ota. "I got yellowed paper, peeled from the shoji of the house I was staying in and the houses of acquaintances in the village, toilet paper, two or three pencils. Death was breathing down my neck. If I was to die, I wanted first to fulfill my responsibility of getting the story written down.

"My pen did not take in the whole city. I wrote only of my very limited experience of the riverbed." Ota had been living at her mother's house and escaped to the river. She lived there, in the *atomu* ruins, for three days.

"Take one episode, reported in the press at the time, that is still fresh in my mind. It is the story of three children, orphaned in that instant on August 6." They entered a camp for orphans outside of Hiroshima. "The three said they wanted to become monks and dedicate

117

their lives to the spirits of their parents and to the spirits of other victims of the war." They were taken to a temple in Kyoto. "There they took the tonsure and wore the shawls and robes of priests." These stories "flood my heart with tears. I am a writer; but even so, I wanted first and foremost to wrap my arms around those small children and weep. I wanted to be a writer able to do that with good grace."

Ronin wrote his stories on scraps of paper, tickets, notices, hotel stationery, advertisements, and several brochures from the peace museum, in honor of the courage, the unbearable dedication of Ota Yoko.

Ronin sorted his notes and scenes into several random bundles during the month he lived in Matsue, Japan. He posed as a direct, native descendant of Lafcadio Hearn and moved into the museum residence of the author. Ronin told the director that Hearn, in his late twenties, had lived for a summer with his grandmother on the White Earth Reservation in Minnesota. None of this was true, of course, but the director was taken with the romantic association of woodland natives.

Miko mailed these original literary shards and ledger notebooks to me in several tattered cardboard boxes. Nothing was organized, dated, or in any obvious order, except that the remnants were in layers by paper size, but the notes and scenes were not directly related one to the other.

The Hotel Manidoo became the center that deciphered his scenes, teases, and descriptions into an elaborate catchword guide and chronicle. Night after night the native veterans unraveled with great respect and humor the scraps of stories by the incredible son of Nightbreaker.

Ronin is clearly the literary artist, author, and inspiration of the ultimate assembly of his stories, but the native ghost decoders made it possible for me to connect the scenes and narratives of *Hiroshima Bugi*.

9 Ronin of the Ainu Bears

The Atomic Bomb Dome, as you know, is my Rashomon. My kabuki haven, my kami gate in the ruins. Oshima came out of the rain, the memories of black rain, the waves of atomu poison, and we have lived here since the start of this manuscript.

Hiroshima is my bugi dance, the peace pond my fire, origami cranes my tease, the park roamers, ravens, mongrels my strain, and the Peace Memorial Museum is my *Hiroshima Mon Amour*.

I changed the name on my museum tee shirts and decked the main entrance to the museum with the name of the movie. The noisy paper banner had a worthy audience for about three hours today. The guards, who recognize me and who liked the new name, were ordered by the director to cut it down.

Hiroshima Mon Amour Museum.

I lectured some twenty tourists who had arrived by bus that the new museum is named after the movie *Hiroshima Mon Amour*, and then assumed the role of an official tour guide in the museum. I pretended to be two decadent characters in the movie, a moody hafu architect and a seductive actress with green eyes. My voice was pitched and heady. The tourists listened, frowned, one or two smiled by doubt, but they seemed to like my style.

I summoned the tourists to that case of plastic miniatures with nuclear wounds. They were pained by the hideous representations, and some turned away. My *Hiroshima Mon Amour* act was in front of that diorama of aesthetic victimry. I shouted at the simulations, figures in the atomu ruins, and ridiculed the miniature woman in a kimono. The trees were bare and yet the figures were dressed for the museum tourists.

You saw nothing in Hiroshima.

I saw everything.

Atomu 12, the time is summer, twelve years after the atomu bomb incinerated Hiroshima. I played the parts of two characters in *Hiroshima Mon Amour* by Marguerite Duras.

She said, "Four times at the museum."

He said, "You saw nothing in Hiroshima."

She said, "The people walk around, lost in thought, among the photographs," contorted beams, broken bricks, a "bouquet of bottle caps," a wristwatch with dead hands, and a tricycle. "Human skin floating, surviving, still in the bloom of its agony."

He said, "You did not see the hospital in Hiroshima. You saw nothing in Hiroshima."

She said, "Hiroshima was blanketed with flowers. There were cornflowers and gladiolas everywhere, and morning glories and day lilies that rose again from the ashes with an extraordinary vigor, quite unheard of for flowers till then."

He said, "You made it all up."

She said, "Like you, I know what it is to forget."

He said, "No, you don't know what it is to forget."

She said, "Like you, I have a memory."

He said, "No, you don't have a memory."

She said, "Like you, I too have tried with all my might not to forget. Like you, I forgot. Like you, I wanted to have an inconsolable memory, a memory of shadows and stones."

He said, "What are you doing in Hiroshima?"

She said, "I'm playing in a film."

He said, "What's the film you're playing in?"

She said, "A film about peace. What else do you expect them to make in Hiroshima except a picture about Peace?"

You saw nothing in Hiroshima.

Morning glories, horseweed dumplings, the fate of black rain, and the injustice of chance. What is remembrance, and how do we resist forgetting?

Bugi in the simulated ruins.

Hiroshima Mon Amour is my bugi movie tonight, because the new war on simulated peace starts right here in the museum. The nuclear nights never end in a diorama of victimry. The tourists backed away. I never lived by lies, but there is so little time to overturn the persuasive dioramas and fakers of peace.

The tourists listened to my movie voices and my tease of solemn chitchat, but only one person, a retired nurse, reacted to my soliloquy, contradictions, and irony. She shouted back, "Sir, you may have lost your sense of peace."

You saw nothing in Hiroshima.

I abandoned the tourists near the pillar of promissory letters, the scene of my last crime against the simulations of peace. The pillar was shrouded in heavy, velvet drapes. The melted, decomposed letters had been removed, and a sign nearby explained that many new peace letters would soon be mounted on the column, but not a word about my wily assault on the memorial catchwords of the peacemongers. That scene should be in my new version of *Hiroshima Mon Amour*.

Virga teases children in the park.
Ravens convene on solemn monuments.
Roamers sound the peace bell.
Oshima waits at the river near the ruins.

Miko rushed to the hotel sauna to see, for the fist time, the invisible morning glory on her back. The Tea and Cocktail Lounge was not busy, so she left work early. She carried a mirror, moved sideways on the bench, she told me, and waited for the invisible tattoo to emerge. There were three men in the sauna, and one said he was a journalist. Naturally he was interested in the invisible tattoo. Miko told him the flower was my creation, a secret, shamanic art taught by the Ainu in Hokkaido.

Ainu shaman?
Secret, invisible tattoos.
Yes, osoraku yakuza?
Maybe yakuza?
Yes, shaman yakuza.
No crazy kabuki.
Yes, bakuto traces?
No gamblers.
Yes, oyabun yakuza?
No kobun.
Yes, yubitsume?
No cut fingers.
Maybe nationalists?
No, maybe so.
Yes, osoraku bushido.
No, maybe so.
Yes, praise the emperor?
No, maybe never.

Miko invited the journalist to meet me at the ruins the next morning. He was earnest, and very eager, a man of many praises, none his own. He bowed several times and presented his embossed business card, *Asahi Evening News* in Tokyo.

Richie, a nickname he adopted in honor of Donald Richie, was nervous, awkward, shy, and he covered his mouth when he smiled. His teeth were crooked and diseased, but more than that, his breath was smelly, truly sour. He wore a black shirt with a high neck and black trousers and shoes, the pose of an imperial raven.

I had my doubts that he was a journalist, because anyone who interviews people every day must take better care of their teeth, but as a police maniac there was nothing for me to hide in the atomu ruins. Virga watched him from an escape distance. Later, we had breakfast with the journalist at the Andersen Bakery.

Richie had read my entries in the museum dialogue book, but he told me that he was convinced the author was not real. Maybe a police maniac, he told me, but not a peace terrorist. Miko, however, inspired him to consider my story. She presented her new tattoos in the sauna, and that erotic, floral connection was more persuasive than a voucher of authenticity.

I was tricky and evasive at first, and especially when he tried to record my comments. Richie was obsessed with my mother and her praise of the emperor. I avoided his peculiar interest in my parents and resisted his curiosity about native cultures. He was an obvious racialist, troubled by communism and the menace of a hafu culture, but eventually he turned his attention to my ideas of peace, nuclear weapons, and my connection to Ranald MacDonald.

Richie, as a child, heard the story of MacDonald and dreamed of retracing his journey back to a native culture in British Columbia. Nightbreaker, my father, was inspired by the narrative and planned to shadow MacDonald in Japan. The war recast his adventures, and my father served as a military interpreter with the occupation in Tokyo. Richie was touched that my father inspired me to carry out his vision of the journey.

MacDonald was in custody most of the time he was in the country, so my rove was on the paths he and my father might have taken, first with the Ainu in Hokkaido, and then the ghost parades in Hiroshima.

Richie mentioned that he once visited the Ainu in their new homeland nation, Ainu Moshiri, on Hokkaido. He said the leaders are very active in politics. I told him the anishinaabe and the Ainu share a sense of natural reason and similar stories of animal creation and presence. Bears are honored in both cultures. He was curious and encouraged me to tell him more about my journey in the name of my father and Ranald MacDonald.

You sail boat?

Rishiri Island to Soya Bay.

Many winds.

Gale tore the sails.

Ainu save you?

Yes, just like MacDonald.

Ainu communists?

No, no, bear shamans.

MacDonald was a sailor on the *Plymouth*, a whaler in the northern seas of Japan. By agreement with the captain he pushed away in a small boat and sailed to several islands. Near Rishiri Island he capsized his boat on purpose, to present a state of distress at sea. On July 2, 1849, he saw smoke on the island and was rescued by the Ainu. They cared for him, and then he was turned over to the Japanese on Hokkaido. My boat was overturned by a sudden wind in the very same month, more than a hundred and fifty years later in Atomu 53.

I washed ashore, abandoned my makeshift sailboat, and slowly made my way south, a route of spas that my father might have taken, first to the Toyotomi onsen near Horonobe, Hokkaido. My backpack was light, only a change of clothes, scant toiletries, and three wet books, *Narrow Road to the Far North*, a haiku journey by Matsuo Basho, *Glimpses of Unfamiliar Japan* by Lafcadio Hearn, and *Japan: Story of Adventure* by Ranald MacDonald.

Noboribetsu was the second great onsen on my route, a volcanic, sulfurous, natural hot spring in the mountains south of Sapporo. The Daiichi Takimotokan Hotel provided a wide selection of natural mineral baths and other services, but is was much too expensive. I stayed only one night and used the hot baths for two more days.

Many sulfur pits.

Steamy, sulfurous winds.

Yes, many suicides.

Richie was creased too close to the bone, and he leaned to the dark side of reason, but he always smiled, even about suicides, and, of course, covered his mouth to hide his crooked teeth. His smelly breath, however, could not be covered. He gave more thought to the emperor and communism than to the kabuki ghosts in the ruins. Miko sat back to avoid his breath over breakfast at the Andersen Bakery. Dark or not he was eager to hear more about my time in Noboribetsu.

I told him that the vacationers were curious and wanted to hear my stories about Ranald MacDonald. One man, a lonesome professor, had studied the cultures of the Ainu. Seikichi taught literature at Tohoku University in Sendai. Later, he revealed an invisible tattoo of an elegant bird in flight on his shoulder. I could not believe that a bird tattoo came alive with a mere blush, and was otherwise invisible. He was evasive about the practice but the next day he agreed to drive me to Biratori Village near Tomakomai.

The Ainu were created with golden eyes, and the women wear decorative dark blue tattoos, beauty marks on their upper and lower lips. Seikichi told me that the art of tattoos was learned from a tricky tukusis, a trout, a creature that became a woman. The dark blue color of the tattoos he told me came from herring oil and the soot of burned birch bark rubbed into the incisions.

Virga was at my side.

Oshima drank tea.

Miko touched my thighs.

Richie wrote furiously.

Seikichi introduced me to several elders and mentioned my interest in invisible tattoos. They raised their arms in praise and stroked their great wavy beards. MacDonald described their kindly salutations in exactly the same way.

The Ainu returned my salute.

I told the elders about my father, my hafu parentage, and the adventures of the hafu teacher, Ranald MacDonald. Seikichi must have elaborated on my stories in translation because the elders were amused and wanted to explore the actual journey of MacDonald. They gestured with their hands and mentioned his name several times. That night we sat around an open fire, and the old men told stories. Their generous manner, and the light in their eyes, created a sense of solace. My father was with me, his face wavered in the shadows on the other side of the fire that night. My heart was at peace in his presence. This would have been his great journey.

Seikichi, by coincidence, has the same name as the tattooer in the story "The Tattooer," by Junichiro Tanizaki. The next morning he mentioned to the elders my native interest in invisible tattoos. The elders sat in silence. Seikichi smiled, bowed several times, and then suddenly drove out of the village. That afternoon the elders were on the move. No one invited me to travel with them, but no one resisted my presence either.

The elders drove north toward the Shikotsu Toya National Park. The Ainu were courteous and spirited on the way, and they always invited me to share their meals, but no one indicated to me the actual destination or anything about invisible tattoos.

Later that day the elders parked the trucks and we walked into the national forest toward Lake Shikotsu. The Ainu listened to the swish, hushed soughs, hints, rumors, and ya, ya, ya in the canopy of the giant trees. The iso kamuy, or great spirits of the bear, turned in the shadows. The wind heaved the trees in the ancient rush of creation.

Great brown bears waited at every natural path in the forest. The bears were secure, curious, and tricky, but never evasive or worried about the presence of humans. The bears teased me, and touched me, a gentle bump on the side. The elders were amused and raised their ceremonial worry sticks. The bears ran ahead only to circle back and bump me again. This was once the imperial forest and no one ever dared hunt the bears. They have never heard the sound of a gunshot and had no reason to fear humans.

The Ainu and the anishinaabe honor bears as original totems in their creation stories. Bears are wise, persuasive, and wily. Bears show humor, and bears masturbate. Bear spirits are the trace of humans in the remembrance of the natural world. A family of bears encircled me, nosed my chest, thighs, and the cubs snorted near my crotch. I was tempted to touch their ears but held back because my absolute enchantment would have been risky. The bears laughed, pushed against me, the trees, and licked my head and shoulders.

The elders were doubly amused and laughed with the bears. My presence, the scent of a wild stranger, became a bear bugi in the forest. One of the elders sounded the hyoshigi and the bears slowly walked away. We continued, and the bears seemed to be our constant escort at an escape distance, almost invisible at dusk. The sound of their breath was primal, sonorous, and steady. Another mile or so we arrived at a tiny village of dam tenders and their families who lived on Lake Shikotsu. The dam tenders warmly embraced the elders. They teased each other and then we were ushered into one of the houses. The light of the fire danced around the room. The dam tenders were gracious, and so pleased to see the elders that they overlooked me at the fireside. My father was there in the wild shadows.

Two young women watched me closely. Their eyes were golden, maybe hafu Ainu. They wore leather belts with silver chimes attached by thongs. The elders created a sense of rapture and fancy with their stories. My heart raced, a wild desire, and their murmur was lusty and visionary. Suddenly, one woman burst into an ecstatic song, and the other woman danced near the fire. The dam tenders were enchanted, and the elders raised their hands to honor tusu kamuy, the presence of shamanic spirits. The dancer blushed, and revealed a trace of an invisible tattoo on her breasts. The women aroused me with their great passion, the sound of their chimes, but that sacred moment was chancy.

The dam tenders teased me, and tricked me to swim in the lake. I resisted the bait at first, but then some of the elders removed their clothes and with no hesitation headed for the water. I quickly undressed, ran to the bank, and leaped into the dark water, ahead of the elders. Naturally my bold move was to impress the daughters of the dam tenders.

Lake Shikotsu was dark, deep, and icy from the snowmelt in the mountains. So cold that my feet, hands, and penisu were numb in seconds. I struggled back to shore and shivered into my clothes. The elders continued their stories in the water, and not one of them commented on the cold or shivered. The nature of my presence was set that night by the mountain lake.

The elders told creation and bear stories, and my heart, once again, was at peace. That night we ate together in front of the fire. Nightbreaker was there, a great shadow at my side. He would have lusted after the ecstatic women and told stories about the anishinaabe trickster naanabozho, and his waabi, or vision, of Ranald MacDonald.

My waabi, a lusty vision, was animated by golden eyes and breasts decorated with invisible tattoos. The dam tenders served sweet, cloudy sake to me, and there were many, many salutations. Naturally, they were right to protect their daughters, but that should not rule out the spirit of tattoos.

Later, the elders hushed me, and the dam tenders pushed me down on a tatami near the fire. We sat there in a cozy circle and drank more sake. The elders handed me a piece of thick paper and invited me to draw pictures of tattoos. My vision was a morning glory, chrysanthemum, and wild lettuce on my back, and on my chest the exact time and date the atomu bomb exploded over Hiroshima.

The woman with the trace of an invisible tattoo danced by the fire until she blushed. She turned toward me, bowed, and exposed her rosy breasts. The tattoo was the face of a bear, the iso kamuy, the spirit of the bear. I studied the contours of the image, aware that her breasts were forever protected by a mighty spirit. My lust might be a match with a bear, but only on the rise of a great tease.

The elders removed my shirt, pushed me down on my chest, and rubbed my back with herring oil. Then and there, in front of the fire, the elders, assisted by the lusty women with golden eyes, scarred me with invisible tattoos.

Smelly fish oil?
The scent aroused me.
So much pain.
Breasts above me.
No, tattoos?
Yes, invisible bears.
Ainu tradition?
Breasts around me.

Richie, who was unaware of his own sour breath, pretended to be bothered by the smell of herring oil in a story. I told him my tattoos were forever fishy. I said with a smile, Richie, maybe you were born fishy. Miko laughed and pushed her nose against my back.

No, not really.
Heat me once more.
No, not today.
My body is invisible.
On atomu time.

Miko folded a napkin around her maple kuchen. Richie and his breath ruined her breakfast. She lost interest in food, and the scent of his breath lingered in her nose and on her clothes for several hours. Later she painted scenes of children in the clouds over the peace park.

Richie trailed me back to the ruins. He commented on the rope circle and was worried about the mutilated pictures of the emperor. That seemed to bother him more than anything. He stared at me, and then tried to mend the creases in the picture. The emperor would survive by his care, but a friend might wait in misery. At last he turned away from the picture and admired the hand mirror. He turned the mirror several times to locate his image, and then laughed so hard he poisoned the air in the ruins.

You trick mirror?

Not a trick.

Trick, no reflection.

Phantom trace.

Not there, no there.

Raise a blush.

Why blush?

You are invisible.

Yes, like miko tattoo.

Shinto shamans.

Richie was curious about my interests in haiku, Matsuo Basho, and Matsushima. Miko mentioned my journey to the pine islands in the bay. Basho wrote haibun, or haiku on the road, and the images in his poems are more memorable than the actual place. Picture the whole moon on the rise over Matsushima Bay. Once a natural, magic mirror that inspired poetry, the city has become a heavy, crude facade. Tourists chase the shadows on islands for the mere price of admission.

Matsushima is a great memory.

I continued my stories of the imagined journey to the spas by my father and MacDonald. Seikichi invited me to visit Tohoku University in Sendai. He was moved to see my invisible tattoos emerge in the nearby hot baths. He touched the entire outlines of dates on my chest, chrysanthemum and morning glory on my back. The course of his finger became a ritual memory stick of my time with the elders, dam tenders, and the women with golden eyes. The bears, cold water, rosy breasts, and the pain of tiny punctures on my chest and back were visual memories of that night at Lake Shikotsu.

Seikichi was sworn to secrecy, and he was not certain that the elders would decide to initiate me with invisible tattoos. The Ainu, he told me, inspired him to hear the spirit of bears in a world of mighty secrets. He is a generous, elusive storier, and a connoisseur of fine wine. Sake he drinks only to be diplomatic, and he was courtly only once during my two weeks at his house. He lives near an old military base established during the occupation. Camp Sendai, in fact, is now part of the university. My father might have visited as an interpreter. Our paths cross by chance, and forever in visions.

Takao Shimazaki, professor of literature and chairman of the department, invited me to dinner at his house. He was crudely formal, a pretentious man who reminded me several times that he had studied at the University of Chicago. I told him my degrees were from an orphanage, and he turned away to avoid the taste of my tease. This literary man was a poser and had no sense of irony.

Shimazaki constantly questioned me about my heritage, my identity. His crude, racial cues withered on the sleeve, always unanswered. The Ainu, he declared, were extinct but for a few lost souls on the northern islands. Not so, there are many natives on the islands. So, he shouted, but what is your evidence? Show me the primitive tattoos incised, no doubt, by imposters of that distant race of bear hunters.

Seikichi was embarrassed by the racial overtones, and to cover his shame consumed a liter of sake. He creased his mouth, whistled to the shadows, and then sang hunting songs he learned from the Ainu. Shimazaki lectured about the comparative demise of oral traditions and primitive cultures, and yet the learned chairman was sidetracked by native songs and distracted by any oral practice. The chairman would meet his own demons in the mirror.

I turned the conversation to the war crimes of the emperor and the occupation of Japan. What is your learned position on nuclear weapons, and the ironies of a constitution created overnight by an inspired occupation soldiery?

The Japanese constitution and the occupation provoked his rage and resentment as a nationalist. He leaned over the table and railed against the capitulation of the emperor. Then he suddenly paused, aware of my political snares, removed his tiny spectacles, and once again turned the conversation back to my tattoos and identity.

I heartily declared my absolutely pure blood that night, my very first ascendance to racial purity. I removed my slippers, socks, walked on the low table directly in front of the chairman, and slowly removed my clothes, down to my truly real, hafu naked body. My bare feet squeaked on the polished wooden table. His attentive wife snickered and rushed out of the room, not for shame, but to summon others in the house.

Seikichi watched my presentation with absolute disbelief, and then he started to dance in circles. He laughed so hard he came close to a natural, perfect, comic death. He roared, shouted, waved his arms, and leaped twice over the table.

I faced the chairman, crouched right over his rice bowl, and shouted at him to inspect my pure hafu body for any inauthentic tattoos or racial tags of weakness. I allowed adequate time for his review, and then turned around, my pure ass directly over the remains of his meal, and presented my back for a tattoo inspection. The room was cold, and, of course, my tattoos were invisible. The chairman blushed and retreated to his library for the rest of the night. His wife bowed, and much to our surprise, she served several bottles of very fine sake.

Seikichi embraced the vision of my father, and proposed a tour of nearby onsen, natural hot springs, that would have inspired the hafu teacher Ranald MacDonald. The onsen were marvelous, a perfect union of therapeutic mineral water, heat, health, and private pleasure in a public place. MacDonald was a captive teacher and never saw this part of the country. My father must have envisioned this journey for me to carry out.

The people at the hot springs were mannered, of course, and courteous, almost to a romantic fault. We visited one onsen a day for four days. The first was the Tendo onsen, north of Yamagata. My invisible tattoos haunted a few bathers there, but most were curious and seemed to honor the name, date, and natural images.

The Zao onsen was memorable in a very unusual way. An older man, who we later learned was a retired military officer, moved very close to me in the hot bath, squinted, pointed at each letter, and read the invisible date and time on my chest. He was silent for a minute, understood the message, and shouted the date to anyone he could find at the spa, The bomb, the bomb, atomu one! He had not yet seen the morning glory and chrysanthemum on my back. Suddenly, the hot baths were very crowded that afternoon. Many bathers waded closer to see my invisible tattoos emerge in a blush of heat.

The Akayu onsen is in the mountains south of Yamagata, near Yonezawa. There, alone in the hot baths, we mocked the manner of the chairman, a racialist and nationalist. And how could he see with those tiny spectacles?

Seikichi, on the last day, drove to the Tsuchiyu onsen located between Mount Asuma and Fukushima. There, we encountered by chance several stout, worried bathers. The men watched me with awe and aversion, as the chrysanthemum and morning glory arose on my rosy back. They were haunted by the images and rushed out of the onsen. We decided not to contribute to their osore, their fear, and drove back that night to Sendai.

Seikichi was certain that my father and MacDonald would have visited the Kusatsu onsen, located east of Nagano in the very heart of many great natural hot springs. Mount Asama, nearby and to the south, rises above eight thousand feet. Seikichi told me the Kusatsu onsen is eminent, one of the oldest in Japan. The mineral waters are curative, but he warned me about the netsuno yu, the bath of great heat.

I arrived by train a few days later and saw my name printed on a placard in the station. The bearer of the placard explained that my transportation was outside. I protested, not me, there must be some mistake, when two strong men escorted me out the station door. There, at the curb, was a sedan chair. MacDonald was with me, but not the soldiers. Once seated the bearers raised the poles and carried me from the train station, around the town center to the Kusatsu onsen.

Ranald MacDonald was an outsider, a foreigner, in a strict, closed country. He was guarded by soldiers who escorted him from the ship to the dock. The bearers carried the hafu teacher in a sedan chair through the streets of the crowded town. Seikichi had reserved the sedan chair for me, a great surprise, after he read the narratives of MacDonald.

Kusatsu is in the mountains, surrounded by great trees. That mineral scent of natural hot springs was in the air. Seikichi was right about the great heat bath. The water is so hot that bathers must answer to the bath master. I entered the water very slowly with many other bathers to avoid the rush of extreme heat. My body turned red at the critical line of the water, thighs, stomach, and then by inches my invisible tattoos emanated on my chest and back. The other bathers were distracted by the shouts of the bath master and did not notice my invisible tattoos. No one could stand the severe heat for more than a few minutes, and it was then, as the bathers came out of the water, that they saw my tattoos. Atomu One has never been brighter.

Richie covered his sour mouth.

Virga moved closer to me.

Oshima turned away.

Kitsutsuki beat his wooden leg.

Seikichi wrote to me later that he heard stories about a hafu stranger, a hibakusha, who poisoned the mountain water with the invisible words and flowers on his atomu body.

Ronin read the screenplay several times but said he never saw *Hiroshima Mon Amour*. The only movies he ever talked about were those directed by Akira Kurosawa. *Rashomon*, of course, and samurai stories were his favorites, especially movies with his hero, the stouthearted Toshiro Mifune.

Akira Kurosawa "examined the relative nature of truth" in his movie *Rashomon*, observed Stuart Galbraith in *The Emperor and the Wolf*. "Its very title has entered our consciousness, its name synonymous with contradictory versions of reality."

Rashomon was released in Atomu 5.

Mitsuhiro Yoshimoto wrote in *Kurosawa* that *Rashomon* focused on the "nature of social chaos. What leads humans to destroy themselves is egotism. At the same time, what saves humans comes from themselves, too. Egotism must be countered by human compassion, honesty, and altruism. Otherwise, the world would become like the dilapidated Rashomon gate, from which, according to the commoner, even demons have fled because they are horrified by humans."

Ronin besets the egoism of the peace museum, the deceptions of governments, and the contradictions of history. The Atomic Bomb Dome is his Rashomon. The names, stories, and memories of thousands of children, burned to faint shadows, unnamed, and lost in the cryptic egotism of peace.

Hiroshima Mon Amour was released in Atomu 14. The movie, directed by Alain Resnais, won the International Critics Prize at the Cannes Film Festival. The original screenplay for the movie was by the novelist Marguerite Duras.

Resnais had invited her to write the script, and they both agreed that the movie would not be a "documentary and the nuclear apocalypse would not be the primary theme," wrote Laure Adler in *Marguerite Duras*. "Without going to Japan, without researching the subject, without preparation Marguerite worked flat out day and night."

You saw nothing in Hiroshima.

That memorable line starts the movie, and since then that line has been heard around the world. "I saw everything. Everything," she responds, and he answers, "No. You saw nothing in Hiroshima."

The hospital, for instance, I saw it.

You saw nothing in Hiroshima.

Duras, in a radio interview at the time, explained that "you will never see anything, you will never write anything, you will never be able to speak about the event." Later, in a rather pretentious, plural voice about the production of the movie, she wrote, "We have endeavoured to bring Hiroshima back to life through a love story. We hope it will be unusual and 'full of wonder' and that having happened in a place so accustomed to death people will believe in it a bit more than if it had occurred anywhere else in the world."

Adler pointed out that the movie was "exclusively premiered in Paris for six months, then London and then Brussels." *Hiroshima Mon Amour* was "voted best foreign movie in New York, Los Angeles and Chicago."

The Peace Memorial Museum was built on pillars so the view of the park was not obstructed. The building was completed in Atomu 10. Forty years later the museum was expanded to include more displays on nuclear war, peace, and victimry. There were, however, only minimal references to Japanese militarism and the cruelties of the colonial occupation of Asia. The simulated *atomu* dome and pillar of peace letters were located in the new addition to the museum.

Ronin destroyed with chemicals, as you know, most of the etched letters on the pillar of peace. Several weeks later he mounted a standard over the entrance and changed the name of the museum to the movie, *Hiroshima Mon Amour.*

The museum guards were ordered to remove the banner, but many tourists who had seen the movie thought it would be a proper name for the new museum. That, of course, because the name of the movie, and the obscure, erotic touch of two lovers was much more memorable that the abstract and deceptive notions of peace.

Ronin is a shouter, at times, a visionary practice that he learned from a native teaser and hunter on the White Earth Reservation. He named the old woman *miishidoon*, an *anishinaabe* word that means "moustache." Younger women on the reservation thought she was a man, and the men thought she was an accident with a nasty bear.

Miko heard these stories, that *miishidoon* shouted at animals and scared them into surrender. She shouted at shamans, shadows, and tricksters for the same reason, and always at men. Ronin was one of the few natives on the reservation who shouted back at her, and for that she embraced his spirit. He seldom shouted once he left the reservation because the shamanic practice was misconstrued.

Ronin told me he could not restrain his shouts when he acted as a tour guide in the museum. Once more he summoned tourists to the plastic, miniature figures in the "diorama of aesthetic victimry." He first shouted about the simulated, melted bodies, charred lunch box, and flesh hanging from the arms and hands of a woman with disheveled hair, dressed in a black ceremonial kimono stained with blood.

Ronin roared about the kimono, and about the white shirt on one plastic child, singed and dirtied by a background fire in the diorama. The trees were charred, leafless, burned branches, twisted beams, bricks cracked and broken, but the kimono survived the destruction. The diorama only teased the horror with cultural manners.

"The skin of some people appeared to be glistening in the sun but, when I looked closer, I would see that the skin had peeled off like that of a ripe peach and was hanging loosely," wrote Toyofumi Ogura in *Letters from the End of the World.* "I saw one person whose entire facial skin had peeled off, from the hairline down," and there "were objects that appeared to be lumps of flesh lying on the ground. Some of these squirmed from time to time, like exhibits in a freak show at a fairground."

Ronin shouted that thousands of children were incinerated and firestorms burned the tender heart of the city. He shouted and roared at the peace fakers who created dioramas of aesthetic victimry. The tourists, shied by his intrusive shouts, turned away, unlike *miishidoon* and the animals on the reservation. Naturally, the tourists were relieved to buy commemorative tee shirts in the nearby museum souvenir shop.

There were more than seven thousand casualties "among the younger students, who were helping to create firebreaks, and their teachers," wrote Ogura. The many corpses were laid out in the schoolyard. "All had been burned terribly." The trousers of the boys were in tatters, and the blouses of the girls "were scorched and stuck to the skin in patches. Many girls wore *monpe* pants" that were "sliced to ribbons; others only had on underwear." And there were many adult bodies in the schoolyard.

"A girl who looked to be about a sixth grader came close to me, carrying a child" said Takeshi Yamaguchi. "I saw that both of them were naked. Half of their hair had been burned, and the child's eyes were closed and covered with sores. Another girl walking before them had her wrists bent in front of her chest like a ghost. The skin on her arms was loose from her elbows, and was hanging down in flaps at her wrists, as though she were trying on a pair of long gloves for ladies. She was walking in a daze, and her cries and tears seemed to have been utterly spent."

Naomi Shohno pointed out in *The Legacy of Hiroshima* that the "atomic bombs were not dropped on battlefields but on thriving urban centers." Hiroshima became a city of death. "Most of the children abandoned amidst the ruins were infants, children too young to tell their own names."

Many *hibakusha* grieved that their government provided no assistance to survivors or the families of victims. "The atomic bomb victims in general have been suffering from three psychological problems," wrote Shohno. "They are afraid of contracting atomic bomb disease; they occasionally vividly recall the bombing itself; and they feel alienated and shut out from society."

Ronin shouted at the peace tourists.

You saw nothing in Hiroshima.

Richie was an extreme nationalist, not a journalist. He was a secret agent and his only interests were imperial politics and the revision of the constitution. Tonase, the police interpreter, or someone else in the administration, provided the nationalists with information about a *hafu* police maniac who set fire to the peace pond and promoted nuclear weapons. Ronin, in fact, told the agent that he supported an amendment to Article 9 of the occupation constitution of Japan.

Article 9 provides that the "Japanese people forever renounce war as a sovereign right of the nation and the threat or use of force as means of settling international disputes," and to accomplish that constitutional power, "land, sea, and air forces, as well as other war potential, will never be maintained." The renunciation of war does not leave the country vulnerable. The Japanese have the right to defend their homeland from military invasion, and the government relies on a joint security treaty with the United States.

Richie and the ultranationalists were convinced that the *hafu ronin* would be useful to their cause, and, by constant flattery, they could easily overcome his resistance to the emperor. Ronin was

136

invited to attend the formal ceremonies later that summer at the controversial Yasukuni Jinja in Tokyo.

The *yakuza* are gangsters who are members of secret societies. The name is derived from the words for three numbers, *ya*, "eight," *ku*, "nine," and *san* or *sa*, "three," an unlucky score of twenty in *hanafuda*, a card game similar to blackjack. Some historians trace the *yakuza* to the *kabukimono*, the "crazy ones," of seventeenth-century Japan. These were the crazy, outrageous, violent, loyal *ronin*, or samurai with no masters.

The leaders of the *yakuza* have connections with politicians, the police, military, and other agencies of government, "which makes their elimination by the police very difficult," noted Louis Frédéric in *Japan Encyclopedia*. The *yakuza* engage in gambling, extortion, fraud, and murder. "Their groups have a strict hierarchical order, demand total devotion from members, and require each new member to have his little finger cut off at an initiation ceremony," observed Yoshio Sugimoto in *An Introduction to Japanese Society*.

The custom of *yubitsume*, or cutting off the last joint of the little finger, is also performed as an apology to the *oyabun*, the father or head of the *kobun*, who are the followers, the "children" of the *yakuza* family. The *yakuza* have found some protection in ultranationalism.

Japan is famous for *onsen*, natural hot springs or spas, in the many mountains and surrounded by hotels and *ryokan*, inns with traditional tatami mats. The tatami, compressed, braided straw, were first used to cover floors in the seventeenth century. Frédéric noted in *Japan Encyclopedia* that there are more than two thousand volcanic *onsen*, "according to estimates made by the geology department," and some "have hot sand and lakes of hot mud that are used for medicinal purposes." The Kusatsu Spa has a *netsuno yu* bath. The word *netsu* means "great heat," or thermal energy, and *yu* means "hot water," in other words, greatly heated water. The *sento* is a public bathhouse, as in the hotel near the train station in Hiroshima.

The Ainu tease their origins in the presence of *kamuy* spirits of nature, not racial theories, and create in their stories a culture of survivance. The Ainu *moshir* is a homeland of the spirits and nature that provides the shadows, smoke, fish, animals, salt, tattoos, dance, and songs to the people.

The *iso kamuy* is the spirit of the bear, the soul of humans and their survivance. Ronin wrote that he was teased by the bears and

137

shied by the invisible bear tattoos on the breasts of the women of the dam tenders. The Ainu have many stories of tattoos, but there are no historical records of invisible tattoos. Ronin is elusive and obscure about the practice.

The Ainu *iso kamuy* are the "supreme deities," wrote Emiko Ohnuki-Tierney in *The Ainu of the Northwest Coast of Southern Sakhalin*. "Their power as deities is a generalized one, providing food and looking after the general welfare of the Ainu. More than any other single behavior of the Ainu, the importance placed on the bear deities is most succinctly shown in the cultural complex of bear ceremonialism."

The Ainu and the *anishinaabe* tease a similar spirit in their bear stories. The *anishinaabe* are visionaries and storiers of creation. The *makwa*, or bear, is a *manidoo*, a spirit, and one of the original five spirit totems of the people.

Nightbreaker was an *anishinaabe* member of the bear totem, and his son, a *makwa* adventurer, continues that totemic association of creation stories. Ronin told me the bear was in his heart and that he wanted to be buried with a bear near the headwaters of the Mississippi River.

Ronin was tormented by trickster stories on the White Earth Reservation, and, at the same time, he was enriched by liberation and survivance. No terminal believer, monotheist, causation native, or otherwise could endure the tease of trickster stories without the pleasure and humor of natural irony. The *anishinaabe* trickster of creation is named *naanabozho* in stories. This compassionate trickster figure created the earth, natives, animals, evil spirits, death, humor, and surely casinos as the eternal tease of sovereignty.

Ronin carried three books, as you know, on his visionary journey: *Glimpses of Unfamiliar Japan* by Lafcadio Hearn, *The Narrow Road to the North* by Matsuo Basho, and a photocopy of *Japan: Story of Adventure* by Ranald MacDonald. Ronin was inspired for various reasons by these three authors. Hearn, intuitive and selective, created an interior, aesthetic vision of contradictions in Japan. Basho created an elusive sense of presence in nature, the winsome impermanence of motion, memory, and the seasons. MacDonald created the lonesome trace of unrealized adventures.

Basho, the seventeenth-century poet, had visited Matsushima, near Sendai, and wrote about the natural beauty of the pine islands in his *haibun* travel prose. Basho dreamed about the whole moon "rising over the islands of Matsushima."

Basho was a haiku visionary, and by his adventures in the mysterious north he created a memorable literature of presence and natural unity. Nobuyuki Yuasa wrote in the introduction to *The Narrow Road to the North* that "Basho was in possession of a magical power to enter into 'the spirit of place.' Even the people he met on the road are given characters, each different from the others, so that they have enduring impressions on the imagination of the reader."

Ronin was inspired by *haibun*, the imagic poetry of the road, and he created memorable characters on his journey. He listened closely to each person he met by chance on the road, lingered to tease, and searched their stories for a trace of Basho, MacDonald, and his father, Nightbreaker.

"I hired a boat and started for the islands," wrote Basho. "Islands are piled above islands, and islands are joined to islands, so that they look exactly like parents caressing their children or walking with them arm in arm. The pines are of the freshest green, and their branches are curved in exquisite lines, bent by the wind constantly blowing through them."

The word *waabi* means "to have a vision." The *anishinaabe* create a sense of presence in visions and stories, a unique, personal association more with birds or animals and other creatures of nature. Ronin, in his *waabi*, associated with the bear, his father's totem and unrealized journey, and with the native adventures of Ranald MacDonald.

MacDonald landed by feat, risk, and chance on the islands of Rishiri and Yagishiri in 1848. Ainu men rescued him from his overturned boat, cared for him, and then reported his presence to the shogunate on Hokkaido. MacDonald was transported under guard to the port of Nagasaki. There he was held in a special residence or prison for about ten months. He taught English to fourteen interpreters, including his companions Einosuke Moriyama and Sakushichiro Uemura, six years before Commodore Matthew Perry arrived to open the ports of Japan.

MacDonald was born at Fort George, Oregon, and lived in Canada. He refused a sedentary occupation and sailed on whalers out of New York. Princess Raven, his mother, was the daughter of Comcomly, the leader of the Chinook Nation. Raven died a few months after MacDonald's birth in 1824. Archibald McDonald, his father, a "reputed graduate of the University of Edinburgh, Scotland," was a trader for the Hudson's Bay Company. Archibald married his second wife, Jane Klyne, in 1825.

Ranald MacDonald discovered much later that he was native. He never knew his mother. He had accepted the native nicknames, "Little Chinook," and "Little Chief," as an affectionate tease, but did not think of himself as a native or mixedblood Chinook. "He stated that it was then he decided to go to Japan, of which he had heard and read, and from which he was convinced that the North American Indians originally came," wrote William Lewis and Naojiro Murakami, editors of *Ranald MacDonald*. "He decided to run away and get to Japan, if possible, and made his plans accordingly. He had an idea, he said, that the Japanese were similar to the Indians and probably ignorant, so that an educated man might make himself something of a personage among them."

MacDonald wrote that the Ainu rescued him from an island near the northwest coast of Hokkaido. "After clearing the small bay which had served me for a harbor, and when I was in deep water between the two Islands, I shook out the reefs, and purposely capsized my craft, with sail set," to simulate his misfortune at sea. He righted the boat and the next morning "started for the large island," and, "being in high spirits hoisted my little flag."

MacDonald saw smoke on one of the islands. Four men launched a large boat and rowed out. "I raised the plug of my boat and nearly half filled it with water," as they approached. "When about a hundred yards from me they hove up and begin to salaam me, throwing their arms, palms up, bowing, stroking their great beards, and uttering a guttural sound in respectful salutation, as indicated by their look and manner." MacDonald saluted the men in the boat, and they "seemed to take it in compliment, in response."

Near shore the "crowd did not appear unfriendly, just intensely curious," wrote Jo Ann Roe in *Ranald MacDonald: Pacific Rim Adventurer*. As MacDonald "alighted from the boat, the men greeted him in the same unusual way as the sailors, rubbing their hands together, stroking their beards and making guttural noises."

MacDonald, unlike lusty Ronin, "was not tempted by the Ainu women, finding distasteful their custom of tattooing themselves," wrote Roe. "Little girls had a small patch on the upper lip, with additional tattooing as they matured." The Ainu women who were shamans "wore a leather belt for ceremonial occasions, from which pieces of metal clanked pleasantly together."

Ronin, inspired by that salutation story, saluted in a similar way when Seikichi introduced him to the Ainu. Ronin wrote that the elders "raised their arms in praise, and stroked their great wavy beards."

MacDonald concluded his narrative, some fifty years after the adventure, that "even now, after the vicissitudes, varied and wearing, of my life, I have never ceased to feel most kindly and ever grateful to my fellow men of Japan for their really generous treatment of me. In that long journey and voyage from the extreme North to the extreme South—fully a thousand miles—of their country; throughout my whole sojourn of ten months in the strange land, never did I receive a harsh word, or even an unfriendly look."

MacDonald finished his narrative, *Japan: Story of Adventure,* the year before he died in the home of his niece near the Kettle River in Washington on August 5, 1894. He was the first native to teach in Japan, and he was there by chance of nature, adventure, and plucky determination six years before Commodore Matthew Perry.

Ronin was abandoned at an orphanage by his mother about the same time, a hundred years later, that Ranald MacDonald was rescued at sea by the Ainu of Hokkaido.

10 Ronin of Yasukuni Jinja

Sergeant Orion Browne, my father, was an interpreter, as you know, for General Douglas MacArthur, Supreme Commander of the Allied Powers in Japan. Shortly after the first occupation soldiers arrived my father visited the Yasukuni Jinja in Tokyo.

> Nightbreaker and five other soldiers were photographed as they walked abreast under the huge torii at the main entrance to the controversial shrine. Six unarmed occupation soldiers entered the sacred space of the kami spirits in Atomu One.

The Yasukuni Jinja is dedicated to the more than two million warriors who died in domestic and foreign wars over the past century. The shrine was misused by the emperors and then by the militarists to unite the nation in colonial wars.

> Nightbreaker wore his summer uniform, khaki shirt, cravat, bloused trousers, polished combat boots, and a helmet. I march with him in a vision under the torii of that shrine. His uniform and blue cravat are mine, and his memories are awakened in me, his only son, as we salute the bears and once more invade the Yasukuni Jinja.

August 15, Atomu Fifty Seven.

> Hibiya Park is the heart of my Tokyo. I first saw this park in a woodblock print, "Moonlight over Hibiya Park," by Tsuchiya Koitsu. The print is a winter scene, heavy snow covers the ancient trees, and the bright, round moon shivers on the blue pond.

I was enchanted by that print and imagined the natural grace of the park. I wanted to live in that park as a loyal samurai, but my mundane escape was contrary, the ruins of the occupied imperial city. I soared in a vision of kimonos and humane shoguns, and then ran away, as you know, from the Elizabeth Saunders Home.

> They caught me on the Ginza.

Mount Fuji was my first vision in black feathers. The ravens crashed through my window at the orphanage and together we soared around the country. I circled the sacred mountain, scenes of an obscure past, and then soared over my parents at the imperial moat. My father was smartly dressed in his khaki uniform that crucial summer of my conception.

My mother wore chrysanthemums.
My father his blue cravat.
Observe the end of the empire.
My nights are traces of a great vision.

The Imperial Hotel, Kabukiza Theatre, and Hibiya Park were my special sanctuaries by day. The mysterious terraces and many levels of the hotel, memorable scenes of the *Genji Monogatari* and *Chushingura* at the Kabukiza Theatre, and the natural heave and mighty roots of trees in Hibiya Park. My three nights on the run were given to memories of my parents on the grassy banks of the moat near the Imperial Palace.

The imperial ravens stole my lunch. I was sitting on a bench in the park when a palace raven soared from the crown of the Ministry of Justice building and, with a perfect, silent dive, snatched the last piece of my bento sushi. My mouth was wide open, but suddenly my chopsticks were empty. That daredevil raven perched on the back of a nearby bench and ate my lunch. Two other ravens caught the sticky grains of rice that broke loose in flight.

I cursed the raven that stole my sushi, and actually thought about the imperial pilots who were trained for only one mission, a kamikaze attack on the United States Navy. Naturally the ravens were wiser, a theater of coup counts over lunch in the park. I was determined the next coup would be mine.

Tokyo was firebombed at the end of the war and the ravens quickly moved to the secure trees of the Imperial Palace. The more guttural ravens of the industrial areas, nearby docks, and remote sections of the city, resent the imperial strain, their haughty relatives, the palace ravens who survived the war as aesthetic victims.

The palace ravens search the restaurant trash at first light, and then, in smart teams, they raid the parks. By dusk they return to their roosts in the imperial sanctuary. My bento sushi became one of their stories of the day.

I watched the ravens descend at great speed from nearby buildings, a trace of silent black motion, a perfect flight, and snatch a cracker from a child, a rice cake from a schoolgirl, a sandwich from a tourist, with impunity and no moral responsibility. These ravens are a tribute to a criminal empire, the great, tricky warriors of Hibiya Park.

Nightbreaker and my mother sat in this park, probably on his very bench with a view of the sunken garden. The slender, delicate kosumosu, the autumn cosmos, were in full bloom, the other flowers were slighted by the pink and white blossoms.

Miishidoon, the native shouter, told me that my father teased the ravens with simulated meat, a slice of cardboard between two crackers. Sometimes, to amuse my mother, he wrote the words "delicious meat" on the cardboard, a native practice on the reservation during the great depression. Food was scarce at the time, and even the palace ravens were grateful to be teased with stale crackers and military rations.

Naturally, my father wore his military uniform in Hibiya Park. My mother, no doubt, proudly wore her chrysanthemum print dress in honor of the emperor. This very bench, this strain of ravens, and his uniform have now become my story.

I sheathed my wooden sword, cocked my helmet low over my brow, and marched north on Uchibori Dori, along the eastern moat of the Imperial Palace. The Palace Guards at the Otemon Gate were wary of my sword, no doubt, and by my determined, military pace. They were alert, held an imperial distance, and would not return my salute. One guard watched me through binoculars.

I circled the north moat on the other side of Kitanomaru Park and rested on a bench between the Fairmont Hotel and the Indian Embassy. The air was heavy, moist, and the great trees were silent and moody that afternoon. The tourist rowboats were moored, no one was on the dock or the moat. Suddenly, more than a dozen cats crept out of the thicket. The cats waited for a woman to arrive with their daily meal, served on several saucers in front of a bench. She smiled and assured me the cats were not dangerous and then told me the names of every cat near the moat, but not her own name.

Cats are cautious.

Yes, leery.

Nasty sometimes.

Yes, palace guards.

Cats know my nickname.

What name?

Mine, neko okasan.

Yes, cat mother.

Natural nickname.

Sometimes.

Ronin is my name.

No cats by that name.

Surprise me.

Dogs must follow you.

Virga, at a distance.

Dogs want to be cats.

Only at meals.

Yes, never cautious.

Daily, neko okasan carried two plastic bags of food to the shady paths above the north moat. The leftovers came from a waiter at the pasta restaurant in the Fairmont Hotel. The Indian Embassy nearby was eager to provide leftovers, but the cats would not eat curry. She said the cats were insecure about their meals and would not tolerate late service. Most of the cats perched on the benches, raised their tails, and meowed at each other.

Lafcadio Hearn mentioned in *Glimpses of Unfamiliar Japan* that cats were mischievous, cursed, and ungrateful, but dogs were not. "Feed a dog for three days," he quoted a proverb, "and he will remember your kindness for three years; feed a cat for three years and she will forget your kindness in three days." Neko okasan shunned the notions of a cat curse and brushed aside the idea of canine memory. Dogs were loyal, she told me, only because they lacked imagination. Cats clearly demonstrate a sense of natural sovereignty.

Sadly, neko okasan was a widow, and she served wild cats to heal a worried heart. She told me her husband had been run over by a train, probably suicide. She had no income, no family, and was evicted from her tiny apartment. So, she moved to the park with three cats.

Do your cats live here?

Yes, very shy.

Please, show me.

There, behind the bench.

What are their names?

Kisu, Tojo, and Chrysanthemum.

Marvelous names.

Tojo is my hero.

Truly, empire cats?

Yes, this is our palace.

The imperial moat.

The emperor is my family.

Kisu, she told me, was so named because he sucked on her neck. The cat mother reminded me of the old woman with cloudy eyes who wore a black shirt, tied at the waist, bright red hakama trousers, and made her home in Hibiya Park. The students told me that she was hibakusha, lived in the trees, and never revealed her name. She sold red umbrellas and dented aluminum dishes for picnics in the park. She might be a trickster, or a comic ghost, and, no doubt, she has lived alone in the park since the end of the war.

Yesterday she moved close to me, pointed and laughed at my father's uniform and the chrysanthemum seal painted over Atomu One on the front of my helmet liner. Her eyes were clouded by atomu cataracts, but she could see that my rank was the seal of the emperor. She might have teased my parents in the same way, and probably laughed at those huge empire blooms on my mother's best dress.

Ginkgo became her nickname in the park. The police teased her by that name because she decorated the ginkgo trees with her clothes and trivial possessions. She raised several string baskets on the branches to display her wares at lunch. Ginkgo lived on a lovely wooded path near the Imperial Hotel.

Most tourists were amused by her manner and enticed by her constant, generous laughter. She praised the great trees by shouts and gestures, but should someone pause to share the moment in conversation she would beat her brow with the edge of a metal plate. The sound was familiar in the park, and some students teased her with a salutation only to hear the distinctive beat of that plate on her brow. Consequently, her brow was thickly calloused. A park warden told me that she has laughed, waved to the trees, and beat her brow for more than two generations. The mood and tone of that beat changes with the seasons.

Ginkgo laughed at me this morning in the park. I bought a red umbrella and commented on her bright hakama. Naturally, she beat her brow. So, I beat on my head with the umbrella. She stopped, smiled, stared at me in silence for a moment, threw the plate in the air, and laughed even harder. Ginkgo moved closer and touched each one of my father's service medals. She admired my uniform, saluted me, and then turned away in laughter. That old woman was the ronin of the old Imperial Hotel.

The Indian Embassy became by chance a bird sanctuary. The feral cats would not enter the grounds because of the dogs and the scent of curry. Mongrels would taste any cuisine, but cats must be trained to savor spices. I found this out when one of the dogs trailed me at an escape distance to the main street. I returned to the embassy, the dog followed, and the guard told me the dog was a moat mongrel that liked the taste of leftover curry.

No home, no name.

No visa?

Not for mongrels.

No passport?

You tease.

Natural reason.

The guard turned away, and that moat mongrel smiled at me. He trailed me once again to Yasukuni Dori. Curry, his natural name, sniffed my boots and trousers for the scent of cats, sneezed twice, and then returned to the embassy. He ran close to the ground, a cross between a basset hound and a wirehaired terrier. Minutes later, however, he decided that my fate was with mongrels not cats and marched at my side into Yasukuni Jinja on Kudan Hill.

Curry looked at me once or twice, but otherwise he sensed the beat and marched with me to the sacred shrines. He watched the white doves on the road but never broke ranks. Curry was a pukka soldier, and a diplomat. He must have been trained by either the British Army or the Indian Embassy.

The Yasukuni Jinja is haunted forever by the atomu ghosts of Hiroshima. The shrine honors the warriors, the kamikaze, even six war criminals, but the shrine priests never mention the thousands of children who were incinerated in service to their emperor.

The imperial ravens mark their distance from the sacred trees, the ginkgo and cherry, and the monuments, but several times a week they dive on the passive, incestuous white doves that nest at the shrine. These raven sorties arouse the tourists.

Four ravens landed on the huge torii at the entrance to the shrine. They cawed out to warn the doves and ancient soldiers of my arrival in uniform. Curry was wary and watched them bounce overhead. He had gone to war with many imperial ravens over garden dinners at the Indian Embassy.

I marched directly under the torii into the sacred space of the war dead and raised my wooden sword, a command to present arms in the tradition of the military. Several tourists were surprised by my military manner and paused to watch my bold maneuvers. The Japanese covered their mouths with their hands, a gesture of embarrassment and shame, and others frowned at the crude breach of sacred traditions at a national shrine. The American tourists, however, were astounded at my comic march into the kami spirits of the war dead, and broke into nervous laughter.

> My father's uniform was tight around my waist, but the cuts and creases were authentic, and the ribbons on my shirt honored his military career. The spontaneous humor, no doubt, was more about my wooden sword and the chrysanthemum seal on the front of my helmet liner than the historical menace that my occupation uniform represented at the main shrine.

I marched with my sword raised at point, smartly commanded eyes right, then eyes left, and saluted with my sword anyone who paused to notice my military presence. Only some of the children returned my salute. One Japanese child was about to challenge me with his plastic dayglo sword, but his worried parents distracted the wee samurai with something sweet. The plastic sword vanished in a sleeve.

> Curry marched at my side.

Takeo Shimazaki, the nationalist and professor of literature at Tohoku University, was about to leave the shrine but reversed his course when he saw me in uniform and on the march. Takeo was dressed in his empire uniform, a black shirt and trousers, the formal costume of the nationalist escorts, toadies, and priests. Aiko, his wife, waved to me, and laughed once more over the memory of that sensational dinner at their house in Sendai. Takeo surely scolded her later for the friendly gesture to me.

> Memorable sake.
> Nice uniform.
> My father's occupation.
> Loyal dog.
> Curry diplomat.

The honden, or main shrine, was the sacred space of the kami, the spirits of more than two million dead soldiers. The entrance to the shrine and the inner sanctuary was decorated with the seals of the emperor on a great chrysanthemum cloth. The hewn cedar beams and polished, wooden panels created a sense of eternal peace and a natural presence, an imperial reverence and silence that inspired ravens, mongrels, and tricksters.

I rinsed my hands and mouth with shrine water to chase away any traces of mortality. The sough and tease of spirited undertones, the hushed beat of a drum, and the murmur of water and heavy cloth were the sounds of the kami warriors. The imperial mirror, sword, and sacred objects of kami creation were in the shrine.

I clapped my hands at the altar.

The sounds of the ancient spirits were my summons to the main shrine over the altar and oratory of the haiden. The children of the atomu ruins must be enshrined with the kami spirits of other children in the main sanctuary, and by their presence, virtue, and decency, the nationalists would be shamed for their dominance.

My natural way to the chrysanthemum altar of the main shrine was blocked by several shrine guards. The kami spirits of the atomu ruins were with me, but my father's uniform, cravat, and the loyal mongrel at my side were considered a desecration of the enemy.

I clapped my hands once more.

The imperial ravens mocked my moves.

Curry barked at the guards.

Yasukuni Jinja is a shrine of eternal peace and honors the war dead and warriors of the emperor, a museum of kami war memories, but the promises of peace are undermined by the war criminals that are venerated as kami spirits in the sanctuary. Tojo and the remains of other war criminals are protected by the shrine priests and the rant of nationalism.

The children of the atomu ruins forever haunt the emperor and the Imperial Palace. The emperor and shrine priests dare not tease or abandon the kami spirits of atomu children for the eternal shame of war criminals.

The emperor was never indicted as a war criminal. He was protected not by the honor of the crown, or by his moral courage, or by the kami spirits that created his ancestors, but by occupation expediency.

I clapped my hands and shouted at the elusive kami spirits of the war criminals. Come out of that shrine you cowards, come out under the torii and face the thousands of children you sacrificed at Hiroshima. The atomu children deserve to be honored more than you or any emperor. Tojo, come out and face my sacred sword or forever hide behind the hakama of the shrine priests and the black shirts of the nationalists.

Curry barked at my side.

Many tourists considered my rout.

Petros Komuso surprised me once more in his huge straw hat. He was at the souvenir booth near the main shrine and listened to my protest and dare of the war criminals. He bought several woven charms to protect his friends from the absence of sex, earthquakes, fire, flood, evil, war, and, of course, fake peace.

> Mister peace charmer.
> Smart uniform.
> Trouble at the shrine.
> War medals?
> My father.
> Great shrine lecture.
> Who listens?
> War criminals.
> No, tourists.
> More charms.
> Peace protection.
> Tojo is about.
> Nasty war ghosts.
> Chrysanthemum seals?
> Peace mockery.
> The empire crown.
> Leper's memory.
> New mongrel?
> Trained at the embassy.
> Diplomatic corps?
> Curry of the shrines.

> Petros tied two peace charms to the handle of my wooden sword. Naturally, one would protect me from fake peace, and the other was a promise of more sex. Curry backed away, concerned, no doubt, that a charm was collar of domination in disguise.

I was doubly charmed at the souvenir booth, first by a peace protection ornament, and then by a seductive attendant, the miko shrine maiden who sold war memorial souvenirs. I teased her about the charms, and charmers. She blushed, a wide, rosy beam down her neck, and only pretended to resist my attention to her body.

Petros raised his hat and reached out to decorate the mongrel with a peace charm. Curry barked at his floppy hat and circled the souvenir booth to avoid his charms. The shrine maiden laughed nervously, touched my sword, brushed my arm, and then hinted at something hidden in her other hand. She pressed a tiny tenuki statue into my hand, and turned away. The tenuki trickster had an enormous penisu and testicles.

Petros never mentioned the trickster talisman, but there was no need because he was outcharmed at the souvenir booth that afternoon. I raised the tiny ivory figure close to my eye, petted the testicles with my little finger, and turned my smile to match the face of the tenuki trickster.

The Japanese national anthem was broadcast over and over from the speaker mounted on the souvenir booth. The counter was stacked with simulated war trinkets, plastic samurai swords, books, tee shirts, photographs of the emperor, kamikaze pilots, war criminals, kokka hata, or national flags, propaganda, and other museum memorabilia. The most popular book sold at the booth was *The Alleged 'Nanking Massacre.'*

Kimigayo, kokka anthem.
Lost waka poem.
Emperor reigns.
Never a mighty stone.
Yes, great rock.
Lost the natural moss.
You tease me.
Peace protection.

That lusty shrine maiden touched each of the war ribbons on my shirt. Nightbreaker was enticed in my name. She smiled, boldly reached inside my shirt, and pinched my nipples. The seduction started with minor pain. I lowered the wooden gate over the counter and secured the door. She asked about my uniform, race, culture, and was very pleased to learn that my father was a native from the White Earth Reservation.

Amerika Indian?
Maybe.
You know banks?
What banks?
Dennis Banks.

Banks?

You know?

Maybe.

Banks babies.

Dennis Banks, the native radical, published an autobiography in Japanese. She read his romantic story, attended his protests and lectures on nuclear peace, and the more she heard the more she wanted his baby. She was haunted by the romance of the native warrior and wanted to conceive a baby by Amerika Indian. Sadly, she told me her father would not allow her to see any man, and he obligated her to serve as a shrine maiden at the war memorial. The souvenir booth was a much better way for her to meet men.

The shrine maiden removed my helmet and shirt and unbuttoned my trousers. Naturally, she was astounded to see the faint traces of my invisible tattoos. The more she touched the clearer the atomu date on my chest.

You ghost?

Not yet.

Atomu One?

Peace promise.

By who?

Dennis Banks.

No baby.

Peace, Amerika Indian.

I untied her crisp white shirt and touched her breasts, moist and rosy. She quickly removed her hakama trousers, underclothes, and leaned back on the narrow bench behind the counter. She touched my thighs, and then pulled me closer, but my penisu was shied by the loud music, the constant broadcast of "Kimigayo," the Japanese national anthem.

The instant that shrine maiden stopped the anthem my penisu arose for duty. She was young, firm, moist, deep, and emitted a mysterious, distant moan. Every motion on the bench, every sound, touch, and rush was ecstatic. Truly, she was a kami spirit, inspired by wild lust, and the heat of her passion shook the foundation of the booth. She shouted louder with every tease, pause, and thrust, so loudly that a crowd had gathered around the booth to listen. Curry barked to warn me, a loyal embassy mongrel.

I was prepared for the black shirts and inserted my own tape, a recording of "Stars and Stripes Forever," and "Semper Fidelis" by John

Philip Sousa, and that was followed by the United States Marine Corps Hymn, "From the Halls of Montezuma." Two other favorites were on the tape, "Yankee Doodle" and "Praise the Lord and Pass the Ammunition."

The erotic shouts of the shrine maiden could not be heard over the music. The nationalists, however, were outraged by the invasion of enemy music so near the main shrine. They beat on the gate, and that gave us time to button our clothes. The black shirts had surrounded the souvenir booth and beat on the sides in a rage. Finally, they raised the unlocked gate, and found a rosy, ravished shrine maiden, who read out loud a revisionist story about how the Japanese soldiers liberated the Chinese in Nanking.

Three nationalists cut the wires on the loudspeaker and ended my favorite military march, "The Stars and Stripes Forever." Shimazaki was in that fascist crowd. He peered over his tiny glasses and then crushed my chrysanthemum helmet liner with a tack hammer. There was no time for humor because they pulled me across the counter by my father's shirt and were about to beat me with my own sword, when a familiar voice broke the savage fever of the black shirts.

Richie, the journalist?

No, not today.

My kami time at the shrine.

Dreadful music.

The anthems?

No, occupation tunes.

Got an audience.

Dangerous games.

Your game or mine?

Shrine maiden?

Studies Amerika Indian.

Another mongrel?

My envoy.

From where?

Curry of India.

Baka, nonsense.

Semper Fidelis.

Richie, the fake journalist, was actually an ultranationalist, an aficionado of Hideki Tojo, but his bold intervention saved me from a ferocious ruck of black shirts. Later, a newspaper reported said the ultranationalists were Neo-Tojos.

Richie warned me that the music and crude sex in a shrine could have been the end of me. I corrected his notice that we had sex in a secular souvenir booth, but he frowned and waved me aside. The shrine maiden blushed, snickered, and covered her mouth with both hands. Then she raised a copy of *The Alleged 'Nanking Massacre'* in one hand, a tee shirt with the catchword "We Shall Win," in the other hand, and mocked the black shirts. Curry, my envoy, was at my side with a kami dog charm tied around his neck. He bared his perfect teeth and growled at the nationalists. That was a glorious moment.

I recovered and sheathed my sword, bowed twice to the miko shrine maiden, bought four "I Am a Glorious Cherry Blossom," and four "We Shall Win" tee shirts, a copy of every book on the counter, several peace charms, a rising sun hata, and with my crushed helmet under my arm, marched out of the black shirts and shrine souvenirs.

I shouted the tune "Yankee Doodle."

Curry panted at my side.

Ronin is an *atomu* warrior of the ruins, a roamer of shrines, peace parks, and museums, and, as you know, he is an inspired native contrary. His teases and word cuts are an original kabuki style, and he forever maddens the silky posers, sacred and otherwise, with erotic boasts, ridicule, and trickery. Ronin mocks the insinuations of the peacemongers with more delight than a warrior at the Little Big Horn River.

I salute this *hafu* visionary.

The Shinto Yasukuni Jinja honors the spirit and memory of more than two million warriors and soldiers who died in domestic and foreign wars. Yasukuni means "for the peace of the empire," noted Louis Frédéric in *Japan Encyclopedia*. The notion of peace is a contradiction in the context of militarism, colonialism, and thousands of indicted war criminals. The word *heiwa* means "peace," or freedom from war. Jinja means "shrine."

"The Yasukuni Shrine represents a peculiar concept of peace, one that is shrouded in over fifty years of an even more peculiar controversy, obscuring, in some ways, more than it explains about modern Japanese," observed Joshua Safier in *Yasukuni Shrine and the Constraints on the Discourse of Nationalism*. "For many younger Japanese their knowledge of the Shrine is dominated by political debates and international recriminations, resulting in confusion or indifference."

Shinto shrines were once situated in nature at the actual site of the *kami* spirits, or deities, such as mountains, rivers, and other sacred places. Today there are thousands of sacred sites and at least eleven styles of wooden shrines. The Ise Shrine, for instance, is constructed in the *shimmei* style with the entrance on the wide side of the structure; the entrance in the *otori* style is at the center of the gable.

The *honden*, the main shrine, is the inner sanctuary of the *kami* spirits. The *haiden* shrine is the place of public prayer and offering. The *torii* is a huge, distinctive arch at the entrance to the main shrine of Yasukuni Jinja. The *torii* marks the border of secular and sacred space.

157

Yasukuni Jinja was founded as Shokonsha in 1869. The name was changed a decade later. The shrine is a mark of militarism and has been controversial since the end of the war. Thousands of old soldiers in military uniforms gather at the shrine to honor the war dead on the anniversary of the surrender of Japan, August 15, 1945. Even now the main controversy is over the nasty war criminals enshrined as *gunshin*, or deities of war, at Yasukuni Jinja.

Hideki Tojo, the severe militarist and wartime prime minister, and many other political and military leaders were convicted of war crimes against peace and humanity and sentenced to death by the International Military Tribunal for the Far East.

Antonio Cassese pointed out in *The Tokyo Trial and Beyond* that the "indictment charged the defendants with over thirty counts of crimes against peace, the first of which was a charge for having participated in the conspiracy to dominate East Asia and ultimately the world." The tribunal considered crimes against peace, or war of aggression, conventional war crimes, and crimes against humanity, which included murder, extermination, enslavement, and other inhumane acts.

Chief Prosecutor Joseph Keenan asserted that those accused of war crimes were "plain, ordinary murderers." Tojo was one of the convicted war criminals venerated by shrine priests at Yasukuni Jinja.

That indictment of "murderers" included "four prime ministers, three foreign ministers, three economic and financial leaders, two ambassadors, four war ministers, two navy ministers, and numerous senior military officers," wrote Tim Maga in *Judgment at Tokyo*. The "Tokyo War Crimes Trials remains an emotional one, even after the fiftieth anniversary of the event. It should be. The crimes were horrible." The indictment mentioned the plundering of property, destruction of cities without "military necessity," and "mass murder, rape, pillage, brigandage, torture and other barbaric cruelties," and other crimes against civilians and prisoners of war.

"Shortly after the surrender, there was speculation that as many as fifty thousand Japanese might be indicted for committing crimes against prisoners as well as atrocities against civilians in the areas their forces occupied," observed John Dower in *Embracing Defeat*. "A year later, it was estimated that roughly ten thousand such suspects had been identified for possible trial. Eventually, around fifty military tribunals were convened at various" locations in Asia. "The tribunal essentially resolved the contradiction between the world of colonialism and imperialism and the righteous ideals of crimes against peace and humanity by ignoring it. Japan's aggression was presented as a criminal act without provocation, without parallel, and almost entirely without context." The prosecution, at times, "seemed literally blind" to the reality of Asia.

Tojo denied the indictment of war crimes. He wrote in his prison diary that "Japan had made honest efforts to keep the destruction of war from spreading and, based on the belief that all nations of the world should find their places, had followed a policy designed to restore an expeditious peace between Japan and China." Japan, he wrote, was "contributing to world peace," and "fought in order to ensure its own survival and also to establish the proper survival of the people of East Asia. In other words, it sought true civilization for mankind."

Ronin clapped his hands twice at the main shrine of Yasukuni Jinja and shouted at the spirits of the war criminals. "Come out of that shrine you cowards, come out under the torii and face the thousands of children you sacrificed at Hiroshima. The atomu children deserve to be honored more than you or any emperor. Tojo, come out and face my sacred sword or forever hide behind the hakama of shrine priests and the black shirts of the nationalists."

Tojo and more than a thousand other convicted war criminals were enshrined at Yasukuni Jinja in 1978. The shrine priests honored and protected these war criminals as *gunshin*, war spirits or deities of the shrine.

The Foreign Press Center reported that the "Yasukuni Shrine changed a great deal following Japan's defeat in World War II. State Shinto was abolished," and the government was no longer directly connection to the shrine. "The shrine's relation to the imperial family also underwent major changes following the war. Imperial visits to the shrine began with the Meiji Emperor and became a customary part of annual festivals. There is a record of the Showa Emperor visiting Yasukuni Shrine in 1952 immediately following the restoration of Japan's sovereignty at the end of the occupation by Allied Forces, although the current Emperor has never visited the shrine." Prime Minister Junichiro Koizumi was harshly criticized for his recent visit to the shrine.

There is some public sentiment to restore government support of the shrine to honor the war dead of the nation. Those who fear the return of militarism, however, resist any public promotion of the war memorial and shrine. Consequently, there are discussions by the government "to create a new war memorial where the prime minister can pay tribute to the nation's war dead without religious and international implications," wrote Yosuke Naito for the *Japan Times*. Some eight million people a year visit Yasukuni Jinja.

Professor Takao Sakamoto, Gakushuin University, on the other hand, argued "that there is nothing wrong with Japanese leaders paying tribute to the nation's war dead enshrined at Yasukuni, which they describe as the 'spiritual center' that honors people who died for their country." Sakamoto is conservative and a historical revisionist who does not accept the "denigrating" views of militarism in Japan.

The Japanese Communist Party declared that "Prime Minister Koizumi's visit to the shrine has caused immeasurable damage to friendship between Japan and neighboring Asian countries." The Yasukuni Shrine has "served as the spiritual mainstay of Japan's war of aggression and militarism; it enshrined those who died a heroes' death for the emperor's sake as deified war heroes."

Hibiya Koen, or park, is located near the imperial palace. The huge park, created a century ago, has a sunken garden, concert hall, extensive flower gardens, lakes, and many varieties of trees—maple, cherry, and ginkgo.

The Imperial Hotel is situated on the east side of the park. The Ministry of Justice, Family Court, and other government buildings are on the west side. The Imperial Palace Plaza and gardens are on the north side of the park across the Hibiya Moat.

Ronin first discovered Hibiya Koen in "Moonlight over Hibiya Park," a woodblock print by Koitsu Tsuchiya. The framed print was mounted in the reception area of the Elizabeth Saunders School at Oiso on Sagami Bay. Ronin was enchanted by the bright, clean winter scene and imagined his presence in the park. Later he ran away to that place, and now he considers the park one of his many natural homes as a roamer. He either sleeps in the trees or on a park bench. His favorite bench under a ginkgo was home on the shrine and van nights in Tokyo.

Hibiya Park was no garden sanctuary on September 15, 1905. The prime minister declared that the Treaty of Portsmouth, a victory over Russia, was "a great moment in the history of modern Japan," wrote James McClain in *A Modern History of Japan*. Thousands of workers gathered in the park to protest, not praise the treaty. "To their way of thinking, the government had not extracted nearly enough concessions from Russia, rather, 'clumsy' and 'weak-willed' negotiators had settled for a 'shameful' peace." At the end of the demonstration many participants marched from the park toward the nearby Imperial Palace.

The tension mounted, "tempers flared, and fights broke out." The police were outnumbered, swords against thousands of clubs and stones, and rioters destroyed government property. Martial law was declared the next day, but by the time order was restored some three hundred fifty buildings "had been destroyed, five hundred police and at least an equal number of protesters had suffered wounds, and seventeen demonstrators lay dead."

The Hibiya Park rioters were patriots who had affirmed "their place in the national polity." That protest was the rise of modern nationalism. The emperor and militarists would take advantage of the patriotic vitality. The *kokutai no hongi*, for instance, summoned the "absolute obedience" of nation to a divine emperor.

The Imperial Hotel was designed by Frank Lloyd Wright, and the construction was completed in 1922. Ronin was enchanted by the many courts, terraces, and levels. The modern, masonry hotel survived the Great Kanto Earthquake of 1923. The hotel was systematically demolished in 1967.

The new Imperial Hotel towers were completed a few years later. Ronin and Ginkgo regularly use the grand lobby and stately public toilets of the hotel. Each toilet enclosure has a solid wooden door and a heated toilet seat. The towels are thick cotton, and the mirrors create a deceptive image of entitlement, ease, and taste as a suave face shimmers in the tinted, indirect light.

Miko is an artist, habitué of the Andersen Bakery, as you know, and a *hosutesu* at the Ana Hotel in Hiroshima. The *miko* shrine maiden of the souvenir booth is not the same name. The first is a personal given name, and the second is a representative shrine name.

Petros bought several charms from the souvenir booth at Yasukuni Jinja. He tied two charms on Ronin's wooden sword. Curry resisted any tie or tether around his neck, but the charmer prevailed with two charms. Later, he tied similar charms around the neck of the obstreperous Margarito Real.

161

The Japanese *omamori*, a charm or talisman, is trusted as protection against both extreme situations, or curses, and ordinary uncertainties such as social and personal problems. Ronin even bought *omamori* to protect his heart and humor from the sponsors of fake peace.

Ginkgo, the old woman of Hibiya Park, and the cat mother, *neko okasan*, are not uncommon roamers in Tokyo. Thousands of men and women with lost relatives, worried hearts, and descriptive nicknames live in the parks, in the woods near the moats, and in the millions of secret seams and creases of the city. Many roamers must fight with the imperial ravens over leftovers at restaurants early in the morning.

Ginkgo may be *hibakusha*, an *atomu* fugitive, and she may have been exposed to the intense light of the atomic explosion in Hiroshima. Many older *hibakusha* have *atomu*, or atomic, cataracts on their eyes. The "most notable disease among atomic bomb victims is atomic bomb cataract," noted Naomi Shohno in *The Legacy of Hiroshima*. "The first case of atomic bomb cataract was observed two years after the bombing."

The Japanese chrysanthemum, or *kiku*, is the crest or seal of the imperial family. Four seals are on the chrysanthemum cloth at the entrance to the main shrine at Yasukuni Jinja. Nightbreaker and five other soldiers were photographed under the *torii* with the same seals in the background, three chrysanthemums on the cloth over the shrine entrance. Ronin painted that seal on his helmet liner.

The Imperial Palace, a huge plantation surrounded by moats, walls, and stone bridges in the center of the city, was constructed on land that was once the Tokugawa Edo Castle. Emperor Meiji moved the imperial family from Kyoto to Edo in 1868, the very same year the United States government established by treaty the White Earth Reservation in Minnesota. The emperor changed the name of the city to Tokyo.

"The emperor was the spiritual leader of the nation and the supreme Shinto priest," wrote Louis Frédéric in *Japan Encyclopedia*. The new postwar constitution ended the supreme imperial status of the emperor as the head of state. The emperor became a symbol of the nation, "the guarantor of the country's integrity and unity, and he plays a representative role in all national events."

The cat mother, *neko okasan*, lives in the dense woods on the northwestern side of the palace moat, across from Kitanomaru Park. Twice a year she tours the imperial gardens, but she has never seen the emperor or a cat at the palace. The imperial ravens chased the cats to the north moat.

The Fairmont Hotel and the Indian Embassy face the woods and the moat. The paths are remote, and only the nearby residents, hotel visitors, and embassy staff use the benches by day. The woods are a natural sanctuary for the cats. Few strangers ever visit the area at night. The Yasukuni Jinja is only a few blocks away.

Emperor Hirohito was never indicted as a war criminal, and yet he followed closely every "military move, read diplomatic telegrams, read the newspapers daily, and often questioned his aides about what he found in them," wrote Herbert Bix in *Hirohito and the Making of Modern Japan*. "As the commander in chief who had sanctioned the capture and occupation of Nanking, and as the spiritual leader of the nation," he was clearly responsible for the moral breakdown and atrocities of the military.

The *kokutai no hongi*, an ideological discourse on the divine benevolence of the emperor, was distributed to schools in the late thirties as a spiritual mobilization for war. "Eventually more than ten million copies were sold nationwide." Bix observed that the *kokutai* "stressed the absolute superiority of the Japanese people and state over all other nations" and "implanted the image of the emperor as a military ruler and 'a living god who rules our country in accordance with the benevolent wishes of his imperial founder and his other imperial ancestors.' All Japanese subjects had the duty to give Hirohito their absolute obedience."

Bix argues that the "country had taken on the identity of a fascist state," with forced labor and rationed food in a "total war economy," and policies "designed to increase war production by lowering living standards; in the emperor's name all open dissent had been squashed."

That ruinous notion of a divine emperor and militarist was justly terminated in a mundane and inglorious radio broadcast to the country. The emperor renounced his godly stature in the surrender of Japan. General MacArthur was moved by romantic sentiments of a mythic emperor, and, at the same time, sensible about the national entity. He reasoned that any prosecution of the emperor as a war criminal could undermine cultural unity at a time when the country was close to political and economic breakdown. MacArthur became the emperor of the occupation and, at the same time, he protected, desacralized, and separated the defeated emperor from any direct government authority under the new constitution.

Ronin has indicted the emperor, and he shouted at the spirits of the war criminals, "Come out of that shrine you cowards," come out of that sanctuary and "face the thousands of children you sacrificed at Hiroshima."

The Japanese national anthem, "Kimigayo," is derived from a *tanka* poem in the *Kokinshu*. The somber, nostalgic music was created by Hayashi Hiromori. "Kimigayo" was "played for the first time at the imperial court in 1880," noted Louis Frédéric in *Japan Encyclopedia*. This is a translation of the poetic anthem: "The reign of our lord shall last eight thousand and one generations, until stones become boulders and are covered with moss." The tanka is a short imagistic poem in five lines. The *Kokinshu* is a collection of early poems, the first of many imperial anthologies.

Ronin broadcast two marches by the composer John Philip Sousa, the Marine Corps Hymn, "From the Halls of Montezuma," and two other songs from the souvenir booth near the main shrine at Yasukuni Jinja. The consequences of such a bold, tricky move, and, at the same time, vouched by sex with a *miko* shrine maiden in that narrow booth, could have been fatal.

The nationalists, or black shirts, had gathered at the shrine to protest liberal appeasement on the anniversary of the surrender, August 15, 1945. Ronin confronted the black shirts with patriotic military music and survived the enemy torment, and tease of cultural wounds, by the grace of a fake journalist. Richie was an imposer, but he was an honored leader of the Neo-Tojos.

The *miko* shrine maiden raised a nationalist tee shirt, "We Shall Win," and a copy of *The Alleged 'Nanking Massacre'* to distract the black shirts. The book was published by Nippon Kaigi, a revisionist, conservative, nationalist organization, as a "rebuttal to China's forged claims."

"Japan has kept silent whenever and however we were falsely accused of this problem," noted Nippon Kaigi. "Here, we would like to break the silence for the first time. We will not scream like the Chinese, but set forth our views purely and fairly as an accused standing in the dock of a courthouse, speaking in a low tone of voice, asking the fair judgment of the readers." The documents are elusive revisions, the conceits of ultranationalism.

"The Chinese have apparently a special liking for talking about the cruel methods of murder used by Japanese soldiers at Nanking," wrote Akira Nakamura, professor of history, and director of the Research Institute of Showa History. "But all of these atrocities are what the Chinese soldiers have been using for centuries past, but unknown to the Japanese." Nippon Kaigi and the nationalists have supported the publication of public school textbooks that censor any mention of military atrocities or war crimes.

Toshiaki Matsumura, executive secretary of Nippon Kaigi, argued that the goals of the organization are to create a new constitution with respect for the emperor, improve the military, conduct public relations in support of nationalism, and present the "real Japan, with a correct view of history," according to Nippon Kaigi. "That 'correct view,' of course, continues to provoke debate," wrote Annie Nakao for the *San Francisco Chronicle*. The nationalists would revise the article in the constitution that renounces the establishment of military forces.

Dennis Banks and an Amerika Indian baby were likely on the mind of the *miko* shrine maiden, and she might have conceived a child over the military hymn, "From the halls of Montezuma, to the shores of Tripoli, we will fight our country's battles, in the air, on land and sea." That erotic moment in the booth could have been the rise of a shrine *hafu* and the incredible start of another story.

The Marine Corps Hymn, "From the Halls of Montezuma," was derived from an aria in French. John Philip Sousa reported that the melody of the hymn was borrowed from *Genevieve de Brabant*, a comic opera by Jacques Offenbach, in 1868.

Sousa was the leader of the Marine Corps Band in the late nineteenth century. He created about a hundred and forty marches and patriotic music for military bands, including the official Marine Corps march, "Semper Fidelis," in 1888, and the very popular "Stars and Stripes Forever" in 1897.

Ronin broadcast "Yankee Doodle," a song created during the American Revolution, and the popular Second World War song "Praise the Lord and Pass the Ammunition," by Frank Loesser.

Richard Schuckburg, a British Army surgeon, may have written "Yankee Doodle" to ridicule the Americans a generation before the Revolutionary War. Some historians, however, argue that the tune is a variation of the nursery rhyme "Lucy Lockett." American colonists, in spite of the ridicule, carried that tune to war, every war since the American Revolution.

General George Washington won the Revolution at Yorktown in 1781. General Charles Cornwallis surrendered his army to the Americans, who apparently played "Yankee Doodle," a spirited, double ridicule returned in victory. The British military band played the march "The World Turned Upside Down," over and over again. That tune was heard as "Derry Down," and by several other titles, in England.

Ronin whistled the tune and chanted the chorus of "Yankee Doodle" on his meander from the shrine booth to the war museum. "Yankee Doodle, keep it up, Yankee Doodle dandy, mind the music and the step, and with the girls be handy." Ronin minded the music and was indeed handy.

Ronin was moved by the shrine maiden's gift of a tiny ivory *tenuki* figure. The *tenuki* is a trickster, a spirit that poses as a badger with a huge *penisu* and testicles. The trickster might be the figure of a raccoon or a dog. Ronin saw a similar *tenuki* trickster on a small ivory cosmetic case in a museum. The intricately carved ivory *tenuki* was about an inch high and was seated in the center of the round lid on the ivory box.

Dennis Banks is a member of the American Indian Movement. He and other radical natives chased racial simpletons and paranoid separatists from one end of the country to the other. Banks has become a very ambitious capitalist agent in the past two decades, and he has been active in Japan. His romantic autobiography was recently published only in Japanese.

11 Ronin of the Ginza

The actual war museum is located east of the main shrine of Yasu-kuni Jinja. The kaiten, or suicide submarine, is mounted on a pedestal, a merciless memorial to the kamikaze sailors who became human torpedoes. The restored tanks and dive-bombers, swords, guns, and other military hardware are a pathetic spectacle of a defeated colonial empire.

> Outside, the statue of a kamikaze pilot is a trivial representation of bushido, the loyalty of a warrior. That great tradition of the samurai was cornered by the emperor and abused by the militarists and war criminals.

My march was over. The black shirts and war criminals heard my indictment and protest. I draped the hata around my shoulders, rising sun on my back, and meandered past the main shrine to the war memorial. Inside, a tiny old man saluted the picture of a young kamikaze pilot holding a baby. Lieutenant Uemara Masahisa, the suicide pilot in the picture, sat near a window in perfect light and looked down at his puffy daughter with thick black hair. The old man and the lieutenant were both in uniform.

> The old man turned from that grievous picture and saluted me. He wore thick glasses and probably did not recognize the uniform of the occupation enemy. I returned his salute, bowed, and folded the hata with care. I was silent as he studied the picture, saluted once more, and told me the lieutenant was a kamikaze pilot of the Special Attack Corps. He died on a mission shortly after his daughter was born. The old man was not related to the lieutenant, but he admired his courage and saluted him several times a week. The old man served the emperor as an officer, but he was rejected as a suicide pilot because of his poor vision.

Curry was at our side.

> The old man gave me a tour of the new war museum and told me stories about the aircraft and weapons that were on display. The placards were revisionist war histories, of course, but he never once mentioned the enemy, the atomu bomb, the end of the war, or the occupation of Japan. He told stories about war adventure, honor, courage, and loyalty, but never defeat.

Nearby in a new section of the museum a group of war veterans, tiny old men in military uniforms, watched a continuous video presentation on a combat fighter plane, the Mitsubishi Zero. They were moved to tears day after day by war memories, and sang along with the patriotic sound track on the video docudrama.

Curry waited by the old men.

What namae?

Ronin Browne.

Nai, no, no.

Amerika Indian.

Hai, samurai.

Your namae, name?

Bogart.

Nai, no, no.

Bogart movie man.

Hai, *Casablanca*?

Bogart namae.

My mother loved Bogart.

Afurika Queen.

Bogart the emperor.

Nai, jodan.

Hai, my joke.

Mother emperor?

You joke me.

Amerika Errol Flynn.

Baka, *Operation Burma*.

Hai, stupid movie.

Bogart was amused and spirited by our kabuki conversation and invited me to ride along with him to the Ginza district of Tokyo. Hibiya Park and the Imperial Hotel were nearby, and a van was much better than crammed bodies on the subway or a sweaty march in late afternoon traffic.

The van was parked near the museum. I asked him about the driver but he never answered me. I had assumed the old man was not able to drive because of his poor vision. Bogart was a determined soldier and he would not stand for any speculation, hesitation, or debility.

The huge, black van had mirrored windows that menaced anyone on the road. Bogart started the engine, cleaned his glasses, lighted a cigarette, and drove slowly, at first, and then he accelerated once the van was out of the lot. He swerved at high speed between cars and trucks. Everyone seemed to avoid the van, and rightly so because it was immediately recognized as another noisy propaganda machine of the ultranationalists.

Bogart took the expressway exit near the Tokyo train station, slowed down, and turned south on Showa Dori. Suddenly, he was in no obvious hurry. The reason was clear once he started a compact disk of patriotic, military music and loud, nasty diatribes that attacked liberal pacifists and foreign deceptions, and always closed with veneration of the emperor. The van was an instrument of fascist torment. The black shirts abused the ears as a revolutionary strategy. The broadcasts of the nationalists were hardly more enlightened than the lyrics at an acid rock concert. The sound of the music and nationalist propaganda was so violent that some people covered their head and ears. Most people, however, disregarded the very presence of the black vans. I did the same whenever the vans circled Hibiya Park.

The van was insulated to reduce the sound of the speakers, but the music was too loud to even hear a fierce conversation in the front seat. The nationalists are elusive and protected by politicians and the police. No one dared stop a van for any traffic or noise violations of the law.

Curry covered his ears.

Bogart marched to the museum several times a week to salute the picture of the kamikaze lieutenant. The nationalists were so impressed they hired him to drive a broadcast van three times a week around the Ginza district. He was trusted as a war veteran, but he was not a nasty black shirt nationalist. "Kimigayo," the kokka, or national anthem, was his next selection on the compact disk, the same music the shrine maiden played at the souvenir booth.

Bogart could hardly hear my shouts. I pointed, gestured, and shouted over the anthem to stop at the next corner near the music store. The music in the store was almost as loud as the anthem in the van. I bought a compact disk of godly hymns and patriotic music. Naturally, my scheme was to terminate the military van music and see if anyone on the street would listen to gospel music by Mahalia Jackson.

The van was slowed in heavy traffic on Showa Dori a few blocks north of Higashi Ginza. I inserted my new compact disk and selected a track to play as we approached the intersection at Harumi Dori.

"Go tell it on the mountain."

Mahalia Jackson's magnificent voice reached out and teased every seam and crease on the crowded streets. She touched every heart with the sacred blues, "over the hills and everywhere." Many Japanese turned to listen for the first time to a broadcast from a black van.

"Hallelujah Lord."

American tourists could not believe their ears, and hundreds of people on the street started to move with the beat of the music. Many people clapped their hands as if they were at a shrine, and others sang along, "Go tell it on the mountain that Jesus Christ is born."

> Traffic came to an absolute standstill near the Kabukiza Theatre, and several hundred people surrounded the van to hear Mahalia Jackson, "He's got the whole world in his hands." The song was recorded live at a concert, and it started with audience applause. The response of the concert audience inspired the people on the street and they clapped their hands to the music, "He's got everybody here right in his hands."

The Americans danced in the streets, and traffic was blocked in every direction at Higashi Ginza, the intersection near the Kabukiza Theatre. The Japanese clapped their hands, sang along, and created a gospel version of street karaoke.

"Lord search my heart."

Derek Decisis, Margarito Real, and Petros Komuso were at the Kabukiza Theatre and heard the music from outside. They bought only special scene tickets and could easily leave the balcony. "Were you there when they crucified my Lord?"

> Petros told them about my adventures with the shrine maiden, but he missed the trouble that followed with the black shirts and the fake journalist, Richie. Naturally, they were astonished to see me in a black, nationalist van. My Hiroshima friends admired my collection of tee shirts. Real wore "I Am a Glorious Cherry Blossom," and braved an effete pose. Stare could not resist, "We Shall Win," a tee shirt he might wear in court.

> The blues beat the anthems.

> Gospel outshines the nationalists.

Tease a shrine maiden.

Bogart invited my friends to ride along, but the van was already stopped in traffic, and no one really wanted to leave the scene in the streets. We opened the doors and windows, and even the van swayed to the music. The old man watched the musical in the street and talked about the war and the atomu destruction of Hiroshima.

"Didn't it rain children."

Bogart told me he was stationed at a military base near ground zero, and the day before the explosion he was assigned to inspect prisoners of war at a nearby camp. The great mushroom cloud was visible over the mountains to the north. Later that day he was ordered to transport the prisoners for labor duty on the perilous, radioactive streets of Hiroshima. The American prisoners had no idea the war was about to end. Bogart was there when the puny voice of the emperor was broadcast on radio. Hirohito announced the surrender and renounced his divine nature as emperor. Bogart, at that very moment, became a prisoner of war in the atomu ruins of the city.

"Smile when you're happy."

I told the old man that my father was there with a team of military photographs at the very same time, Atomu One. They might have stared at each other over the ruins. Surely, the horror of the atomu destruction was beyond words. Bogart was silenced by my rage over the thousands of dead children, laborers in the streets, incinerated because of their fearful loyalty to the emperor.

>Overturn the war memorial.
>Shout down nationalists.
>Clap out the spirits.
>Shame the shrine priests.
>Oust the war criminals.
>Honor the kami children.

The Ginza was truly liberated by the gospel music of Mahalia Jackson. Thousands of people came together from every direction, from every store, restaurant, and office building to sing, dance, and move with the spirit of the music.

"Trouble of the world."

Many hundreds of people poured out of the subway stations and started to sing and dance as the sun set over Hibashi Ginza. By chance the black van became a kami shrine, the natural center of a gospel occupation, a new blue bugi on the Ginza.

Real boasted in his cherry tee shirt.

Stare lip-synched gospel.

Petros ducked under his hat.

Bogart saluted everyone.

Curry barked with the music.

Bogart surrendered the van, at last, and we contributed the money to buy bento dinners from the basement of the Mitsukoshi Department Store. The prepared dinners were discounted late in the day. He returned a short time later with stacks of decorated bento boxes and several bottles of sake. We told stories about the yakuza and black shirts over a great dinner in the van.

Mahalia Jackson created a spiritual presence with blue swoops, godly moods, and tender tones that lasted forever in the city. Stare was moved by hymns, but he was never without his own collection of blues, country, and rocker music. He was the man prepared to continue the music occupation of the Ginza and Harumi Dori. He inserted a special compact disk into the van player.

Chuck Berry, "Rock and Roll Music."

Roy Orbison, "Pretty Woman."

Johnny Cash, "The Man in Black."

Bogart was at our side, arm in arm, as we sang along with Chuck Berry, "Just let me hear some of that rock and roll music." People on the street were taken over by the rocker beat. Several television crews had arrived to report on the extraordinary spontaneous concert on the Ginza. A young woman pretended to play a guitar and hopped backwards down the street in front of the Kabukiza Theatre.

"Any old way you choose it."

Three older women dressed in formal kimonos, tabi, and getas came out of the theater to the music of Roy Orbison. "Pretty woman, walking down the street," caught them by surprise. They were uncertain about the beat of the music, cautious of the men in the black van, but clearly pleased and, at the same time, embarrassed by the words. "Pretty woman, give your smile to me."

Johnny Cash sang for us the rest of the night. Stare had three compact disks of his music, *The Man in Black, Cowboy,* and *A Thing Called Love.* Johnny Cash in concert on the Ginza. No one would ever forget that night.

Bogart was worried about the music of *The Man in Black*. His nominal association with the nationalists, the black shirts, had been eroded by our teases, stories, and the music of the night, but now he was very concerned that the black shirts were honored in a popular song.

Bogart wondered why Johnny Cash always wore black, and never any bright colors on his back. And why does he seem to have a rather somber tone? Johnny wears black for good reasons, to honor the poor, the hungry, criminals, and to mourn for those who died because they believe in a partisan Lord.

The Man in Black created a new blue mood, a somber tone on the Ginza. "The Ballad of Ira Hayes" moved everyone on the street, and many worried hearts mourned over the miseries of the Amerika Indian. Thousands of people followed the words to "Ring of Fire," "Jackson," and "I Walk the Line," and many shouted out the words to "A Boy Named Sue" and "Folsom Prison Blues."

Johnny Cash, a kami spirit of the Ginza.

The corner marquee projected a giant television picture of Johnny Cash. He was dressed in black, and even the nationalists were moved by the music. Thousands of people waved to him on the screen and danced in the streets. His seductive, melodious voice reached out across the Ginza.

Ginkgo told me, as she beat her brow, that she heard "Rock and Roll Music" and "A Boy Named Sue" that night at the Imperial Hotel and in Hibiya Park.

Ronin and Bogart became the mobile music men of the Ginza and
Hibiya Park. Their unusual union, a bushido veteran with poor
vision and the *hafu* son of an interpreter with the occupation, was
reported on television and in several feature newspaper stories.

The *Native American Press,* a native newspaper with many readers
on the White Earth Reservation, recounted some of the adventures
and tricky protests of Ronin Browne, a generation after Nightbreaker and Bogart in Hiroshima.

Miko told me that for several weeks the two returned to the same
route with the black van and broadcast gospel, blues, and rock music
on the streets. Many people waited at the end of the day for the
mobile concert, and some even waved and praised the black vans.

Hibiya Park was the last concert of the day. The van circled the
park and broadcast "Pretty Woman" by Roy Orbison. Gingko came out
of the trees to beat her brow. She shouted the tune and laughed at the
words. The black shirts heard cultural decadence in the music and
resented the generation of liberty.

Bogart and Ronin were denounced by the nationalists. The mobile
excursions were terminated, but the music continued for a few more
weeks on the Ginza. They bought a boom box and carried their music
around the streets, parks, theaters, restaurants, and department
stores, but the public soon lost interest in the same old blues tunes.
"Go Tell it on the Mountain" was lost in the rush to the subway.
"Rock and Roll Music" was wasted on the street, the rocker beat was
out of mind. "Pretty Woman" caught no one by surprise. "The Man
in Black" was passed over as a ruse of the nationalists. The Ginza
police convinced them that the pleasure was not in the music alone,
but in the original protest of the noisy black vans. They retreated
to the frenzy of pachinko parlors.

Bogart saluted a photograph of Lieutenant Uemara Masahisa, a
kamikaze pilot in the Special Attack Corps. That regular salute of a
photograph in the war museum was the sentiment of a warrior, an aesthetic signature of bushido tradition and a cultural contradiction
of memory.

The Japanese state used the imagistic metaphor of a falling
cherry blossom to "promote the sacrifice of soldiers for the

emperor," wrote Emiko Ohnuki-Tierney in *Kamikase, Cherry Blossoms, and Nationalisms*. The *tokkotai*, or *tokubetsu kogekitai*, Special Attack Forces, "sent thousands of young men to their deaths." Most of them were "student soldiers" and many were the "intellectual elite." The "*tokkotai* operation" of student soldiers "cannot be fathomed without considering the impact of their deaths upon their parents, wives, lovers, siblings, and in very few cases, children." The *tokkotai* is "known as kamikaze outside of Japan."

Ronin was inspired by the samurai traditions of bushido, or courage and loyalty, but he was a *ronin* of native survivance, not of termination or victimry, although he was a dramatic artist of serial, symbolic suicides or figural kamikaze flight. He convinced some of his new friends, in other words, that his sudden absence from time to time was an act of suicide rather than creative truancy.

The word *kamikaze* means "divine wind," a cultural metaphor associated with the *kami* spirits that twice in seven years roused a typhoon to defeat the Mongol forces of Ghengis Khan. The mighty kamikaze typhoons were the *kami* spirits of the "divine wind."

The Japanese stories of divine intervention, mythic kamikaze virtues, and the notable presence of *kami* spirits are the cultural foundations of an ideology of absolute loyalty to the once-divine emperor. Naturally, the *kami* spirits would be summoned by the emperor as a kamikaze force to defeat the third menace to the nation, the conceivable invasion by soldiers of the United States of America.

The Special Attack Corps of kamikaze pilots was created in desperation to defeat another invader of the country. Some four thousand pilots, loyal to the emperor and touched by *kami* spirits, died in suicide attacks at the end of the war. Their spirits are now venerated as *gunshin*, or war deities, at Yasukuni Jinja.

Ronin bought a tee shirt at the souvenir booth with the poetic statement "I Am a Glorious Cherry Blossom" printed on the front, and on the back the imperial crest of the chrysanthemum. Japanese cherry blossoms are a season of delight and a cultural metaphor of impermanence. The delicate spring flowers are "closely associated with the samurai, for whom life was 'as ephemeral as cherry blossoms.' These flowers also became one of the symbols of Japan," noted Louis Frédéric in *Japan Encyclopedia*.

The cherry blossom was a common metaphor of the kamikaze pilots. "The falling cherry blossom became the best known symbol of the young flyers, appearing in their poems, their songs, their farewell letters, and in the hands of the virgin schoolgirls who assembled to see them off on their final missions," wrote John Dower in *War Without Mercy*.

The chrysanthemum, or *kiku*, is the crest of the emperor, and those kamikaze pilots who carried that crest by suicide were venerated as *kami* spirits. The divine emperor impassively honored thousands of dead pilots, but the kamikaze of the divine wind could not stop the Americans. Some pilots resisted the fantastic cherry metaphors, the poetry of service, and the warrant of suicide.

The "young martyrs sensed that their impending deaths would not alter substantially the outcome of the war," wrote James McClain in *A Modern History of Japan*. "Disillusioned, a few plunged to their deaths shouting curses against their unit commanders and the country's political leaders into their radios. Most, however, sent home final poems and letters that expressed a poignant, elemental belief in family, emperor, and nation, values that sustained" many even at the end of the war. "The nobility of youthful sacrifice did nothing to spare the Japanese population from the ferocity" of the strategic incendiary explosives delivered by General Curtis LeMay and the Twentieth Bomber Command.

A *bento* is a box lunch or food that is selected, served and carried in a box. Louis Frédéric thoughtfully pointed out in *Japan Encyclopedia* that *bento* is a boxed meal "prepared in advance and sold to travelers in train stations. Their composition varies by region and town." Bogart bought cuisine *bento* dinners in the basement food service at the Mitsukoshi Department Store on Hurumi Dori and Chuo Dori in the Ginza.

Ronin wrote about three women who wore kimonos to the Kabukiza Theatre in the Ginza. They wore traditional *tabi*, socks with separated toes, and *geta*, shoes with wooden soles. The Japanese kimono is a national, traditional costume worn by men and women. Various fabrics are used for kimonos, but the cut and fashion of materials are similar. Men wear darker kimonos over *hakama*, or loose trousers. Kabuki actors wear the most ornamental kimonos on stage.

The word *kokka* refers to the national anthem, nation or country. The word *hata* means "flag," and *kokki* refers to the national flag of Japan. The circle of the sun, or *hinomaru*, is the national flag. The red circle with red strips radiating from the center was the military flag. The old veterans carry the military flag at Yasukuni Jinja. The flag of the emperor and imperial family is a golden chrysanthemum crest on a red background.

Bogart used the word *baka*, which means "absurd," "a fool," or "a stupid person," in response to the movie *Operation Burma* with Errol Flynn. Ronin said, "*Hai*, a stupid movie." The word *hai* means "yes," and *nai*, "no" or "not."

Pachinko is a vertical pinball machine, and pachinko parlors are noisy, smoky game centers of passive players. "Pachinko parlors offer players row upon row of these machines, and people set their eyes on the balls, forget their work and worries, and empty their minds as they play," wrote Louis Frédéric in *Japan Encyclopedia*.

12 Ronin of Matsue

Curry was undercover in my shoulder bag. My loyal envoy wisely remained hidden and silent on the train, although twice he sneezed, clearly not a human sound. I covered my mouth, smiled, and pretended to blow my nose when several passengers turned around in search of a dog. One woman was not convinced by my gestures. She watched me closely, but luckily did not report her suspicions to the conductor.

Miko was in Matsue, a small city on the western coast, on the Sea of Japan. She had been invited to present her watercolor paintings at a major exhibition in the Hohoemi Art Gallery near the Lafcadio Hearn Memorial Museum.

She summoned me to meet the author at his residence. She read my three books in the ruins and admired my signed copy of *Glimpses of Unfamiliar Japan*. Actually, she knew his signature was faked. The author was dead more than two generations before my edition was published, but she appreciated my connection to the author and my imagination of his stories. Hearn was a hafu in a weird, courteous, and obscure culture. A century later he might have written about me, a hafu ronin in the ruins of Rashomon Gate. Hearn, Ronin, Oshima, Miko, Kitsutsuki, Ginkgo, Bogart, together we are the selective contradictions of Japan.

Miko wisely moved the three boxes of my protest papers from the ruins, and now, once more, she encouraged me to sort out the notes, scenes, outlines, traces, and hints on hundreds of scraps and create a book of adventure stories. She convinced me, even before my march to the war museum, that any association with the memory of Lafcadio Hearn, his residence, and the manuscript collection in his name would inspire me to finish my own stories.

Hearn is my hafu muse.

The shinkansen train arrived on time in Okayama late in the day, too late to catch the slower train through the mountains to Matsue. So, we stayed overnight on a bench in a nearby park. Curry leaped out of my shoulder bag the minute we were clear of the train station and rushed into the bushes. The park was moist, hushed by the consent of shame. The roamers avoided each other, and not one of them related to an animal, trouped an unusual manner, or mocked a right or a song.

Curry waited in the shadows.

Hibiya Park is my home.

The Hakubi Line followed the moody river valleys through the mountains from Okayama to Matsue. Curry sat with me at the window. The shadows were lean, blue on the curves, and the sun was tempered by the morning mist. The great trees moved in a perfect light of ancient memory. The train stopped at every town on the way, Takahashi, Nimi, Hino, Kofu, Kishimoto near Daisen Mountain, Yanago, and at last Matsue on Lake Shinji near the Sea of Japan.

Lafcadio Hearn was very perceptive in *Glimpses of Unfamiliar Japan*. I have that book with me right now. He arrived in Matsue at about the same time, in late August, but a hundred and some years earlier. He traveled through the same valleys, admired the evergreens, the mountains, but not by train. About a year later he departed by steamer for a position as a teacher in Kumamoto in Kyushu.

"It is a lovely vapory morning, sharp with the first chill of winter. From the tiny deck I take my last look at the quaint vista of Ohashigawa," the Ohashi River, he wrote of Matsue. The "beautiful fantastic shapes of the ancient hills" are magical, a "land where sky and earth so strangely intermingle that what is reality may not be distinguished from what is illusion—that all seems a mirage, about to vanish."

The Hohoemi Gallery made arrangements for Miko to stay at the Suimeisou Ryokan Inn. Curry was at my side as we entered the ryokan lobby. The clerk was very nervous about dogs. She bowed, smiled, and kindly announced my presence, and then she summoned the manager.

No inu, out ryokan.

Curry is a loyal diplomat.

No, inu out now.

I bowed, walked out of the ryokan, and turned the corner out of sight. Curry understood the rules of exclusion and jumped into my shoulder bag. I buckled the cover and returned to the hotel lobby. The manager bowed, and then apologized when he found no animal.

Strange, wiry dog.

Wild, maybe.

Yes, many mongrels.

Many good dogs.

The manager smiled, surely aware of the telltale dog bulge in my shoulder bag. Charitably, he looked the other way. Miko came out of the sento dressed in a lovely yukata, with a towel around her neck. Her face was bright, blushed by the heat. I touched her cheeks and imagined the invisible tattoos on the rise of her lusty body. Minutes later we were in her room, naked in a wide lounge chair on the balcony. She scratched my tattoos into sight, mounted me, and shouted out my name over and over. Our bodies were wet and salty. A warm, zesty breeze came across Lake Shinji.

Curry heard my name and rushed to the balcony. He barked in every direction. My loyal envoy warned me once again, and any other person in the ryokan who might do me harm. Nearby guests reported the wild barks to the manager, and soon there was a knock at the door. Curry was back in the bag, and we made our getaway down the back stairs. I walked through the lobby, bowed to the desk clerk, and left the ryokan without a word.

Curry worried about me.

Miko met us later at the Hohoemi Gallery near the Lafcadio Hearn Museum. The gallery was located across the moat from the massive Matsue Castle. I had seen most of her watercolor paintings in the gallery in Hiroshima. This exhibition presented many new paintings. The elusive, transparent traces, shadows, spectral moods, and signature mirrors were there, but the subjects were no longer children in the peace park. Miko had painted the park roamers in wild, natural states of grace. Broad, worried smiles were painted across benches, giant, leprous hands were attached to the rope on the peace bell, and the ravens were overburdened with enormous wings. The atomu dome was decorated with ghostly body parts and faint traces of my invisible tattoos.

Miko is a shaman.

The Lafcadio Hearn residence and museum were about to close, so we decided to return early the next day. Curry charmed the owners of the Yakumo Teahouse and restaurant near the Hearn residence on Shiomi Nawate, in the northern shadow of the moat. There were many historic samurai houses on the streets near the castle moat.

The Yakumo Teahouse enclosed a garden of whimsy. Three cats were perched on the wall in the shadow of the trees. We sat at a table outside, near a pond. Giant goldfish teased the surface of the water. Curry was courteous, never intrusive, and with one eye on the cats he pretended to be shied by the attention of the ladies who owned the teahouse.

I ordered koi, carp, cut and bound with string and baked in a sweet sauce, the singular entree on the menu. Miko order the special Izumo soba. Naturally, we ordered meika sweets and tea at the end of the meal. Curry was given some spicy leftovers at the back of the restaurant. The owners had never heard of a dog that was trained to eat curry.

>Cats never eat spice.
>Not many dogs.
>Yakumo Koizumi ate spice.
>My hafu author.
>You writer?
>Lafcadio is my ancestor.
>Hai, sosen?
>Hai, Amerika Indian.
>Girishajin samurai?
>Greek Amerika Indian.
>You joke me.
>Miko likes my jokes.
>What namae?
>My name is Ronin.
>Nai, not ronin.
>Ronin Hearn of Rashomon Gate.
>You joke me.
>Curry likes my jokes.

Miko insisted that we walk to a new waterfront park on the canal south of the Matsue Castle. Closer, she ordered me to cover my eyes and marched me toward a wall near the water. Curry was always at my side. I heard the sound of a jazz violin nearby. She stopped and told me to open my eyes. I shouted with delight and moved closer. Lafcadio Hearn was against the stone blocks. The bronze sculpture was mounted part way into the stone blocks, an image based on a familiar drawing of the author walking away with a suitcase in one hand, a satchel in the other, and one foot turned out. His hat, coat, and trousers are rumpled and creased. I pressed my body against the cold stone, akin to the halfway statue, and turned one foot out in the manner and swerve of the author.

Miko attended a reception at the gallery and then returned late to the ryokan. We agreed to meet in the morning for breakfast and then visit the museum. Curry was at home around moats, and now canals. He was enchanted by the scent of the sea. The tide was in at Lake Shinji. We stayed overnight near my hafu ancestor at the waterfront park.

Jazz musicians gathered at dusk under the streetlights in the park and created the music that might have distracted Lafcadio Hearn. He turned to gardens, the hush of a sanctuary, precious scrutiny, the romance of tradition and civility. Hearn celebrated the exotic stories of an ancient culture that would cover for militarism and a divine emperor. Jazz and blues might have reversed his literary concentration on a cricket or a smile. Hearn was never a wild dancer, he was shied by accident, a roamer and peripatetic storier.

One musician had recorded a recent Herbie Hancock concert in Tokyo. The music started with a great solo violin performance by Naoko Terai. She transformed two audiences with a marvelous rush, beat, and tease of tones.

The Matsue waterfront audience moved with the recorded audience in Tokyo, an intense, creative union, and the shouts of pleasure continued at the park. The blues, a fusion of wiles, bruises, and cares, bounced on the canal and roused the somber kami spirits of the samurai in the castle. The spirit of every beam and stone of tradition was routed by the beat of a new cultural memory.

Naoko Terai is a new spirit.

Curry was seduced by the music.

Museums are not high on my list of pleasures, as you know, but this museum was a personal association with the author. The Lafcadio Hearn Museum was rebuilt about twenty years ago, a traditional Japanese structure with tile roof and gables. Matsue was the author's home for only about year, so the idea of a museum in his honor was slow to mature. The Yakumo Memorial Society was established, and the first museum was constructed some thirty years after his death. Hearn's favorite desk was the first object received as part of the museum collection.

I stood at his high desk in the museum and imagined the view of his garden, an enclosed sanctuary. I walked around the desk with the author as he wrote *Glimpses of Unfamiliar Japan*. "The second garden, on the north side, is my favourite. It contains no large growths. It is paved with blue pebbles," he wrote in my memory. The pond, "a miniature lake fringed with rare plants, and containing a tiny island, with tiny mountains and dwarf peach-trees and pines and azaleas, some of which are perhaps more than a century old." I posed with the author at his desk. "It is a delight to watch every phase of their marvelous growth, from the first unrolling of the leaf to the fall of the last flower."

I praised his children, my distant relatives, and stood with him in photographs. I turned my head to the side, as he did to hide his blind left eye. Lafcadio Hearn died some forty years before my birth, and yet there was a sense of his presence in the museum and even more so in his residence. I studied the pictorial genealogical charts of his hafu descent, and there was not much chance that he encountered my anishinaabe relatives or any Amerika Indian.

Miko was amused by my poses with the author, and then she joined me in each photograph. My head was turned slightly to the left, and with a downward glance. We might have teased the author out of his tabi and traditions at the ruins. His ghost stories would have been shamed by the atomu horrors of Hiroshima.

Lafcadio Hearn at a ghost parade.

Maybe he was there.

The hafu kabuki storier?

Poetic justice for his romance.

Miko wondered if the author had tattoos, and we imagined the rise of invisible tattoos on his chest and back. The obvious signatures would be the names of places where he had lived and worked, but in some abstract notice of the author. Homer, the hafu Greek, Romaic, Paddy Boy, Dublin 1854, Mattie, Saint Pierre, Matsue 1890, Yakumo, and other names and dates of his travels that we read in the museum. Hearn might have created a new calendar to measure the curious hafu crown of his birth in Greece, and marked his chest with two invisible tattoos, Levkas One, and his death, Levkas 54.

Museums forever bore me.

Never the best stories.

No chance, no irony.

Curry posed at our side.

The Hearn house was mine by right of hafu association and memory. The gardens at his residence were lovely. The ancient peach and azaleas secured the miniature scenes as he had described them in *Glimpses of Unfamiliar Japan*. The title of his first book bears the sentiments of his first encounters, but the actual gardens were familiar. His words touched the elusive nature of his moods and the place.

> Maybe his gardens were always ghostly. Lafcadio watched the rising sun rush over the wall and chase the vapory shadows out of the garden. The breaks of light, tease of shadows, and hints of the seasons were entirely familiar to me. These were the gardens of the empire. Every ancient tree, flower, and cut of wind served the dominion of the emperor. The gardens must have been a blue haunt of the nanazu tricksters.

Japanese traditions were at his gate, the empty tatami rooms, soft shoji light in his study, the blue stones, and miniatures of his garden are common and customary. The comely beauty must have been what attracted him to the old samurai house near the moat, with a guarded view of Matsue Castle.

> Lafcadio Hearn wrote that his new house was the "ancient residence of some samurai of high rank. It was shut off from the street, or rather roadway, skirting the castle moat by a long, high wall coped with tiles. One ascends to the gateway, which is almost as large as that of a temple court, by a low broad flight of stone steps; and projecting from the wall, to the right of the gate, is a lookout window, heavily barred, like a big wooden cage."

Hearn was a literary artist inspired by cages and ancient ghost stories. He would rather capture tree crickets than chase butterflies, and he never tormented the snakes. That garden endured by cultural traces and stories, the coy remembrance of two seasons in the old samurai residence. Memories were barely recurrent, not a scene of visions, but the humors of an understated presence. These rooms are mine forever in stories.

> The samurai house was mine, a union of our stories, a wordy empire. I opened the shoji in my new study and pronounced the garden a familiar memory. Curry watched for the birds, crickets, and snakes, but held his distance.

Miko assured the manager of the residence that we were relatives of the author and shared his many rights and memories. Fumiko was unsure of our connection to the author, but she smiled, bowed, and gestured with confidence.

> Fumiko was generous by manner and hesitant to consider chance connections, which gave me a few minutes to create a four genera-

tion descent story. Rightly, she was worried about me, a hafu descendant who carried a wooden sword.

Curry was told to leave the house. Fumiko objected to his mere presence. She recited the absolute rules and worried that he would dirty the residence. Curry smiled, but she ordered my loyal envoy to leave. Fumiko smiled right back and pointed to the gate. Curry looked to me for protection. I appealed to the manager that the dog was an envoy, rigorously trained as a special agent in the diplomatic service of the Indian Embassy in Tokyo.

> Nai, no inu envoy.
> Loyal envoy.
> No inu in old residence.
> Curry is a diplomat.
> Hearn, no inu envoy.
> You are mistaken.
> No inu mistake.
> He owned many dogs.
> Nai, not here.

I pleaded that my ancestor Lafcadio Hearn had been honored by Amerika Indian on the White Earth Reservation. I mentioned a huge statue of the author with two hafu envoys at his side. Fumiko caught her breath and covered her mouth, truly surprised to learn that a bronze statue of the famous author had been erected at the headwaters of the Mississippi River.

> Why statue there?
> Famous author.
> Hai, Amerika Indian?
> Many wives.
> Nai, Koizumi Yakumo?

Lafcadio Hearn was very secretive about his hafu family on the reservation. Fumiko blushed but could not resist the stories of a scandal and the tease of hafu names. I assured her that most of his ancestors were not critical or judgmental of the author. She agreed that time heals the wounds of abandonment. Japan was his escape, and the only spite that remains to this day is that he never wrote about Amerika Indian.

> Fumiko smiled and turned away.
> Curry waited at her side.

The Lafcadio Hearn statue, created by a shaman, was turned to the side. The shaman was one of his ancestors. She revealed an ecstatic journey to an inu shrine, and there the author appeared as a mongrel in the kabuki play *Chushingura*. Convinced that he could be roused to return to his reservation relatives, she mounted the bronze statue at the headwaters. Thousands of his ancestors have waded across the source of the river in the past century to pray at the foot of the statue. Amerika Indian honor the mongrels, some visitors have observed, more than the author with one eye.

Curry was invited to stay.

Praise the heirs of Lafcadio Hearn.

This is my house by virtue of imagination and association with the stories of Lafcadio Hearn. He owes me this moment to envision his words by the garden, to create his presence by the turn of shadows, to honor his animal poses and tease the snow spirits that haunt his absence in Matsue. I have carried his stories, and now he owes me a spirited comeback at his residence.

Hearn was born almost a century before my atomu calendar, but he rescued me more than once in a story. He turns to the side on a park bench, a hafu fugitive, and the children mock him in the ghost parades of Hiroshima.

I moved into the residence and unpacked my boxes of notes and papers in the study. Hearn at my side, and the rich scent of the garden, inspired me to create my stories. Fumiko insisted that my meager belongings be hidden away with the futons by the time the residence opened in the morning. I protested that at least the author who had ignored his family on the reservation could now encourage my stories in his name and study. My notes, scraps, and scenes were neatly stacked, one by one, around the room.

The mounds of my notes on tickets, hotel stationery, napkins, advertisements, and recent scenes written on brochures from the museum and gallery were sorted by stories of the ruins, museum actions, park adventures, the nanazu, roamers, invisible tattoos, and other visual memories.

Fumiko was troubled by my presence, but she was moved by my strategic stories and assumed an obligation to the ancestors of the author. She decided that the mounds of story notes could be explained to visitors as the original manuscripts of Lafcadio Hearn. She was grateful that a serious distraction had been reversed and told me to continue with my mounds of avowed stories, and, at the same time, pose for the tourists as a literary scholar.

Curry nosed each mound.

Miko had invited many of my friends and roamers to visit our new residence in Matsue. Oshima, Virga, Kitsutsuki, Petros, Bogart, Real, Decisis, and Ginkgo, that marvelous roamer of Hibiya Park, arrived by train over several days. Oshima and Virga were the first to enter the gate.

Fumiko smiled, blushed in silence, broke into a sweat, and then backed away from Oshima. The fake peace of the museum residence had ended with the arrival of my friends. Fumiko was terrified by leprosy and sorry for the mongrel at his side. The secure count of tourists was over with the consent of my presence, the roamers, mongrels, and leper stories.

Bogart and Ginkgo traveled by train together, Kitsutsuki carried an extra wooden leg, Petros was under his straw hat, as usual, Real posed in his rubber gloves, and the others arrived later that day. Fumiko was utterly unnerved by leprosy, wooden legs, big hats, rubber gloves, and by glimpses of unfamiliar, invisible tattoos on my chest. She wrote a formal letter to inform me that she would be away for a week and pleaded that the residence must be vacant on her return.

Lafcadio Hearn wrote about glimpses of the exotic, the elusive manners, ghosts, and unusual spirits, but surely he never imagined that such strange characters as the roamers might actually occupy his old samurai residence. Hearn was here for the stories, and so were we, but no one ever stayed very long.

Miko arranged a tour of the Hohoemi Gallery. Real, naturally, wore the gloves for the show, and he asked about every detail in the paintings. His questions were tedious and turned to notions, doubts, and reservations about the watercolor scenes. He cocked his head and sighed with fake reticence that the "smear of body parts and ghostly distortions were too obvious, mere horror movie truisms."

Curry moved closer, cocked his head at the painting, turned and barked twice at Real. Ginkgo beat her brow and pretended to bark with the other roamers. "Really," shouted Real. That whiny sound of sanction and entitlement provoked the roamers and caused a friendly fracas in the gallery of smiles. Kitsutsuki kicked the whiner and his wooden leg came undone. Bogart shouted the orders and we wrestled the grouser to the floor. Ginkgo beat him on the head with a red umbrella. Stare read him the termination of his rights to freeload and complain. Petros tied two charms around his neck. Virga licked his neck until he pleaded for mercy. Miko disposed of his rubber gloves. I poked him in the belly with my wooden sword. The gallery manager smiled and called the police, and by the time the officers arrived we were weakened by laughter over our own scene.

> Curry barked at the police.
> Kitsutsuki arose with his leg in hand.
> Bogart saluted everyone.
> Stare recited "A Boy Named Sue."
> Miko blushed and pointed to her paintings.
> Ginkgo shouted "Pretty Woman."
> Petros ducked under his hat.
> Virga licked the toes of the manager.

The police studied the comic scene, a wooden sword, carved leg, weird art, charms, a leper, an old woman under a red umbrella, two mongrels, and they decided to remain silent. Their sense of humor, however, could not be wholly contained by the serious pose of questions.

The senior officer smiled, bowed, and asked if we had ever met before the gallery fight. Naturally, we looked around the gallery and denied any knowledge of each other. Real teased the police that the entire scene was sexual. "That man over there," he said, and pointed at me, "truly tried to measure my penisu with his wooden sword." The manager smiled, raised her arms, and turned away.

> You, namae?
> Yes, Real.
> How you real.
> No, Real.
> Why charms?
> Fear of the dark.
> Real dark?

Petros pushed his hat back and intervened. Real is decorated with charms, he pointed out, because we need protection from his cocksure, whiny truisms, and sexual mouth persuasion. There was much more, of course, but the point of the charms was made clear. The senior officer directed his assistant, a young woman in bright orange socks, to prepare forms for his signature. We were each presented with an official, ironic certificate that declared we were "police maniacs."

Miko continued our tour to the Matsue Castle. We crossed at the Somon Bridge and meandered around the gardens and rested in the shade. Real was coerced, because of the trouble he caused in the gallery, to buy everyone a bento lunch. Later we climbed the six stories of wood stairs to the watchtower, a spectacular view of Lake Shinji.

Oshima raved about the marvelous views of the city. He was inspired, liberated, and teased me in stories about the park roamers, my ironic tours of the peace museum, and my invisible tattoos. He was at his very best that afternoon, a loyal storier of the castle.

Oshima turned from personal to traditional stories. Urashima Taro, the young fisherman, was his favorite, and he animated the story with voice tones, hand turns, and face gestures. His creative power as a storier actually increased as tourists gathered around to listen. No one seemed to notice his leprous face and hands. The watchtower was hushed by his emotive performance. He bewitched the tourists and enchanted their children with the familiar story of a young fisherman. His voice changed under the sea, and in flight as a crane.

Urashima Taro was a modest boy who lived in a small village with his mother in southern Japan. The sea was wild and rough that autumn, and he could not launch his boat. So, he walked along the shore and noticed several boys who had captured a turtle crippled with leprosy. They teased the silent turtle with sticks, threw many stones, and cruelly tormented the turtle. Urashima Taro shouted, "How dare you tease my ancestor the turtle." He convinced the boys to release the turtle and told them never to torture their relatives, the animals and creatures of the sea.

Urashima Taro was on the shore the next day and watched the turtle poking his head out of the waves. "You saved me from those cruel boys," said the grateful turtle. "I would like to reward you with a visit to the castle of the dragons." Urashima Taro was honored by the invitation but he could not leave his old mother home alone. The wise turtle assured him that the visit would not take long. The young fisherman agreed and climbed onto the back of the turtle. Suddenly, they were deep in the sea. Soon they came to a castle that shimmered with gold and silver.

A princess emerged from the castle with several other young women and many gorgeous fish. Urashima Taro was invited to a banquet at the castle. He was enchanted with the beauty of the place, and then suddenly realized that he had been there for three years. He pleaded with the princess to allow him to return home to his mother. She agreed and gave him a splendid gift, a hand-carved ivory chest with three drawers, and told him that if he was ever in serious trouble, "please open the chest." The turtle returned him on his back to the shore that he had left three years earlier. He was surprised to see withered trees, and the mountains and rivers were not the same. Nothing was familiar.

Urashima Taro introduced himself to an old fisherman and asked him what had happened to his mother and their house. The fisherman said that when his grandfather was a young man he told stories about a young man who saved a turtle and was taken to a castle deep in the sea.

Urashima Taro did not know what to do, but then the gift from the princess came to mind. He was indeed in trouble, so he opened the top drawer of the ivory chest and found a crane feather. When he opened the second drawer white smoke poured out, and minutes later his hair turned white. He had become an old man, and in the third drawer he found a mirror. He could not believe how suddenly he had become an old man.

Urashima Taro could not understand how this could have happened to him. At that very moment the wind carried the crane feather to his back, and he became a crane. He raised his wings and flew high into the sky. The turtle was truly the princess, and she waved to him as he circled above the sea.

Margarito Real moaned, waved his hands, and declared the story was sentimental, even stupid, and played more to time and royalty than chance, irony, and ordinary associations. "The Japanese have humor, you see, but no sense of irony."

Lafcadio Hearn, however, was drawn to the traditional sentiments of this story of poverty, temptation, pleasure, return, magical flight, and the mystery of the great sea.

Matsue is one of the oldest cities in Japan. The city was built on a peninsula, developed a singular, historical culture, and in the eighth century became the capital of Izumo on the Sea of Japan. This new province was later overcome by the civilization of Yamato.

Matsue is a reserved castle town with moats, rivers, canals, many teahouses, and old samurai residences. Lafcadio Hearn is the only outsider, a *hafu* foreigner, who is honored by statues and museums in the city. He arrived as a teacher and married Koizumi Setsuko of an old samurai family. Lafcadio assumed a new name, Koizumi Yakumo, derived from the family name of his wife and a poetic word that means "eight clouds," or the origin of clouds.

Lafcadio first lived in a tiny house, "dainty as a bird-cage," near the Ohashi River and the lagoon, or Lake Shinji. "I was sorry to lose the beautiful lake view, but I found it necessary to remove to the northern quarter of the city, into a very quiet street" near Matsue Castle. "My new home," he wrote, "is shut off from the street, or rather roadway, skirting the castle moat by a long, high wall coped with tiles. One ascends to the gateway, which is almost as large as that of a temple court."

That old samurai residence is now a museum, and nearby is the formal Lafcadio Hearn Memorial Museum. Ronin mocked the poses of the author in exhibition photographs, and he imagined Lafcadio's presence behind his favorite high desk.

"Hearn insisted that the great gains in his life resulted from 'disillusion' rather than from friends. Some of his disillusion must have come from his treatment of friends," observed Carl Dawson in *Lafcadio Hearn and the Vision of Japan*. Ronin surely would not have been one of his many disillusions. The *hafu* roamer would have teased him from the start, a natural defense of disenchantment.

Miko was honored by an exhibition of her recent watercolor paintings at the Hohoemi Gallery. The word *hohoemi* means "smile," and the name of the gallery was derived from "The Japanese Smile," an essay in *Glimpses of Unfamiliar Japan* by Lafcadio Hearn. The manager of the gallery presents art as an ancient sentiment of the smile, no matter the elusive, moody, political, odious, or loathsome content

193

of the creation. "We smile in the face of contradictions, and so we celebrate the countercultural renunciations and dissension of art," declared the manager of the gallery.

"To comprehend the Japanese smile, one must be able to enter a little into the ancient, natural, and popular life of Japan," wrote Hearn. The smile is moral, and "to some extent aesthetic." The etiquette is a cultural sensibility. "A Japanese can smile in the teeth of death, and usually does. But he then smiles for the same reason that he smiles at other times. There is neither defiance nor hypocrisy in the smile." The smile is not a "weakness of character," but rather a native custom, a "silent language." Some outsiders consider the constancy of the smile as "insincerity." The Japanese observe the converse, the "angry faces" of foreigners. Hearn seldom smiled, and was shied by a blind eye.

Ronin was surprised when he found his notes and papers in the residence of Lafcadio Hearn. Miko was determined, and she was convinced that an association with the author would inspire Ronin. He created many mounds of connected notes, dialogue, and impressive scenes, as you know, but he did not complete his stories as a manuscript.

Miko protected the creative mounds of scenes, and she mailed three boxes to me. Ronin instructed me to complete the stories from his notes and papers and provide an envoy with information about the scenes in the stories. The actual, final draft of the manuscript, as you read it now, was created by the favor and scrutiny of many veteran residents at the Hotel Manidoo.

The Lafcadio Hearn statue, halfway into the stone, is mounted at the new waterfront park on the canal near the Ohashi River and Gensuke Bridge. Hearn lived nearby for a short time when he first arrived in Matsue. The bronze statue is a back view of the author based on a photograph of a sketch by an artist named Weldon.

The statue and the photograph "shows a small man walking away from the camera," observed Carl Dawson in *Lafcadio Hearn and the Vision of Japan*. "His suit is loose and ill fitting, his hat broad brimmed, his arms weighted by a satchel and an old suitcase. With one foot pointing outward and his body slightly bent, the man looks uncertain or off balance as he moves toward the port."

The Gensuke Bridge was a recent construction, but the ancient structure was not stable. The pillars were carried away by the tide. The remedy, at last, was a human sacrifice to distract the evil spirits. "A man was buried alive" near the center pillar, wrote Hearn in *Glimpses of Unfamiliar Japan*. The "bridge remained immovable for three hundred years."

Gensuke was unaware that he would become the chance nomination as he crossed the river. He was sacrificed to secure a section of the bridge. Ghostly fires have been reported on moonless nights at Gensuke Bashira, the center pillar of the bridge.

Ronin mentions another statue of Lafcadio Hearn at the headwaters of the Mississippi River, near the White Earth Reservation in Minnesota. Fumiko, the manager of the museum residence, was rightly suspicious of his earnest pose as a descendant of the author. There is no record of any statue with two mongrels at the headwaters. Hearn does not write about any contact with the Amerika Indian. He truly loved children, and surely would have noted responsibility for a *hafu* child on a reservation. Ronin's pose and notion of ancestry, however, is plausible, at least based on the chance encounters of travel.

Hearn traveled by train from Montreal to Vancouver, and then boarded the steamship *Abyssinia* on his way to Japan. He might have stopped along the way at Winnipeg or Medicine Hat, or he might have had contact with natives on the train. Surely he would have written about his experiences. He has been described as shy, and he seldom expressed in his private letters or publications much about sexual situations or episodes, other than his adventures with prostitutes.

Lafcadio, "morbidly shy," waited at a distance, as "his gregarious friend approached the decorative girls at the open doors of the various premises and chatted them up, then drew his companion inside toward the sound of music and laughter," wrote Jonathan Cott in *Wandering Ghost*.

The Yakumo Teahouse shares the same name with Lafcadio Hearn or Koizumi Yakumo, the name he adopted when he married and became a citizen of Japan. Yakumo is derived from a word in early *waka* poetry. Miko and Ronin order *koi* and *soba*, specialties of the teahouse, and *meika*, a delicious sweet cake. The word *sosen* means "ancestor."

Ronin opens the shoji screens to the garden in the old samurai residence. The shoji are sliding doors or windows covered with a rice paper. The translucent paper creates a soft light in the room. The tatami are braided straw mats used to cover floors, as in the study of Lafcadio Hearn. The tatami are specific, traditional sizes, always twice as long as they are wide.

195

Urashima, the young fisherman who discovers paradise in the mysterious depths of the sea, is a popular story in Japan. There are many versions, of course, but the same sentiments are expressed by the adventure, pleasures, mortality, loyalty, and consequences in the lives of Urashima Taro.

Lafcadio preferred this legend over other traditional stories. He might have seen himself by metaphors of the sea in the adventures and pleasures of Urashima. The young fisherman "sails away from home and, because of an act of kindness, wins the love of the daughter of the god of the sea," wrote Carl Dawson in *Lafcadio Hearn and the Vision of Japan*. "For an illusively short time, he lives contentedly with his beautiful wife in what becomes his native element."

Urashima is in exile, but he "imagines himself in an apparently timeless world, far from the sufferings of ordinary mortals, enjoying what Hearn elsewhere calls 'the silence of the great water.' He is the analogue of Matthew Arnold's mermaid and the many Western myths of escape and separation, love and betrayal."

Dawson observed of Lafcadio Hearn that, apart from the time he was "alone writing, he seems to have been at his happiest when he could swim, day or night, out into the ocean, losing himself like the legendary fisherman," Urashima.

13　Ronin of Lafcadio Hearn

Oshima continued his stories at the museum residence that night. His miseries were overcome by humor and the honor of memorable stories. The chrysanthemums at the leprosarium are his most wretched memories, but his new stories traced the spirits of those who nurtured the giant blooms. He created a sentiment of liberty. The spirit of his friends became lepers of survivance, not victimry.

> Miko spread the futons around my mounds of notes in the study. The shoji screens were open wide and the sounds of the garden rushed into the room. The crickets created a natural chorus in the old samurai house.

Lafcadio Hearn sat in the very same room and wrote about the same sounds, the crickets in the garden. Miko told the roamers that the songs of crickets summon the dead to return. "Listen," she said, "the crickets convene in the name of the author." Yes, we listened for almost an hour to hear the name of Lafcadio Hearn. Ginkgo said she heard his name, and so we tried to mock the cricket songs.

> Lafcadio, rafucadu, rafukadu.

The "Japanese tree crickets are much more extraordinary singers than even the wonderful cicadae of the tropics" he wrote in *Glimpses of Unfamiliar Japan*. The tree crickets "are much less tiresome" because there are various species. Hearn fancied the tsuku tsuku boshi because "this creature can have no rival in the whole world of cicadae: its music is exactly like the song of a bird."

> Margarito Real was the first to search the mounds of my notes and episodes. He selected a few scraps of paper, read several notes in silence, and then returned the papers to the mound. Clearly, he was interested in my stories, but not in random scenes.

Bogart, curious about my practice, reached into a mound, picked a movie advertisement, and read the notes on the back. Ginkgo, on the other hand, selected scraps of paper from several mounds and shouted out each episode. The scenes, by force of her voice, seemed to be connected at least by sentiment.

> Three old women, formal kimonos, tabi, and getas, come out of theatre. Music of Roy Orbison. "Pretty woman, walking down the street," caught by surprise. Uncertain about beat of music, cau-

tious, men in black van, but clearly pleased, embarrassed by the words. "Pretty woman, give your smile to me". Ginkgo beat her brow, heard "Rock and Roll Music" and "A Boy Named Sue" that night. Imperial Hotel and Hibiya Park.

Ronin, that was some other woman.

Ginkgo continued the stories.

The ocean, another chance, lasting presence in world. My heart beats with waves, bony clouds race to sea. Nearby, four ravens strutted the beach, teased me, garrulous croaks. Sun warms the sand, my hands, drew me to natural pocket of solace stories.

Suddenly, strange animal, mongrel, webbed feet, soft, stole my sword right out of my hand. Ran down beach to trees. There, mongrel changed, sandy coat to shades of pale green, vanished in luscious blues, hues of the forest.

The ravens borrowed your sword.

Ginkgo was a generous reader.

Virga, eternal shadow, tricky trace, motion, natural reason. Could be my mother, always a distance, never escape. Reached out many times to touch, heal, secret wounds, slight and separation. Circled back once, catch my shadow, chance, she constantly evades me. Virga bear at dusk, hafu shadow, always, same mongrel by morning.

Virga barked at the reader.

Ginkgo was so pleased with the response to her selections that she wanted to read more and shout a tribute to the Imperial Hotel and Hibiya Park. Bogart, Kitsutsuki, and others, however, were eager to read their selections. Oshima was their inspiration that night.

Bogart read my note about death.

Death, morning vision. Master said, We are separated from sense of presence because, fear of death. Consider instance, nuclear wounds, morning, fear of death vanishes. Samurai warrior never shamed by fear, death.

My first death chance, high fever, orphanage. Huge ravens crash windows, burst of light. Suddenly, feathers, turned black, soared over paddy, circled Fuji. Second death seven years later, visions of ravens, night after night. Could not resist, lust and wonder, ran away to Tokyo. Shanties gone, streets cleared. New buildings obstruct Mount Fuji. Camped three nights, memory of parents. Appeared in death dream as raven. Many soldiers, bugi dancers, moat that night.

Kitsutsuki leaned back on the futon, unfolded three scraps of paper, and turned them around slowly as he read. Two notes he selected were written on the curve of a napkin, and the third was on the back of a peace message form the museum.

Curry was at his side.

Miko covered breasts, hand towel, body bare. Great ravel of black hair on crotch, erotic crest. Sat close on high bench, sauna. Later, men more at ease, nudity, she lowered towel, touched her own breasts. Nipples huge, bloated by heat.

Miko watched atomu date, time emanate on my red chest. Invisible tattoos arise on blush, first she has ever seen. Turned sideways bench, removed towel, uncovered floral tattoos.

Chrysanthemums?

My mother.

Morning glories?

Nuclear survivance.

Wild lettuce?

Fare of ruins.

Chrysanthemums tease my mother, wears print dress, giant showy flowers, conceives me near imperial moat, she was obedient to emperor. She honored chrysanthemum crown and abandoned me for racist war criminal, emperor. Tattoos, empire ironies, hafu native fugitive.

Petros raised his hat to read my notes.

Atomic Bomb Dome, my Rashomon. Kabuki haven, kami gate in ruins. Oshima comes out of rain, memories, black rain, waves of atomu poison, lived here since the start of manuscript.

Hiroshima my bugi dance, peace pond my fire, origami cranes my tease, park roamers, ravens, mongrels my strain. Peace Museum my *Hiroshima Mon Amour*.

Changed name, museum tee shirts, decked main entrance name of movie. Noisy paper banner, worthy audience for three hours. Guards recognize me, liked new name, ordered by director to cut down.

Hiroshima Mon Amour Museum.

Lectured some twenty tourists, new museum named after movie *Hiroshima Mon Amour*. Assumed role of official tour guide. Pretended to be two decadent characters in movie, moody, hafu architect, seductive actress, green eyes. My voice pitched and heady.

Tourists listen, frown, one or two smile by doubt, seemed to like my style.

Stare asked me to select a scrap of paper from the mound for him to read. He moved closer to the garden, and with the sound of crickets at his back read a short scene about Curry and my adventures at Yasukuni Jinja.

The Indian Embassy, by chance, bird sanctuary. Feral cats would not enter grounds, the dogs and scent of curry. Mongrels taste any cuisine, cats trained to savor spices. Dogs trail me, escape distance, main street. Returned to embassy, guard tells me dog a moat mongrel, likes taste of curry.

No home, no name.

No visa?

Not mongrels.

No passport?

You tease.

Natural reason.

Guard turns away, moat mongrel smiles. Trails me again to main street and Yasukuni Jinja. Curry, natural name, the moat mongrel of Indian Embassy. My loyal envoy.

Oshima selected, by chance, an erotic scene.

Miko moved behind, presses thighs close to mine, both hands touches my stomach, unbuckles my belt, pushes me down path to a shrouded bench. No Virga, no one heard, seen, alone.

Buy my soul.

How muchie?

Promises.

Samurai promise?

Maybe so.

Opens my trousers, raises her skirt, mounts me face to face. My penisu, aroused by touch, heave, ducked, wet, swollen, fleshy lips. Sighs, we moan, pushes hard against my thighs. Raises her body, pounds against me, over and over. Thighs smack, erotic sound lasts forever in moist night air.

Miko distracted the roamers with stories about mongrels. She selected several scenes about a production of *Chushingura Inu, The Loyal Dog Retainers*. Lafcadio Hearn is an inu player in her version of my notes, but he is not part of that episode in my story.

Osaka recited awesome story, forty-seven ronin, by sound of her voice same number of mongrels appeared on stage, my dream.

Great billowy clouds moved across painted landscape, simulated trees wave at back of stage.

Inu Shinto Shrine, mongrel memorial, located near river, south of koban. The hyoshigi sound, hafu samurai rinse paws, enter inu shrine. Stage, back of the shrine.

Lafcadio, Mishima, Shinji, Reiko, Kaisoku, Virga, Kenka, Yubi, thirty-nine other hafu samurai, no masters, pose by name on stage. Move in ethereal light. Three mongrels posed as ravens, noisy air, bounce across stage. Lafcadio, one eyed hafu cocker, terrier, is a guard. Kaisoku carries wooden sword. Kenka, hafu toy terrier, odori shaman, acrobatic warrior taunts poses of royalty. Several roamers wore feathers, two ecstatic lepers, covered twisted paws with miniature white tabi, together with other hafu samurai, mighty chorus of tatari vengeance.

Osaka created *Chushingura Inu, The Loyal Dog Retainers,* or the forty-seven hafu ronin, play staged first time in my dream. Shrine a kabuki theater, perfect vision of my own death.

Princess Asagao, wispy, white, hafu borzoi, black teeth, minces under torii, floats down walkway. Ghost, almost invisible, train of hoary kimono creates romantic murmur. The hyoshigi sound, she enters, tsuke beat faster, clack, clack, clack, clack, dramatic sound, enhances magical motion.

Mishima, hafu samurai master, akita, whippet, lurcher by shares, chases princess down walkway, caught her train center stage. Airy material vanishes, mighty paws. Shimmer of light lingers, trace of thin, transparent bones, princess vanishes in cloud waves.

Mishima licks his crotch on stage.

Lord Nox, vowed royal hafu Shih Tzu, insulted by crude manners, obscene pursuit of Princess Asagao. Peevishly insists, proud ancestors loyal to Murasaki Shikibu, author of *The Tale of Genji.* Dubious story of royal authority, hafu samurai ordered to commit suicide, seppuku at Inu Shrine.

Lafcadio Hearn returned that night by the song of crickets. He was troubled at first by the roamers asleep in his study and by the mounds of papers, but when he turned back to the garden the crickets created a familiarity.

Curry and Virga were his loyal envoys.

I walked into the garden and turned back to see the author with his mongrels at the entrance to his study. He observed the slightest motion and searched for the sources of natural sound in the garden. Hearn waited at the shoji border for hours that night, an intense meditation on motion and sound, and never once turned to record a name or make a note.

Lafcadio Hearn was there by visual memories, an ecstatic presence, a meditation and natural surprise. Later, he might have turned to metaphors, or singular words of sight and sound, to create a presence in the garden. The author touched the azaleas, oblivious to the sound of heavy breathing in his study. The roamers twitched like mongrels in their dreams. Kitsutsuki embraced his wooden leg as he slept. Stare almost created the blues as he snored, a burst of emotive breath at times. Bogart wore his uniform but did not salute anyone in his dreams. Real frowned in his sleep, a silent conceit, and held his penisu in both hands. Ginkgo lost wrinkles and the callous on her brow as she wheezed in the corner. She tucked her dirty hands under her cheek.

Miko was the shaman, the artist of visions. The heat of her body filled the study with a lusty light. She waited for me to notice her in the bakery, and she roused me to this garden. Our friends are asleep across the tatami between mounds of notes. There is nothing more for me to tease in this old samurai house. My time has come to vanish. Lafcadio Hearn forever moves away.

The Atomic Bomb Dome is my Rashomon. Oshima is my soul brother. Miko is our shaman of liberty. Virga is my teaser. Curry is my loyal envoy. Death is my vision in the faint light of morning, and this is my chance to run again with a death story.

Lafcadio escorted me to the gate of the old samurai house. He was silent. I turned back at the gate, and he looked away. The crickets roused his name, but he has nothing more to say. He wrote of the smile and buried his own in an unfamiliar glance.

I walked directly to the waterfront park that early morning. The distant sun raised wisps of light on the horizon and moved across the canal. The ravens hurried back from their tour of the restaurants to hear the story of my death.

I undressed for another mortal journey, stacked my clothes, my wooden sword, a nanazu treasure, and a crane feather at the left foot of the bronze statue. Lafcadio was already halfway into the stone, and the feather gave us both wings. Curry and Virga were at my side, and they stood by my clothes at the foot of the statue.

I vanished by the faint morning light. The police might search for my body in the lagoon or far out to sea. The reports might say that a tourist in the city was drowned in the lagoon, but his body has not yet been recovered.

I am a crane, and you readers who want to know more about me must search in the clouds. Lafcadio Hearn is a crane on my wing. Many authors fly this way.

Ronin is a *hafu* native speaker of Japanese. He understood a hesitant manner, the hint and tease of the language, but, other than a few common words, he refused to speak Japanese. English is his sense of presence, resistance, survivance, and source of irony. He is the son of a soldier, a *ronin* of the *atomu* ruins, and death, or strategic retreat, has been his bushido way. He has died many times over the manners and proprieties of an empire nation that would not embrace the *hafu* children of the occupation.

Lafcadio Hearn, on the other hand, was a *hafu* teacher who married and became a citizen of Japan. His "sympathetic trespass" and "authority as a complete witness," rather than his "linguistic accuracy," were persuasive to many readers, wrote Carl Dawson in *Lafcadio Hearn and the Vision of Japan*. "Astounding as it seems, Hearn never really mastered the Japanese language."

Ronin is loyal to the *kami* spirits of thousands of children who died when the atomic bomb destroyed Hiroshima. He has resisted, countered, and accosted those who endorsed notions of fake peace, as you know, and he has obstructed museums in the name of war and peace.

"Death is my vision in the faint light of morning," he wrote on a bakery napkin. Ronin mentioned an unnamed master. That could be a vision of his father, but the veterans at the Hotel Manidoo were not certain. "The master said, We are separated from a sense of presence because of our fear of death. Consider the instance of nuclear wounds every morning and the fear of death vanishes. The samurai warrior is never shamed by the fear of death."

Ronin was inspired by the courage of his father, Nightbreaker, by the *ronin* manner of Toshiro Mifune, by the adventures of Ronald MacDonald, by the haiku images of Matsuo Basho, and by the memorable stories of Lafcadio Hearn. The Japanese, he boldly told me, have always been influenced by the outside, and at the most critical moments in their history. Theater, art, and literature were saved by outsiders. Faubion Bowers, for instance, saved the kabuki theater during the occupation. This irony provided him with a vision and sense of adventure. There were times when he seemed convinced that by shouts, encounters of the *kami* spirits, and trickery he could create stories of human dignity and survivance, rather than the dead letters of tradition, obedience to the emperor, and peace poses.

Miko mentioned that the songs of crickets summon the dead to return, and the roamers mocked the cricket tenor of Lafcadio Hearn. She was probably referring to the Noh play *Matsumushi*. Crickets, *korogi*, or *kuriketto*, sing back the memories of the dead in the fifteenth-century play, probably written by Zeami. Hearn was a serious student of crickets and their songs. The memory of the author surely returned that night to his old samurai residence.

Lafcadio Hearn and Ronin were both inspired by the story of Urashima Taro. They were drawn to the sea and to the vision of magical flight. Ronin placed a crane feather, a metaphor borrowed from the story, on his mound of clothes at the foot of the statue in the waterfront park. He once dreamed that he was a sandhill crane and soared out of sight. Urashima Taro, Ronin, and Lafcadio Hearn are roamers transformed by the spirit of a crane feather in the story. They are drawn to the sea and vanish in magical flight.

Ronin did not mention in his last story that he fastened a tee shirt banner on the back of the statue of Lafcadio Hearn. The police removed the banner later that morning, but the catchwords, "I am a glorious *hafu* cherry blossom," became the headline of a story about the death of a tourist in the canal. Ronin inserted the word *hafu* to the familiar kamikaze metaphor of duty.

Miko mailed the three boxes of notes, scenes, and seven ledger books to me at the Hotel Manidoo. The actual manuscript was completed here, as you know, and published as *Hiroshima Bugi* by the University of Nebraska Press.

Ronin truly vanished at the waterfront park, but the roamers and the veterans at the hotel sensed his eternal presence. Handy Fairbanks declared that he would soon emerge in another story.

Miko visited the White Earth Reservation in Minnesota. She intended to share the grievous stories of his death and the great stories of his manuscript, but she was teased at the mere mention of his name. Ronin was known on the reservation, to be sure, but not the way she constructed the story. She tried many times to honor his memory.

Miishidoon, the shouter, would not listen to any death stories about Ronin. The reason, she shouted, is that he is not dead, and he never has been a dead man. Miko was scolded for spreading death sto-

ries. The shamans were not pleased. Actually, the nasty shouter and
many others on the reservation treated her the same as any stranger
who arrived with wicked stories. She was teased, mocked, and humiliated by Miishidoon.

Miko understood why Ronin would leave the reservation, to avoid
Miishidoon. She smiled, endured the shouts, and tried to avoid the
old woman. Finally, the tribal president invited her to meet with several relatives of Nightbreaker and his errant son, Ronin. Miishidoon
shouted their names, the errant boys who could not bear Japan.

Nightbreaker's many cousins and elders were invited to meet Miko
for a potluck supper at the mission school. She arrived early only to
discover that the invitation was wrong, the potluck had been moved
to a garage near the fire station. Miko decided not to eat because the
food was fried and fatty. She smiled, bowed, moved around the tables,
and tried to engage people in conversations, but no one had anything
to say about Ronin. Actually, conversations turned to silence when
she sat at a table. Miishidoon sat alone in a corner of the garage. She
never shouted over a free meal.

Booty Beaulieu, the president, told her to ease back and wait for
the elders to show some interest in her ideas and stories. Miko followed her advice, but no one said a word to her the entire evening.
She was angry, worried, humiliated, and critical of Ronin. He never
told her about reservation manners and politics, and she regretted
the journey. Naturally, she summoned *kami* spirits, but the native
tease was much stronger. Ronin was a mighty teaser, she knew that,
but he never resisted her *kami* charms.

Miko shouted back at the teasers. No more smiles around here, she
shouted and turned away. Miishidoon shouted that she was a faker, a
deathmonger with no visions of your own. Take your death stories
back to Japan.

Miko shouted right back that the old woman was a demon, erased
dreams, and hated memories. You even hate to hear your own shouts.
Miko found her voice as a shouter on the reservation, but she could
not find an audience to share stories about Ronin.

Booty told me that she won the shout contest later that day. Miko
pursued the old woman and shouted that she was a rock at the bottom
of an outhouse forever howling at the assholes overhead to stop, stop
shitting on me. Not a chance, Miishidoon.

That encounter raised an audience, dozens of people gathered
around for the shout out. Miko earned a natural sense of presence by

shouts. Miishidoon was stunned by the force of the shouts. Miko sensed the power of her demonic stare and stared right back at the old woman. She moved closer and became a *kami* menace.

Booty reported that two shamans had a shout out on the reservation, and both survived. No one forgot the tiny shouter from Japan. The only other person to shout the old woman down, but not out, was Ronin. She loved that boy, and she would not listen to any death stories.

Miishidoon turned away, waved her arms, and then burst into wild laughter. Later she reached out to touch the new shouter on the reservation. Miko could hardly bear the stench of her body, but the old woman was truly warm, gentle, and she emanated the lusty scent of a bear. Miko, for the first time, wondered if the old woman was a man.

Miko earned her voice as a shouter. She lived with the old bear woman and told many stories over several days about the adventures of Ronin. The people were moved by his vision of the *atomu* children and laughed over the scenes at Yasukuni Jinja. The last stories of his death, however, were resisted by almost everyone on the reservation. She learned later that the crane feather was one of his ancestral totem, the signature of his conversion, spiritual motion, and sovereignty of magical flight, but never his death. Miishidoon shouted that he might have vanished, but he never died that morning at the waterfront park in Matsue, Japan.

Miko convinced the tribal president to commission a bronze statue of Nightbreaker, Ronin, Lafcadio Hearn, Curry, and Virga. Dead or not, she reasoned, the statue would honor the association and memory of three *hafu* storiers and their loyal envoys. Miko arranged for the roamers to participate in the tricky dedication at the headwaters of the Mississippi River.

Miko pitched a tent that night.

Ronin was in her dreams.

Miko was alone at the headwaters.

Ronin walked out of the woods and hummed a tune from the "Fanfare for the Common Man" by Aaron Copland. She heard the muted thunder of water drums. Ronin teased her in a dream to beat his brow and cheeks.

Miko watched the invisible tattoos of two mongrels emerge on his rosy cheeks. Suddenly, she said, he circled at a great distance and almost vanished in the dream. She shouted his names, *atomu hafu*, *hafu*, and the invisible tattoos turned to bears.

In the Native Storiers series:

Designs of the Night Sky
by Diane Glancy

Hiroshima Bugi: Atomu 57
by Gerald Vizenor

Lightning Source UK Ltd.
Milton Keynes UK
UKHW011815100922
408527UK00011B/228